IN TOO REAP

THE ACCIDENTAL REAPER PARANORMAL
URBAN FANTASY SERIES, BOOK 3

MISTY EVANS

Beach
Path
Publishing

In Too Reap, The Accidental Reaper Mystery Series, Book 3

©2022 Misty Evans

Print ISBN: 978-1-948686-58-7

Cover Art by Fanderclai Design

Formatting by Beach Path Publishing, LLC

ONE

G hosts and graveyards—I was always dealing with one or both these days.

Huddled in Shepherd's Rest Cemetery behind an elaborate crypt belonging to a long-dead family named Montague (yep, just like those of Shakespearean fame), I shivered and pulled up the hood of my black robes.

The place was quiet except for the murmur of a tour guide and the soft crunch of shoes on frozen ground. Sacred ground, I reminded myself, wondering how many of those buried in the soil, as well as in caskets inside the multitude of crypts, rested here. According to my research, it was one of the oldest burial grounds in Dante's Grove, dating back to the founding fathers.

"Have you seen anything?" A deep baritone voice asked in my ear.

Tucking my cell between said ear and shoulder, I blew on my frozen fingers and told my grim reaper mentor and investigative partner, Killion, "I've sent six earthbound spirits to the great beyond in the past three hours, and avoided a ghost tour, but haven't seen one robber."

He sounded as bored as I felt. "Better things to do on such a night, I suspect."

It was nearing midnight on New Year's Eve. I was hungry and tired, along with being a popsicle. While I was no social butterfly, I dreamed of spending the night at a grand party with champagne and a kiss from a handsome guy at the stroke of midnight. "My toes will fall off when I remove my boots, and it will take me until summer to raise my core body temperature to normal. I'm calling it a night."

His tone turned bemused. "I believe I recommended a warmer coat and a pair of gloves for your stakeout."

Being a vampire, cold didn't bother him. Granted, this was Louisiana and cold was relative this far south, but I didn't need him to rub it in. "Yes, you were right again. All hail the great and powerful Killion." My dog and psychopomp, Ghost, a five-pound mix of long hair and attitude, gave a snort. It was uncanny how she seemed to understand me. "Even with her doggy coat, Ghost is freezing."

"It's forty-seven degrees. While that is chilly, it's hardly—"

"Forty-seven?" My teeth chattered, making my voice tremble. Shepherd's Rest was a good five miles west of his location, but that couldn't be the reason for the difference in temperature. "It's at least ten degrees colder here." I sent him a screenshot of my weather app showing that exact fact. "Regardless, it's New Year's Eve and I shouldn't have to work."

"Do you have a date?"

The prohibition I'd placed on my love life aside, I could have. Two guys had asked me out—one from the hospital and one from my Clinical Pathology class. "In fact I do— with a good book and my bed." Turning down potential dates had been easy. I didn't feel the slightest attraction to either man. My friend, Nita, had invited me and Killion to a party, but I feared what could happen at the stroke of midnight. When it came to the master vampire, I was in trouble.

My growing attraction to him concerned me. A lot. I didn't want to do something stupid in the heat of the moment—like kiss him madly—and ruin not only our friendship, but our working partnership as well.

Then there were the nightmares I kept having. Flashbacks about him nearly killing me. I'd done my research—I had PTSD after a nasty episode before Christmas involving his fangs, but since it involved a vampire sucking the life out of me, I couldn't exactly tell my therapist. "Have you seen anything suspicious on your end?"

"No miscreants so far. A few drunken revelers, along with mystics looking for death omens about the coming year."

"Weirdos." Who thought it was fun to party in a graveyard? Even in high school, the most we ever did was sneak a cigarette or two. And why would anyone—mystic or not—want to see the future? "Does that actually work? The corpse road thing?"

There was an old superstition in these parts that psychics and witches could hang out on a 'corpse road'—one that ran between a graveyard and a church—and see the spirits of those who would die in the coming year.

"You'd have to ask Aurora."

As I peeked around the edge of the Montagues' crypt, the lingering ghost tour was wrapping up. The woman who led the group glanced my way but then proceeded to ignore me. She wore a warm cloak and gloves, and I envied her.

A man with his sweatshirt hood drawn up lingered near

a grave. The beam of his flashlight went back and forth over the name and dates carved into the stone. Seemingly satisfied, he flipped off the light and melted into the shadows.

Double weirdo. Keeping out of sight of the departing group, I journeyed over to the marker he'd been so interested in, Ghost trailing after me. Neither the deceased's name, nor anything else seemed of particular interest, but I snapped a photo for my records. Briefly, I compared it to the pictures of the two graves that had been robbed, and saw nothing similar.

Heading down the incline, my beam illuminated an elaborate double headstone in a raised section off by itself. The names made me pull up short. *Gertrude Grace Elizabeth Reveux, adored wife. Marius Cipriam Reveux, cherished son.*

My heart clenched. So that's why Killion had insisted I take this cemetery. He'd called her Eliza. His son had looked just like him.

A gentle tugging took hold in my chest and the dormant jasmine plant vining around the stones began to turn green.

Whoops!

I moved away in a panic, Death's amulet around my neck springing to action and enclosing me in a sapphire blue bubble—not to protect me from the dead, but them from me. Definitely not disturbing those poor souls, even if I did feel their spirits reaching out to me. It was attached to my magic—the necromancy—and I wanted no part of that.

Nor did I want to accidentally raise Killion's dead wife and child. My magic was two sides of the same coin—I could end a life or resurrect one. I said a prayer for them and jogged away.

Killion had insisted I change my perspective about my necromancy. I wasn't *raising zombies*—my terminology—

but instead *returning life* to departed beings. It sounded better, but to me, they were one and the same.

Skirting an enormous bench in front of a crypt, I considered saying something to the master vampire about what I'd discovered, but it was too sensitive of a subject. The silence between us was comfortable and I didn't want to ruin his night by mentioning it.

My stomach rumbled and gave me something else to think about. "I'm hungry. I should have brought more snacks."

I could hear the smile in his voice. A smile that was all for me. "You are always hungry."

The church in this ancient place had long ago been reduced to its foundation stones by a fire. In fact, the whole cemetery was run down, the perfect setting for a ghost tour. The largest building on the ten acres-plus was a mausoleum resembling a Grecian Temple, complete with columns at the front door. Time had been unkind to the structure, the well-known ancestors of the Banks family, one of our founders, resting peacefully inside. Like their surname suggested, the wealthy brood had been in the banking business, along with cotton and tobacco, and built our city into a thriving metropolis before The Depression hit. There were still a few of their descendants in the area, and the original Banks financial institution had scraped by, eventually rebuilding into a successful enterprise that had branches all over the South.

I bet none of them ever spent a New Year's Eve freezing in a graveyard. "I'm calling it," I repeated. "I'll come back tomorrow night if I don't end up on morgue duty."

"You told me you'd put in your resignation."

"But they haven't found a replacement." My uncle was disappointed I was quitting, since he was the pathologist in charge. Along with completing my fourth year of veterinary medicine, I was re-opening my parents' clinic downtown, and I didn't have time for everything. "Nobody wants a cushy job shuffling paperwork at the bone house, surrounded by dead people. Who knew?"

Killion chuckled. My sarcasm usually made him growl or roll his eyes. This was progress. "Are you in need of a ride home?"

Carless, I tended to walk most places, or call the local ride service. I had a new friend who owed me, and he was a good guy, but I'd promised not to bother Rafael tonight, since he'd be extra busy with drunk revelers. "I borrowed Vera's Prius."

Ghost pawed at my leg to carry her. My scythe, magical and compact, was strapped to my back in its leather sheath. Placing the phone between my shoulder and ear once more, I lifted her, told her she was spoiled, and headed for the car.

"You should buy your own vehicle. You have the money now."

I did, but it felt nice to look at my savings account and see actual numbers there.

Vera's baby was a half a block from this section on the overgrown road that led to the church. The tour had broken up, and most in attendance had already bailed, although the guide kept sending covert glances my way. I waved; she didn't return it.

"I like my current arrangement just fine. But this stuff with the robbers—Death should put up cameras at the different sites and wait to catch the *miscreants*." I emphasized Killion's word choice as a subtle tease. Being three hundred years old, his lexicon included archaic terms that I enjoyed poking fun at. "Come to think of it, the police should do the same. I'll mention it to Officer Rogan when I see him at The Bean on Monday."

"The department is understaffed and overworked. They do not have the technology or funding to play Big Brother. They have more serious crimes to investigate."

Ghost and I reached the next section of plots where the less wealthy were buried. Most were raised beds, since the low water table made subterranean burials impossible. The path was weeds and rocks, and I used the trunk of a tree to balance as I worked my way down the slight incline. "Robbery should be their responsibility."

"SMG has decided it is equally ours, since the dead are being disturbed."

Soul Management Group, along with my boss, Death, had placed me on probation for violating several clauses in my contract. I had a sneaky suspicion graveyard duty was more a disciplinarian action, and a way to keep me out of trouble, than a sincere concern for those trying to RIP.

As the woman glanced my way before she got in her car, I wondered if she actually worked for SMG and was only posing as a guide to check up on me.

As the last of the group drove off, Ghost and I veered past two concrete angels guarding the entrance. One was cracked from his left shoulder down to his heart. The other was missing a wing. "Training tomorrow?"

"At three. We'll be working on controlling your powers. Again."

"My favorite." I fumbled in my pocket for the keys, the Prius looking like my version of heaven—warm and cozy. At least Killion had moved off the idea that he could get me into physical shape with push-ups and five-mile runs. Self-defense training was going better, but at present , I'd had to drink a specialty brew Aurora had made, along with wearing a necklace Death had given me, in order to keep from accidentally raising the dead.

Tonight, I'd downed extra tea and made sure the amulet was secure around my neck. Even with those precautions, I could sense those sleeping in their caskets stirring at my presence.

Up to this point, I had only raised dead animals and a few insects, but recently, I'd been much more in tune with the world, including the millions of corpses buried everywhere.

I felt the soulless, empty containers of the physical bodies whenever I ventured near burial sites. Like, *really* felt them. They were empty shells, their spirits right on the other side of the veil, and many were keen to come back. Too keen for my liking.

Being in the cemetery was risky, but tonight, I hadn't so much as raised an expired squirrel. This was progress, too.

I suspected the amulet was Death's way to keep me under his thumb. Talk about Big Brother. After my dealings with him, I had little trust of his intentions and hated the idea he could track me no matter where I might be or who I was with. He despised Killion and the Undead because they defied the natural order of things. I had a feeling he now felt the same about me because I'd fed Killion to keep him alive.

Our spirits made a contract with the universe before we entered a physical body. That contract had an expiration date, and most people went easily when it came due. Those who tried to cheat the system ended up with a grim like me reaping them. Those who were killed before it was up become shades—a ghost stuck on the earthly plane. Many times they sought retribution or revenge.

Because I'd died several times and brought myself back

to life, thanks to my inherent necromancy, I was considered a "tweener"—able to see and communicate with ghosts because I walked in both dimensions. It was part of my job to help the shades cross to the afterlife.

Killion had been assigned as my mentor and partner, but his contract had been up at Christmas, and because of me, he still walked freely. That was why I was on probation, as was he.

"Do *you* have a date?" I held my breath, hating myself that it came out sounding awkward. "Not that it's any of my business."

"I'm hosting a party. You are, of course, welcome to attend as my guest."

Ghost whined, her head cranking to my left. I glanced over and saw an odd, vibrating gray mass hovering above the road. Like a cloud, it appeared to be moving. "Thanks, but I really should get home. I haven't had a decent... Hang on."

The cloud roiled, the fog moving toward the car. On instinct, I drew my scythe. Was this some type of spirit?

"Is it the criminals we seek?"

"Not sure what it is." Slowly, I moved closer and stuck the tip of the blade into the gray, undulating mass. My whole arm vibrated. Ghost growled.

As if gripped by an invisible hand, it tugged hard on the blade. Gripping the handle tighter, I yanked it free.

The moment it cleared, the fog popped and vanished. I let out a tight breath and backed toward the car. "It's nothing." I just wanted out of this place. "See you tomorrow."

"Happy New Year."

I was about to wish him the same, when a cold, hard body hit me from the side, knocking me to the ground.

TWO

My phone and scythe went flying and the impact knocked the air from my lungs as fast as the weight hit.

Then it disappeared. I scrambled to my feet, swearing, and scanned the area.

A ghost hovered a few feet away, looking as bewildered as I felt. He scrunched up his face. "Chloe?"

Sucking in a crisp breath, I heard the peel of church bells in the distance, ringing in the new year. I took a step back and blinked at the apparition. "JR?"

He patted his hands over his torso. "What's going on? Where am I?"

My stomach dropped. I hadn't seen Jackson Rawlings Banks since we'd graduated high school. He'd left Dante's Grove for Harvard and things had gone sideways for him there. Last I'd heard, he'd become a veterinarian and moved to Colorado, but there had been a time in our younger years when we'd been close friends.

We'd bonded over animals. I'd accidentally given him a

scar over his left eyebrow while attempting to rescue a baby raccoon who'd fallen in a deep ravine.

I scanned his face, and yep, there it was.

Breaking the news to someone that they're dead is never easy. Doing it to a friend, even if we hadn't spoken in years, more so. "I'm sorry, JR." I was the only one he'd ever let call him that. "You're…"

Elongated tentacles from the portal reached for him. I'd never seen anything like it, and I instantly snatched up the scythe from the ground. Ghost growled.

His eyes widened as he looked at the weapon. "What is *that*?"

Before I could answer, the gray portal fingers wrapped around him. He let go a surprised cry. "Chloe! What's happening?"

I had no idea. I rushed forward with the blade. "Touch this," I demanded.

"Why?"

"Just do—"

The fog jerked him back. He clawed at the air, whether reaching for the scythe or me, I couldn't be sure. I lunged, attempting to bring it to him, but the gray fingers swept him into the roiling mass.

"Help!" Terror covered his features. "Chloe, *help me!*"

It was too late. His ghost disappeared as I jabbed the blade into the fog. It was hitting a stone wall. The blade came to a sudden halt, vibrating in my hand once more, and sending a shockwave up my arm.

Jerking the weapon back, I lost my footing and stumbled from the portal's sudden release. Another popping noise and a flash. Shadows spread like a blanket, cutting off the moon's illumination and plunging me into utter darkness.

It was like becoming blind, and the chill that swept over

me had nothing to do with the actual temperature outside. Through the deep gloom, I saw Ghost turning into her psychopomp but she didn't seem to know what to do.

Neither did I. The air in my lungs froze. My ribs turned to ice. Blood congealed. All of it happened in the space of the blackout. Panicking, I tried to suck in air; failed. I blinked rapidly, attempting to see even the faintest outline; couldn't.

Was this it? Was this the end? My body felt heavy, my brain a feather.

It vanished as fast as it came. The moon was once more in the sky over my sprawled body. My lungs expanded and I panted hard. Ghost, back in her puppy form, barked savagely as I coughed and sputtered, my muscles clenched so tight I couldn't sit up.

From my phone, I heard Killion coming from a million miles away. "Chloe! Answer me! Are you all right?"

Stars twinkled in the midnight blue sky. The last peel of the bells faded, my ears ringing. The ice in my body began to melt, but I still shook, my hands twitching and my head banging against the ground.

Above me, clouds drifted across the moon. *That's what space must feel like. Bottomless, frigid, nothingness...*

"Chloe! I'm on my way!"

I snapped out of the stupor. "Ki..lli..on?" My voice was scratchy. The single word came out in way too many syllables, thanks to my chattering teeth. I cleared my throat, Ghost now leaning over and licking my face. With shaky arms, I gathered her to me, soaking in her warmth. "Killion?" I tried again.

"Yes, I'm here!" His reply was tinny, coming from my cell phone where it had fallen. "What happened?"

"Not...sure." Trying to explain it would take too much

energy, and I didn't have any to spare. Releasing the dog, I rolled to my side. The phone lay a few feet away under the car. I reached for it and gasped at the pain that ricocheted through my system.

Gritting my teeth, I dragged myself closer and slowly stretched once more. A cramp hit, buckling my spine and I cried out.

"I'm on my way," I heard him say. "Hang on."

The most I could grind out in response was, "*Huurrrry.*"

Shivering and shaking on the ground, Ghost lying next to me, clearly worried, I had several earthbound spirits decide to drop by for a visit.

The cemetery had far too many of them hanging around, probably one of the reasons the tours loved to bring people here, even though most of the visitors couldn't see or hear them. "Look at the big, bad slayer," one sang. "Out of commission and at our mercy."

He was a noncompliant who'd run from me during my stakeout. His bell bottoms and V-neck shirt, displaying several gold chains along with chest hair, gave me plenty of fodder for a snarky comeback, but it hurt to even move my lips. Plus, I was seriously worried that I'd somehow short-circuited something in my brain, if not my body. "I...will... reap you," I stammered.

He mimicked my threat and laughed, continuing to taunt me until Ghost, who truly did seem to understand far more than even the smartest dog should, morphed into her psychopomp self again. She stood guard over me and gave a hair-raising snarl.

Kill, the death blade sang.

He's already dead, I mentally countered. *But I would if I could.*

The Travolta wanna-be shut his yap and floated backward. The now massive dog picked up my scythe by the mouth and flung it at him.

It sailed through the air with such accuracy, Travolta bolted, but the weapon did its thing and sliced cleanly through his semi-transparent form. Ghost lunged, grabbed him by his white-belted waist, and they both vanished.

She returned a moment later, loping back to me with an evil grin. Lips pulled back, her incisors were fully on display, and the scythe in her mouth. While I knew she was delighted with herself, the other ghosts suspected they were next. They fled.

Returning to stand over me, she dripped drool into my face. I wiped it away, the movement sending fresh pain through me, but I gritted my teeth and patted her big head. "Good...dog."

Within minutes, Killion arrived and Ghost returned to her normal size. He rushed from the limo before it came to a full stop, dressed in a tux and looking for the world like he was on his way to a formal celebration. Over the clothes, he supported an expensive trench coat. A wave of his energy came with him, and I was finally able to breathe through the last of the ice still crusted on my lungs.

The scowl on his face when he scanned me from head to toe told me what I'd suspected. While I'd joked about being frozen earlier, now I truly was.

"Blanket," he barked at Moss, the driver. "Can you stand?" he asked me.

The clouds parted and silvery moonlight touched his hair. I wanted to simply take him in, run my fingers through the thick strands. "Not on your life. Can we just...stay here for a minute?" At least my voice didn't shake. "Every time I move, I want to scream."

"I believe it would be best to get you to a safer location."

The softest material ever landed on me. Killion tucked it around my limbs and then shifted his arms under me. "This may hurt."

Ignoring my protests, he lifted and carried me to his vehicle. A "safer" place than a cemetery, in case my necromancy went wacky.

Inside, he continued to cradle me. I stopped protesting, the pain dissipating in the heated car. Ghost jumped in and Moss placed my scythe and backpack on the seat opposite us, then shut the door. I started to mention I couldn't leave Vera's vehicle, but Killion read my mind. *I will send someone to take care of it.*

Our telepathy was one of the benefits of having shared blood with each other. Typically, it freaked me out, but for once, I was grateful for it. Body limp, I lay my head on his chest. *Thank you.*

"Rest," he said. "when you've recovered, you will tell me what happened."

Would I recover? Something inside me felt different, off. I'd seen my friend's spirit. He couldn't be dead, could he? What was the gray mass that had jerked him back into it, and where had it come from? Where had he gone?

The questions pinged around in my brain as the limo sped off into the night.

THREE

K illion's hold tightened around me, drawing me closer. "Without knowing the details, I can only offer a logical guess as to what you experienced." He'd read my thoughts, "heard" my questions. "You were on a corpse road at the stroke of midnight." I stiffened, but it hurt, so I forced my muscles to relax again, bracing myself for what he was about to say. "You experienced a precognitive apparition."

Jackson's words echoed in my head. *Help me...*

The roiling fog, the way it sucked him in...the way my scythe responded to that portal. I hadn't given much thought to the superstition, but my brain was as tired and achy as my body. I fought to keep my heavy lids open. *What does it mean?*

Killion was silent for a moment. He spoke aloud when he responded. "He's not dead yet, but will perish at some point in the calendar year."

I fought against the idea emotionally, but the truth of it resonated inside me.

"There's nothing you can do," Killion reassured me, tucking the blanket under my chin. "Rest, now."

Unable to resist the call of oblivion, I sunk into a deep sleep, cocooned in the vampire's arms.

When I woke, he was carrying me through the lobby of The Beaumont, the sounds of debauchery and music blasting from the hotel's ballroom. Killion owned it, and lived on the top floor.

I felt sick, and a flash of heat flashed up my spine. A reaction to the hundreds of vampires whose energy rippled through the place. My skin itched, and my throat closed up from it.

I attempted to demand that Killion put me down, but my limbs were dead weights, and my vision blurry. No matter how hard I worked at making a sound, it was lost in the constriction of my throat.

Upstairs in his penthouse, a private party waged. A command from him and the reveling vampires, all sequins and satin, disappeared with heads bowed. "Yes, master," they murmured as they made their escape, scathing glances not lost on me.

He placed me gently on a plush sofa facing the fireplace. Flames danced in the hearth and Ghost sunk into a ginormous bed nearby that he'd bought her .

Growing warm in my limbs, I shrugged off the blanket, and then my robes, while the butler, Pennyworth, brought hot cocoa. He'd added real whipped cream, peppermint pieces, and chocolate shavings. Although I was growing too warm, I sucked it down, the rich drink soothing.

Killion removed his coat and unfastened his jacket's buttons, taking a seat in a chair facing me. He eyed my empty cup. "I assume you feel better."

I did, but the heat from the hearth was growing to be too

much. I rose and lurched away. The liquid had managed to loosen my tight larynx. "Hot now."

Killion followed me to the dining area. The entire table was filled with an impressive array of foods. Any other time, I would have grabbed a plate from the sideboard and helped myself, but I wasn't hungry for once. Only thirsty.

The expansive bar displayed punch, hard liquors, and wine. Blood, too, if my nose was accurate about the coppery tang in the air. My stomach flipped. "Water?" I mumbled, none in sight. I peeled off my sweatshirt. "Ice?"

Sweat beaded on my forehead. Like many times before, Pennyworth instantly appeared with my request. I downed the cool liquid with a sigh of relief, and then crunched on a fancy piece of ice in the shape of...a heart. Lovely. "This is crazy," I said, running a cube across my forehead and top lip. It melted instantaneously from the feverishness of my skin. "I feel like I have a virus—full brown influenza-grade."

Killion took the carafe and refilled my glass. His nostrils flared ever so slightly. "I detect no virus in your body. I believe it to be shock. What, or should I ask who, did you see on the corpse road?"

My blood felt as if it were boiling inside my veins. The name stuck in my throat, shooting flames up into my mouth. I downed the water and flew to the patio doors.

Outside, the rise and fall of music and drunken laughter met my ears. I sucked in a deep, cold lungful of air. Even the light of the moon bathed me in a fire-extinguishing mist, the iron railing of the balcony frosty under my fingertips.

Without hesitating, I stripped off my shirt and pants, letting the air and the moon bring relief to my entire system. In nothing but my boy-shorts and sports bra, I was grateful for the plants that vined over and along the banister. While no one was paying attention to the penthouse balcony, and privacy was the least of my worries at the moment, I didn't like being on display.

The atmosphere changed and crackled with electricity as the master vampire came up behind me. I gripped the iron tighter, every cell in my body now on high alert. My blood did not cool, even though the rest of me now registered a more normal temperature.

I didn't dare turn around. Our psychic connection was too strong—I felt what he felt, often saw and experienced what he did.

Right now? He wanted to touch me in the worst way.

His energy washed over me, sunk into every bone, every organ, every vein. I wanted him to.

I wanted to feel alive. Wanted to forget what I'd seen, how scared JR had been. The irony, of course, was that Killion wasn't technically the model of aliveness. He was half human, but his vampire side was Undead. Yet, since he'd entered my world, life had become so much more...

Well, *more.*

More meaningful. More emotional. More everything.

And the vampire wanted me.

If he read my mind, he pretended otherwise. "The friend is someone you care deeply about?"

I glanced at him over my shoulder, not looking directly at him for fear I'd jump his bones, and where would that leave us? My fingers clenched the iron again, just in case. "He's an old friend, and yes, at one time, we were close."

There was a pregnant pause, and I felt him retract his energy. "I see."

Only two words, but a boatload was conveyed in them. It wasn't that his voice changed, nor was there anything telling in his posture or face when I did finally meet his eyes. Neutral—his entire presence was a carefully cultivated neutral. Yet, that in itself spoke volumes to me. "Are you jealous?"

His stance went even more still, if that was possible. Tension coiled from him. He stood there under the moonlight, impeccable in his designer threads, perfect hair, and violet eyes. They were rich purple, and they studied me with total detachment. "Should I be?"

He was trying to hide, forcing himself to stay removed from any emotion. I knew from being around him the past few months that vampires rarely experienced them the way humans did. Since he was part human, his still could get the best of him, but after three hundred years of practice, he was good at concealing any that wanted to surface.

Vampires couldn't afford to feel anything, since they lived for eons, and people, places, and times changed. They were usually loyal to their master and those in their nest. Power plays were the undermining factor in every Undead community, as Killion had recently experienced. Those closest to him were the ones he couldn't afford to trust.

He trusted me. I told myself that's why explaining about JR had caused this reaction, not the attraction I was struggling with. Turning my gaze back to the city, I thought of my childhood friend. "We were friends growing up," I clarified. "From two different classes, though. In middle school, he was too cool for me and his mother influenced him more than ever. We went our separate ways."

He was curiously silent again. For so long in fact, I checked to make sure he was still there. He was, and his eyes told me more. There was something wolfish—or, more appropriately, vampirish—in them.

My core body temperature leveled out, my muscles went languid. I held his smoldering gaze and felt satisfaction when his energy caressed me once more. I opened my mouth to tell him more about the earlier incident, but something else came out. "You look quite dapper tonight." Dapper? Where had that come from? Had I actually ever used that word before? I hung my head. "I mean, you always look nice, but that suit really..." *brings out your eyes.*

His continued stillness was unnerving. He didn't speak as his gaze started at my legs and rose languorously, taking in my shorts, my bare belly, my bra. I held my breath when his focus caught and held on my neck, before he finally met my eyes. The slow perusal made me tingle all over.

In my head I heard his voice. *You are devastating to my senses.*

Every inch of my skin flushed. It took all my willpower not to throw myself at him. *So not going there.* "Boundaries," I grumbled halfheartedly. I forced myself to recall a nightmare to try and scare myself. "No provocative chitchat in my head. You know we're on shaky ground."

His lust for my grim blood was held carefully in check. One slip on either of our parts could screw up everything.

His eyes went black. If he could have shut down any more, I don't know how. With a scorching once-over, he turned on his leather clad heels and stalked inside.

The air around me fell flat. My body temperature plummeted. Gooseflesh rose on my skin. My socked feet were soaked. Counting to ten to calm my heart rate, I dragged myself from the railing and followed him.

He had flopped down into his favorite chair once more, a fresh drink in hand. He loosened his tie. The fact he wouldn't look at me suggested he was brooding.

Snatching up my discarded clothes, I automatically started to apologize. Instead I grit my teeth, shucking off my wet socks and pulling on my shirt and pants in front of him.

Now starving, I went to the dining table and grabbed a plate of food.

Pennyworth appeared and offered a glass of sweet tea. Once I had that, I took it along with my overflowing plate to the couch. Eating in the charged silence wasn't easy, but if he wanted to brood because I didn't want him flirting with me, so be it. I had to keep these boundaries between us. If I didn't, he could end up dead.

"Thank you for coming to get me." I finished off the last of my meal, wiping my hands on a napkin. "I'm sorry I ruined your party."

Apologizing for that was reasonable and seemed like good manners. A flick of his brows was his only response. That and downing the last of his beverage.

Ghost rose from the bed and jumped up beside me. I took a minute to do a search on my phone for JR. After a few more minutes of scanning his social media pages and not finding any obits, I reassured myself he was still alive. "Alrighty, then." I pushed off the sofa. "If you're giving me the cold shoulder, I'll be going. My bed is waiting for me."

My robes were folded neatly on top of my bag near the door. The butler loved to take care of me as well as his master. I knew he'd tucked the scythe inside, its energy a sweet song in my veins.

"Moss will drive you." The vampire hadn't moved, yet I felt him tracking me.

"I'll get a lift from Rafael." My promise not to bother him would have to be broken.

"Take the limo," Killion growled.

"Pardon the interruption, master." Pennyworth emerged from the kitchen. "You asked to be notified if I heard anything from my source about grave robbing."

Killion came to attention, sitting forward and setting down his glass. "Has there been another?"

"Not a robbery. However, I believe what I heard will still be of interest."

I dropped my bag strap over my shoulder. "What is it?"

"A grave has been disturbed, but not by thieves." He held a tablet in his hand and raised the screen for us to see. "A ritual has been performed in St. Joseph's." As we both moved to get a better look, my breath caught at the sight. "A young woman has been murdered."

FOUR

Neither of us said much on the ride to the cemetery. When I asked about Pennyworth's source, Killion replied, "I have many acquaintances in this town. Friends, and those who owe me favors, or seek to stay on my good side. They report to him."

"They listen to police scanners and notify the butler about crimes?"

A shaft of light cut across his face as Moss took the highway north. His features were grim. "Among other things. I have contacts inside the department who, shall we say, pass on items of interest. They consider the grave robberies a nuisance more than anything, but those who have lived as long as I have remember a time when a string of such deeds precluded an epidemic."

"You didn't tell me that."

"Until now, the current robberies bore no resemblance to those. However, if the culprits graduated to human sacrifice for their purposes, we have a much more serious issue at hand."

A chill swept through me. "You think the murder was a sacrifice?"

"We shall see."

The flash of blue lights cut through the tinted windows as we neared St. Joseph's. Police cars lined the road. An ambulance had been called, but the medical technicians slouched next to an unused gurney between them. They chatted and stomped their feet against the cold.

While there were few places Killion's limo couldn't access, the entrance had been taped off and two officers stood duty to keep non-officials out. As we drew near and Moss slowed, turning down a side road, a news van drew the attention of the cops. A dark-haired woman exited, and when blocked, began asking questions and shoving a microphone at one of them, then the other.

Killion waved his hand and a pulse of magic covered the limo, causing it to become invisible. "Pull over up ahead," he instructed Moss.

The driver did so and we idled. The three-foot stone wall around the aging graveyard with its iron fleur-de-lis posts blocked much of our view, but it was the overgrown bushes and draping moss hanging from the skeletal trees that hid the rest.

"We need to get closer." I reached for the door and Ghost bounced on the seat, ready to go.

Killion placed a hand on my arm to stop me. "You cannot simply walk into a crime scene."

"I can if you toss your invisibility cloak around me." I always had a Harry Potter reference to throw out. "Make me invisible."

"You may not like what you see."

From the photo, I knew the up-close-and-personal

would be ten times worse. "I work in a morgue. I'm used to dead people."

"It is not the same as viewing the results of a murder."

He was right, but I couldn't let my squeamish stomach stop me from investigating. "Whether or not this is tied to our assignment, I need to find out who did this and why."

He studied my face, his in shadows. Seemingly resigned, he nodded. "I will accompany you, but you must remain absolutely silent and stay close. The farther you are from me, the harder it will be for me to keep the glamour in place."

"How will I see you?"

"You will hold my hand."

Not the worst thing in the world, and it would be cool to walk around like the Invisible Grim.

Moving as one, he and I exited the backseat. Ghost tried to join us, but I gave her the command to stay.

Killion stepped to the tree line and held out his hand. "Should we become separated, return to the car. Do not proceed on your own."

His skin was cooler than mine, but warmer than the night air. My blood spiked at the contact, the current of our mutual attraction running up my arm and electrifying my heart. I knew he could sense my galloping pulse. As he tugged me closer, our bodies went wavy, then faded out.

A shimmering glow outlined his and I canted my head, examining the silvery light. I couldn't always see magic, but when I could, it never failed to give me pause. His outline hummed and shimmered, and I could have stared at it forever. "You're glowing."

His voice went low, seductive. "As are you."

His fingers intertwined with mine and I saw a gold outline around my hand and wrist. The soft silver of his aura merged with the threads of brilliant gold. "Is that mine?" I'd never seen it before, and I didn't believe I even had magic, per se. My grim powers were...unusual. Not like his or any other supernaturals I'd encountered.

"Beautiful, isn't it?"

It was, but I felt as though it was entirely him creating the artistry. Whether it was his magic or a combo of ours, I lit up inside, happy. I remembered the first time my dad gave me a sparkler on Independence Day. I'd twirled it through the night air and giggled uncontrollably.

My aura twinkled. I was glowing from head to toe. "Whoa." For a breathless moment, I simply stared, bathing in the braided gold and silver threads as they danced together. Blissful waves washed through me and I laughed softly. "This is amazing."

"Coroner's here!"

Startled, I whipped around and unintentionally broke the connection. Instantly, the magical lights disappeared and I became somewhat visible.

"Killion?" I whispered frantically, waving my hands toward his now dimmer outline.

I breathed a sigh of relief when he caught them in his. "I've got you."

We both lit up again. Parts of my anatomy began to warm and I stepped closer, bringing myself within kissing distance.

The master vampire spoke quietly but with iron command. "Do not tease, Chloe."

A part of me liked the fact he lusted after me, yet the other, more rational side was always there to remind me it was my *blood* he desired. If not for that, would he still be attracted to me?

"I just…" My mouth was dry, my heart conflicted. I wasn't only captivated by Killion—I was falling for him.

That was a horrible, terrible, worse than Botox idea.

My parents had taught me to be responsible, dependable, loyal. My feelings for the master vampire made me wild, reckless. I'd seen death in a different way tonight on the corpse road, and it hit me all over again—none of us were guaranteed another day, another sunrise, another breath. If I didn't take what was right in front of me, would I regret it?

Letting my recklessness guide me, I tilted my mouth up, my gaze searching for his lips. I couldn't see the sharp lines of his cheekbones, his square jaw. I couldn't look into his violet eyes or discover what was hiding behind them.

But I sensed what he felt because our blood bond allowed me to—when he willed it. He was doing so now, and the rush nearly made me moan. I ached to kiss him. Was there more than bloodlust to all of this?

A lone, furtive howl went up, eerie in the chilled air. Once again I jumped—the wolf was close. Killion held me firmly so we didn't lose the connection. "Was that…?"

"Yes," he grumbled. "I can smell him."

The wet dog scent hit my nose right before Andy, the shifter I'd harvested and brought back to life, slid into view from behind a magnolia tree in his animal form. His golden eyes flashed as he joined us.

"What are you doing here?" I whispered. The scent of burnt herbs tickled my nose, redolent and familiar. I glanced toward the shadows. "Aurora?"

The air crackled and I saw the twinkling flash when she changed from panther to witch. The blue color of her transfiguration's eyes morphed to her normal green, as she, too, came to stand next to us. "This is bad," she said under her breath, glancing toward the gathering inside the yard.

"Wait, you can see us?"

"Your aura," she clarified, stroking the wolf's mane. He stood as tall as her chest and panted as he scanned the temporary lights and the people moving around the scene. "We heard about it on the scanner. We were patrolling to see if the culprits might still be here, watching."

Killion dropped my hand and allowed our invisibility to fade, drawing the shadows around us instead. "Do you know what happened?"

"I fear it's starting again," she said, almost remotely.

"What is?" My gaze flicked to the shadows around us. "The epidemic?"

"The witch hunt." She met my eyes. "The sacrifices."

"Witch hunt?" I sent my attention to those gathered around the desecrated grave. There was a familiar figure among them, Uncle Morty. "I don't see the victim's ghost hanging around."

"I will move in for a closer look," Killion said. "Stay here."

He became invisible once more, but I could still make out his glow. He easily hopped the low stone barrier and advanced toward the temporary lights.

I moved to a crumbling section of wall and angled my head to get a clearer view. Aurora joined me but our line of sight was blocked by a concrete crypt. Not being as nimble as Killion, I hoisted myself up and sat on the top, the cold of the ancient stones instantly seeping through my pants and into my skin. I brought my knees up and swung my legs around, easing down on the other side near the grave of a woman many decades gone. I crouched, peering around her enormous headstone as Aurora landed beside me.

A layer of crime scene investigators and police blocked my view of the body. Killion's glow moved here and there in a swift dance to avoid running into any of them as he crept close enough to observe. With all eyes on the crime scene, I felt safe venturing to a small mausoleum with an owl statue perched on the top. The blank eyes looked on and his counterpart, nearly as tall as I was, perched beside the crypt's door. Sneaking around the corner, I ducked behind the giant owl and watched the proceedings, catching snatches of conversation.

Officer Pete Rogan, a regular at the coffee shop, blew on his cupped hands. "When can we release the body?"

My uncle Morty stepped out of the perimeter he'd established around the victim and snapped on a pair of latex gloves. "I need to be sure we handle the scene carefully and don't miss anything." He removed a thermometer from his black bag and instructed a tech to get a picture of something on the ground nearby. The woman did so, dropping a numbered yellow marker on the spot. "Could be a while."

"Chloe?" Rogan's partner, Dave Loomis, was staring in my direction.

Busted.

My uncle, layered up in several worn jackets, pivoted and followed the officer's gaze. "Chloe." His tone was less surprised and more disgruntled. "Do I want to know what you're doing here?"

There was no hiding now and I wondered at Loomis' eyesight. Stepping forward, I forced a smile and waved, as if showing up at a cemetery at nearly two in the morning was normal. "Hey. I was out with some friends and saw the lights."

Killion's aura paused and shifted as if he were looking at

me. I could sense his concern and annoyance. I expected a mental lecture, but he remained silent.

"You shouldn't be here," Rogan said.

Uncle Morty stared at me, before glancing at the body. "Actually, I'm glad you're here," he said, motioning me over. "I can use your help."

Quicker than I could breathe, I noticed Killion's aura returning to Aurora and Andy. All three disappeared.

Great.

There was no avoiding my uncle, so I complied, keeping my focus off the victim. "I'm not sure what I can do."

Uncle Morty's expression said he would chastise me later. I'm sure I'd get that from Killion, as well. He rummaged in his black bag and held out a hand. "Glove up."

I chanced a glance at the corpse and my stomach flipped. I staggered backward, but butted up against Rogan and came to a hard stop. The victim was young and female, a look of sheer terror frozen on her face. "I don't know how to..." I motioned at the mutilated woman and held my breath.

"I'll handle the body." My uncle's eyes softened when he cut his attention to her, and I knew he was saying a silent prayer. "You assist. That's all."

"What about Mary Lynn?"

The morgue attendant helped my uncle with identifications and autopsies. "She's an inebriated mess. You're filling in."

Stomach queasy, I accepted the gloves and swallowed hard. "Any idea what happened?"

His eyes were sad when they met mine. "We stick to the facts the body gives us. No theorizing or conjecture, no guessing. Got it?"

The sign he'd hung in the morgue flashed through my mind.

We speak for the dead. Respect and honor them.

Stick to the facts, and do not suppose you know what their life was like.

In the end, we are all the same – none of us gets out of this world alive.

This was how we did business. We had to stay detached, yet show compassion and kindness to every person who ended up in our care.

He didn't wait for my reply. Handing me a tablet with "Unknown Female" and the date listed at the top he started his initial examination.

He instructed me to enter the location and time, then rattled off a description of the body, approximate height and weight to be confirmed at the autopsy, and used his temperature gauge. "Time of death is between one and two hours ago."

Midnight. Shivers ran down my spine, the memory of the corpse road experience still vivid. Keeping my eyes on the screen, I entered the details as he continued to circle the body and examine it. The woman had sigils carved into her forehead, palms, and soles of her feet. She was naked, except for the layer of blood covering her from a central wound. There seemed to be a circle carved into her belly.

Were those letters inside it? Against my better instincts, my curiosity won out and I leaned forward to examine her more closely.

Aurora was right. As I stared at the gory display, the message became clear: W-I-T-C-H.

It appeared someone was, indeed, on the hunt.

FIVE

"Tell me about the witch hunts."

Aurora stared at me groggily from inside her secret lair.

That's what I'd started calling her home, hidden away inside a mausoleum in the Evil Eye graveyard on the outskirts of town.

She blinked and yawned, obviously woken from her bed. "It's four a.m."

I pushed through the door. I'd been at the morgue with Uncle Morty until he'd gotten Randy Jarvis, a hospital tech with a healthy interest in me, to take my place. My uncle had sent me home in a cab he'd put on the hospital's tab, but even after a shower and Killion assuring me Ghost and my raven, Corvus, were safe with him, I couldn't sleep.

Figured. The first time in months that I'd had the bed all to myself, and my body, brain, and gag reflex were overloaded. Mr. Sandman refused to bring me anything more than horrible memories of our witchy Jane Doe, whose body kept flickering across the backs of my eyelids each time I closed them.

"How can you sleep?" Plunking down on my favorite stool at her large workstation, I rubbed my eyes. "Someone is hunting your kind."

Moving like a slug, she stopped on the other side of the counter. "Someone always is." Putting the kettle on to heat, she produced several ceramic jars of dried herbs. "My apologies about the disappearing act earlier. The vampire and I thought it wise to stay out of the fray."

"He told me." The cops would have been suspicious and latched onto them for questioning if they'd showed themselves. "Why would our grave robbers up their game to murder?"

"People have disturbed the dead for various reasons throughout history." She gathered two mismatched cups. Her black cat eyed us lazily from its perch near the hearth. "Stealing jewelry or artifacts, using the cadavers, or parts thereof, for study—no longer necessary for actual medical students these days—and in the magical world, corpses have been dug up by their enemies to curse them, or to harvest specific organs and rituals. Even to eat."

"Gross!" I hadn't even had any of her awful tea, and I already felt sick. "They're embalmed."

"Not all are, and the last wave of disturbances and killings took place ninety-nine years ago. It was less common then."

"Killion mentioned sacrifices, but you said they were witch hunts. Our Jane Doe had the word 'witch' engraved on her torso."

"Killion told me."

"Up to now, our robbers have stolen a few necklaces from the gravesites, but none have killed for them. Why her, and why now? Was she just in the wrong place at the wrong time? Maybe interrupted them while they were working?

Are they using her as a diversion to throw the cops off? Or is her murder completely separate?"

"You've been mainlining coffee again, haven't you?" She yawned again and took the kettle off the burner, pouring steaming water into the cups. "In answer to all of that—I don't know."

Had I ever heard that out of her mouth before? "Don't you have some ancient book or a spirit you can ask?"

She ignored me, returning the kettle to the stove.

"Did you recognize her? Is she for real a witch?"

"I didn't get a good look at her face, so I'm not sure."

This was getting me nowhere. Pulling out my cell, I brought up the woman's autopsy headshot. I hated having it, but if it helped me figure out who she was, I'd push past the 'eww' factor. I showed it to my friend. "What do you think? Look familiar?"

Her glance was brief before she looked away. "I know most magic practitioners in the area, but there are some who keep to themselves. I don't know her. She may not belong to a coven, or she didn't openly display signs she practiced."

Accepting one of the mugs, I blew gently on the liquid, buying time before I had to taste it. Surprisingly, it smelled good—mint and roses. I might be able to stomach it. "Let's assume, whether she was a witch or not, that they purposely killed her. Could she have been a sacrifice?"

She sipped her tea. "Sure, but to carve the word on her seems more like a warning." My questioning brow spurred her on. "When the epidemic hit all those years ago, there were witches under suspicion of stealing from the dead— organs and other organic material they used in spellwork. From what I know, most of those in this area avoid such castings. They always have. But there are some who will leave their home territory and go elsewhere to retrieve what they need. However, that was a dark time in our town's history and the church hyped up the great desecration to rouse fear in our citizens. Vigilante justice took hold and anyone who looked or acted even a bit different was seen as a threat. People died from the epidemic, innocent witches, too."

The sadness in her voice suggested she had lost someone dear. While she appeared my age, I knew she'd lived far longer, and had possibly seen as much as Killion.

"I'm sorry," I said, giving her a moment. She fiddled with her jars. When she was done and had returned to her drink, I delved deeper. "Who was it? A fellow witch?"

She seemed to steady herself with a deep breath. "My grandmother."

Oh, jeez. Reaching for her hand, I squeezed it. "If she was anything like you, I bet she was a real badass."

This brought a fleeting smile. "She was, but she had nothing to do with the robberies. She was the gentlest, kindest person you could know. Made salves and lotions to help folks. She had the sight, and knew they were coming for her because of it. She decided to take the blame, hoping the hunters would believe she was working alone. She thought she could spare others from the horrible killings. Unfortunately, the fear mongers got a taste for it. Her sacrifice was for nothing."

"She was incredibly brave."

Aurora stared into the liquid in her cup, a million miles away. "The grave where the body was found...that was hers. It's a message. I owe it to her memory to stop this before the huntings get out of control again."

My heart ached for her. If the person or persons responsible had purposely killed tonight and left the woman at her grandmother's burial site, was it someone who remembered the previous witch huntings? "What you need to do is stay safe. Let me and Killion handle this."

Her eyes snapped to mine. Determination fired in them. "I'm helping—don't try to push me out. You need me."

"I do, but you can't help me if you're dead."

Her expression turned cunning. "You have the power to bring me back, Grim Zero."

"Sure, if you want to stay in panther form." I sipped my tea and shook my head. "Don't even go there. You're not using our friendship as an excuse to take unnecessary risks. They're hunting witches, not grims or vampires. If you promise to stay here, I promise to share everything we uncover, and seek your advice. Okay?"

Her features hardened. "I don't take orders from you."

Andy had groused repeatedly about her stubbornness. This was a battle I couldn't win. If I let her work with us, I could lose her to these killers. If I didn't, she'd go off on her own and get killed anyway.

On the other hand, she was smart, resourceful, and one extremely powerful magic worker. She hadn't survived without being shrewd and wise. "It's not an order, it's a plea. You're my friend and mentor. I just found you, and I can't take a chance I'll lose you."

"Playing the friend card. That's low."

"You played the Grim Zero one. We're even."

Her sigh was dramatic. So much so, even the cat cracked open a hooded lid to eye her before resuming his sleep. "I can't sit on the sidelines, Chloe, and don't act like you would if the situation were reversed. Neither of us is a fainting wallflower. We kick magical butt and bring justice where there is none."

I gripped my cup, digging for patience. "You're making

this hard for me. How can I focus on bringing justice if I'm worried about you being sacrificed?"

She swept around the table and took my hands in hers. "You are the first real friend I've had in years. I worry about you every day. But I've seen what you can do. I believe in you. You can protect yourself, and I'm the same. I'm no martyr like my grandmother. I *will* use caution."

Compelled to give in—not by any magic, but common sense—I relented. "Can you spread the word among the local covens and warn them to be on alert? I don't want to incite panic, but they need to be on guard until we stop whoever is behind this."

Returning to her side of the counter, she withdrew her cell from a pocket in her robe. "I'll send a blue code to the heads of the covens and explain the situation." Her fingers flew over the keyboard.

"Blue code?"

"It's a warning that the police are looking into a homicide that may involve a witch. I'll be sure to explain our suspicions. Go home, Chloe. There's nothing for you to do for now."

"Can't you peer into a crystal ball and tell me who killed that girl?"

She gave me a *really?* look. "Let's regroup later today, okay?"

My limbs didn't want to move. I wished I could crawl over to the hearth and sleep next to the cat. "Don't do anything, or leave the sanctuary, without me, promise?"

Her eyes were serious as they met mine. "I—"

Before she could finish, an explosion rocked the cemetery.

SIX

The ground shook. Aurora grabbed the counter and I went sideways, the stool toppling.

"What the...?" The cups chattered and she grabbed them before they fell to the floor, but one of the jars did, busting into a dozen pieces and scattering its contents.

I gained my feet, untangling an ankle from the rungs of the stool. Under us the ground vibrated and shifted, and I clutched the edge of the wooden counter. "Earthquake?"

"Seismic activity here is rare and always of low magnitude."

I'd never experienced one, but what else could it be? A cup jumped and sent liquid splashing over her hand. Bits of plaster rained down from the ceiling. I turned toward the entrance.

"This place could come down on us." I pointed at the door. "We need to get out of here."

"Nothing can destroy my wards." Her face was fierce, but scared. "This room will hold."

"Good. Stay here." I pushed away from the worktable and did a dance toward the door.

"Where are you going?" she yelled.

Particles from the ceiling fell in my eyes and I blinked, trying to clear my vision. Hands splayed, I wobbled one way and then the other. "I'm going to see what's happening."

The exit was only a few feet farther. The cat was there, scratching frantically at the exit and leaving marks in the wood.

"Wait for me," Aurora called.

How long did an earthquake last? It seemed this one would never end. "Stay there!" If this was abnormal, it meant magic was involved. "Somebody could be out here."

The heavy door groaned when I pulled on it. The hinges were always sticky, the weight a challenge to move. With barely three inches of opening, the cat shot out like its tail was on fire, squeezing through with a meow of terror.

I grunted and yanked harder, dragging it enough I could squeeze through myself. The rumbling grew louder in the outer area of the large crypt. The stone walls groaned and creaked and dust filtered from the ceiling.

This anteroom was lit by a single sconce. I put my back against a wall and used it for support as I slid my way around the chamber to the exterior door.

The concrete caskets nearby shifted and rolled. With her magic, Aurora had used them to provide a barrier to her inner sanctum, in case someone managed to get past her wards outside. The monstrosities pinged around like pinball paddles. I didn't want to be the ball.

The cat had disappeared and I wondered if he had a secret way in and out. The exterior door yielded more easily, and throwing my weight into it, I fell through the opening and into the night of the graveyard.

The shaking and noise immediately ceased, leaving a hollow ringing in my ears. The earth felt solid under my feet, although my equilibrium was still off, and I grazed a headstone and went down on one knee.

"There you are," a deep voice with a rich Australian accent said. "Figured you were with the witch."

Aurora emerged and rushed to my side. With her help, I got to my feet and brushed frosted dead grass from my pant leg. "You created an earthquake to get me out here?"

Death, in his extremely tall and buff human form, gave a bemused smile. "I'm certainly not entering the witch's hiding place."

Aurora's hands went to her hips. Color rose in her cheeks. "This witch has a name, and you mean you brought Chloe out here because you *can't* enter my home."

His eyes glinted, even though there was no moonlight to reflect in them. Clouds hung low in the night sky, seemingly ready to rain thunder and lightning at his command. With a final glare at the witch, he purposely turned to me and motioned to the man next to him. "Meet your new necromancy teacher, Neymar Stormfinger."

"My what?"

The lanky guy wore a bowler hat, long coat, slacks, and shoes, all in black. A thin mustache quivered over his lips as he scanned me from head to foot. "You're sure she's worth training?" he asked.

"Pompous much?" I stepped forward. "I don't need a teacher. What I need is to get rid of the necromancy."

Aurora linked her arm in mine. "And I'm helping her with that."

"She's wearing my amulet," Death countered. "That's what is controlling it."

Stormfinger sniffed, eyeing my throat as if searching for the necklace. "Clever. And it works?"

"Of course, it works." Death glowered at him. "It's mine."

A nod. "The witch has the gift?"

My boss looked bored. "Yes, but she is of no concern."

"Now, wait a minute," I said.

At the same time, Aurora threw out her hands. "Is that so? Let me tell you who's of no concern!"

The ground began to tremble again, but it was concentrated at the section surrounding us. I felt the dead shifting in their graves, calling to me.

If I didn't do something—and quick—this showdown was going to raise a bunch of zombies.

I grabbed her hands and lowered them. "They're not worth it," I whispered. "Let the dead rest. We have more important things to focus on."

The ground stopped. She lowered her hands, giving me a disappointed glare.

"Ready?" Death asked me. "Time's a-wastin'."

I held onto Aurora, more so I didn't raise a few corpses than to chase him away. "For what?"

A breeze of irritation teased at strands of his blond hair. "Training. Are you even paying attention, Chloe?"

My grip tightened. "I don't have time. Aren't you listening? I'm investigating a murder."

"I don't recall that being part of your assignment." He scanned me from top to bottom. "There was quite a disturbance in the soul timeline earlier tonight. Had your fingerprints all over it. Were you trying to save one of your friends again? Did you forget our deal already?"

Killion—Death held his Undead life over me like a bolt of lightning ready to strike. If I reneged on our deal, the vampire's soul contract was forfeit. "I haven't forgotten anything, and I certainly haven't tried to save anyone." The memory of JR rushed back to me. "Are you talking about what happened at midnight?"

"He certainly isn't concerned about a dead witch," Aurora grumbled.

Death glared down his nose at us. "So you *were* the cause. What exactly did happen?"

"I didn't do anything, I simply saw a portent. Someone who is supposed to die this year." His focused attention zapped me right down to my toes. He would love nothing more than to rescind his deal and force me to reap the vampire. "I swear."

"You saw a soul who hasn't died yet?" Aurora's face paled. "You were on a corpse road?"

"I was investigating the robberies and it just sort of happened."

Everyone looked at me like I'd started Armageddon. Death loomed, invading my personal space. "And you tried to intervene, didn't you?"

"I told you, I didn't." I stood my ground, regardless of the fact I would definitely have attempted to save JR if it had been possible. Not to spite my boss, but because it was my natural instinct to help people. I had no idea what was happening to my old friend, nor why everyone was so freaked out about it. "His soul was caught in some in-between place. He seemed terrified."

Death tilted his head, his supernatural eyes continuing to bore into me. "Your scythe crossed the void."

Was that an answer or an accusation? "What are you getting at?"

"Is she daft?" Stormfinger asked, then gave me a perplexed expression. "Why would you split the void with your reaper's blade?"

"Holy hexes," Aurora whispered. "Did you do that, Chloe?"

I flicked a glance at her. "There was this swirling fog. I didn't know what it was, so I used the blade to sort of...poke it. That's all."

A tension-filled silence descended as all three gaped at me.

My breath clouded in the air, a different kind of cold spreading through my body. "What's the big deal?"

"Why were you carrying your scythe?" Death asked. "You're on probation, prohibited from reaping anyone until your last assignment has been reviewed."

"You think I'm going to spend New Year's Eve in a graveyard hunting criminals without it?"

"You had your stun gun," he countered.

And how did he know that? "It doesn't work on ghosts."

Stormfinger rocked on his heels and shook his head. "You warned me she was a rule breaker, but you left out that she was also a moron."

"Shut up," I said to him, and then to Death, "I don't know what the problem is. I haven't seen my friend in years, and I did nothing to interfere with whatever is going on with his soul." It wasn't a total lie. Yes, I had tried to keep him from the grabby fog fingers, but it hadn't worked. "If you don't like the fact I carried my scythe to the cemetery, fire me and find another grim you can bully." I grabbed Aurora's arm and turned us toward the safety of her place. "In the meantime, whether I'm employed by SMG or not, I have a murder to investigate."

Marching to the lair, I dragged my friend through the door and slammed it.

SEVEN

I wanted to discuss the witch hunts, but Aurora insisted on hearing about JR. She kept quiet during the story, asking a few questions, but mostly just looking distressed.

"Sounds like you were exposed to a timeline fracture," she said, flipping through pages of one of her ancient volumes of books. This one had the distinct look of a grimoire. "That would explain the extreme reaction you experienced afterwards."

My mint-rose tea was gone, my eyelids felt as heavy as weights. "I don't understand what you just said, and I'm not sure I have enough brainpower to handle anything more."

She bundled me in a blanket, and as the sun came peeking through her skylights, put me on her couch. I fell into a deep sleep and only woke a while later when she waved coffee under my nose.

Blinking and rubbing my eyes, I untangled my legs from the soft cotton. Coming out of such a heavy exhaustion made my movements slow. It took a minute for me to remember why I was at her place.

She cupped my hands around the coffee, then handed me a piece of toast. "Time to go. Your ride is here."

I sucked down the liquid and made a face. Chicory. "Blech." Handing it back to her, I took three bites of toast, ravenous. "You messaged Rafael?"

My boots were near the hearth and she brought them over. "Happy New Year."

Like a sudden summer downpour, the previous night's events came back in a rush. I could barely feel my legs and my fingers didn't want to work well. "Did you drug my tea?"

She traded me the boots for the half-eaten toast, plucking the cup away as well. "You were exhausted after what happened. You needed sleep."

I continued to throw questions at her, and she dodged each and every one of them while helping me with my coat. Once that was on, she handed me the rest of my food, then slid my backpack over my shoulder and shoved me toward the door. "Everything I could find on the witch hunts is in here." She patted the bag. "I'll query the covens today and let you know if I learn anything." She wiggled her fingers and the heavy door opened easily. Sunshine streamed through the overhead skylight and made the fine lines around her eyes and mouth appear deeper. "Stay away from that sorcerer."

"Who?"

"The man with Death." She handed me the toast. "He's a soul dealer."

I'd been called something similar. "Like me?" I still didn't understand.

"He's *nothing* like you." She pushed me into the front chamber of the crypt and shut the door behind me. When I glanced back, a line of sparkling magic had sealed off the entrance.

What the devil was that all about? Muttering to myself, I shook my head and shivered under my coat.

The winter sunlight blinded me as I emerged from the shadowed interior. The air was warmer than the previous day, and the frost had melted. I shaded my eyes and took the narrow path to the gate, the synopses in my brain beginning to fire in the clear, fresh air.

My body felt lethargic and I had no idea the time. As I walked, I pulled out my phone and checked. Noon. Twelve hours since I'd seen JR's ghost...or rather, *future* ghost. I was still unclear how it all worked. *A timeline fracture?* Is that what she'd said?

His apparition had known me, had begged for my help. Yet, according to my research, he was still alive and well. Had I actually seen the future? If so, how was he going to die?

My heart was heavy as I trudged to the iron gate, ignoring the ghosts who were part of Aurora's camouflage. JR had always been so vibrant. He'd had much to offer the world.

A loud bark shook me from my thoughts and I glanced up to see Ghost rushing to greet me. I kneeled down and she leaped into my arms, managing to snag the last bit of toast, which she put away in a single gulp before licking my face. "Hey you," I said, laughing. "How did you get here?"

She bounced away and I stood, watching her dash up the path toward the open gate. A limo idled at the curb.

My pulse picked up and so did my stride. Killion leaned against the black vehicle, one ankle crossed over the other, and a white to-go cup from The Smoking Bean in hand. His jet black hair seemed to suck up the sunshine, and he wore dark, reflective sunglasses.

I licked my lips.

I told myself my rush to get to him was because of the coffee, not my sudden need to touch him.

What a lie.

Fingers clenched so I wouldn't grab him and kiss him, I forced my footsteps to slow. This...whatever it was...was getting out of hand, and I didn't know what to do about it.

If it weren't for the nightmares, I would have already made a fool of myself.

Once I cleared the entrance, laughing at Ghost's antics, he held out the magic elixir. "Your favorite. Nita made it just the way you like it."

The first taste of the caramel mocha latte nearly made me swoon. "You're my hero."

The corner of his mouth twitched. "Setting the bar high, I see."

In the lenses, my own reflection stared back at me. "Actually, I am." I downed more sugar and caffeine, then surprised him by giving him a hug.

For a heartbeat, he did nothing. A statue. I upped the ante and laid my head on his shoulder.

It worked, one of his arms wrapping around me, his hand slipping down my spine to rest on my lower back.

Everything in me exploded, and I bit my bottom lip to keep from purring. Or maybe moaning. Both wanted to come out.

If only we were a *normal* couple.

Ghost danced at our feet and barked. Killion kept his hand where it was, but I sensed a change in his body. He'd read my mind. "To what do I owe this display of affection? Bringing you coffee hardly seems worthy of your heart."

He said it with an off-handed tone, but I suspected he really wanted to know.

"I'm not taking you for granted." Leaning against him was a relief. He was steady, secure, and well...safe.

I heard him laugh in my head. *I'm a dangerous master vampire.*

I mentally scoffed and hugged him tighter. I could not risk losing him. JR had been a good friend long ago, but as my boss kept telling me, I couldn't save everyone. The contract was the contract—people had to die when their time was up. "Thank you for always taking care of me."

Gently, he peeled me off his chest and lifted his sunglasses. "Are you unwell?" He removed a leather glove and laid the back of his hand on my forehead. "What did Aurora do to you?"

I playfully smacked his hand away. "I mean it. Life is unpredictable, even for a vampire."

His steady gaze held mine. "It is that." Something ancient and mysterious burned in that look. It was gone before I could breathe, yet I held onto the sensations it sent spiraling through me. He opened the car door. "Shall we get to work?"

Ghost jumped in and I followed. Neither the hotel nor my apartment was where we landed. Instead, Moss drove into the parking lot behind the vet clinic.

"What are we doing here?" I asked.

"You open next week. There's much to accomplish."

"We're working the grave robberies, and that murderer—"

"Will still be there after our afternoon spent preparing for the grand opening."

"I thought we were training at three."

"Let's see how much we get done here first."

The interior smelled of fresh paint. Boxes of supplies were stacked on the floor awaiting unpacking. Ghost sniffed at everything, and I wandered through the backroom and the kennel area, the surgery suite and check-up rooms. Someone had been busy sprucing the place up, and I thanked Killion. He gave me a smile and a nod. While I knew he hadn't done all this himself, I was grateful he'd had his minions or whoever do it.

As I let the truth of it sink in—the place was truly mine—I smiled at the memories of spending so much of my childhood here with my parents.

Killion shed his coat and rolled up his sleeves. Together, we inventoried and organized the supplies, making sure each exam room was well stocked.

Soon, I was out of coffee and my toast had deserted me. Moss brought lunch prepared by Pennyworth, and I coached him and Killion into rearranging the waiting room furniture.

At three, I heard a knock on the front door. We were in the back, updating the software for the lab and x-ray machines. "Who could that be?" I asked.

"An interview I arranged." Killion brushed off his hands. "Dr. O'Leary looked over this man's résumé and determined he would be a good candidate for our second veterinarian. You have final say, of course."

I followed him to the waiting room, Ghost on my heels. Dr. O'Leary would be our lead vet, and we had three techs lined up, including Andy who would work the evening and night shifts. I still needed office staff to answer phones, make appointments, and order supplies. I would float between working the counter and helping with patients, but I needed to get serious about filling the gaps in my employees.

Killion's body blocked the glass door as he unlocked it to

let our applicant in. "Welcome," he said. "Glad you could make it."

The man was backlit. The two shook hands. I wanted our second vet to be female, simply because I'd witnessed many animals being frightened of men. Already predisposed to that, I tried to hide my disappointment. Dr. O'Leary knew his stuff—if he felt this was the right veterinarian for us, I needed to give the guy a chance.

"I'm Killion." The master vampire moved aside and motioned at me. "And this is Chloe, the owner."

My mouth fell open and I froze, not believing my eyes.

"Chloe bear." JR Banks grabbed me and drew me into a tight hug. "It's so good to see you."

EIGHT

"JR?" It came out strangled, my face pressed into his shoulder. Pushing back did little good, his embrace crushing. I managed to get my head up, however. "What on earth…?"

He held on tight and buried his nose in my hair. "I've missed you."

Over his shoulder, I spotted Killion, who'd gone still as a statue. His violet irises turned red and his upper lip trembled.

Oh boy.

Guess he hadn't planned on us knowing each other. I'd never told him JR's name.

My old friend lifted me off the floor and laughed. I couldn't breathe in his vise grip.

The tips of Killion's fangs peeked out.

Double on the *oh, boy.*

Ghost danced on her rear legs and whined, wanting to join in.

Patting JR's shoulder when he lowered me to the ground, I

pried myself loose. His palms slid down my arms when I took a significant step back. He caught my hands, keeping me from going too far. "I can't believe you're reopening the clinic," he said. "Look at you. All grown up and filling your dad's shoes."

I broke free from his grasp with some effort and picked up the dog. "I didn't realize you were back in town. What are you doing here?"

"Applying for the job." He gave me a big smile—the one filled with charm that had suckered Dante's Grove women from five to eighty-five. His blue eyes sparkled. "It's time I came home."

There was nothing in his face suggesting he remembered our encounter the previous night. Although relieved about that, I was nevertheless concerned. He was in serious peril, especially from the vampire behind him. Killion whipped around, staring out the window rather than at the two of us. His magic was all kinds of protective as it flowed around me.

"Your parents must be thrilled," I said, trying not to twitch from it.

JR scratched Ghost's ears, the smile fading. "Mom's sick. Cancer. Early stages, but we don't know if the treatment will... She's been taking care of everyone else all these years, and now she needs help. Dad can't do it all."

For a brief second, I thought I saw a worm-like shadow flow around his chest, but when I blinked it was gone. The memory of the fog fingers surfaced and I cleared my throat. "I'm sorry. I had no idea."

He put on a brave smile, but sadness clung to his eyes. "You never did climb on the town gossip train." Fishing in his coat, he removed an envelope and handed it to me. "A hard copy of my resume. I've worked for my uncle on his horse ranch for the past two years. He and my aunt have the rescue, remember?"

He started to glance over his shoulder and I caught his hand, keeping his focus on me. Accepting the envelope, I tried to think of what to say. "That must have been interesting. Did you enjoy it?"

"Absolutely. Horses are marvelous creatures, but I've always thought a small animal practice suits me better." He chucked Ghost's chin. "When I saw the posting, I jumped on it. It's like it's meant to be, right? I hope you'll consider me for the position."

He winked, as if it were already in the bag.

Killion strode past us, keeping his face turned away. "Chloe, may I speak to you in the other room?"

"Of course." I handed the dog to JR. "Feel free to look around. I haven't cleaned the office yet, but the exam rooms are nearly ready."

Ghost promptly licked his nose and he chuckled. "Take your time. And, hey?" I paused and glanced back. "Maybe we can have dinner tonight? Catch up?"

Killion heard the offer, of course, and his magic raged around me, making the hair on my arms tingle. I raised a finger. "Hold that thought."

The master vampire waited for me in the storeroom. His hands were braced against a shelf of bandages, his focus on the floor at his feet. "Is that the man whose spirit you saw on the corpse road?"

"Reading my mind again?" When he didn't respond, I leaned on the wall next to the doorframe. "It is."

His voice was a growl. "For someone you haven't seen in years, you are exceedingly affectionate. I suspect I know how he will die."

I chuckled. Yep, I knew exactly what he was suggesting,

but I couldn't help myself. I played dumb and asked in an innocent voice, "You do?"

Before I could blink, he was in front of me, his irises a deep amethyst. His fangs were still on display and my blood surged.

"Yes." His gaze went to my mouth and he placed his hands on each side of my head. "Because if he touches you again, I will kill him."

He lowered his mouth to mine, the kiss swift and deep. His tongue pushed past my lips, stealing my breath.

One kiss and I was ready to melt. He broke away, a question in his eyes. He must have read my answer and he descended on me again, all the while keeping his hands on the wall.

Our lips and tongues danced, his mouth teasing mine with the sweetest, yet most demanding, of kisses. He licked into my mouth, ran the tips of his fangs over my sensitive lips.

I moaned.

The rest of his body stayed agonizingly far away, and I knew he wanted me to feel free to stop him.

I didn't want to. All I could do was revel in the feel of him as I snaked my arms around his neck, drawing him closer.

His body slid against mine, and it was heaven. He was solid and real under my hands. I wanted more. *So much more.*

"Sure is great to be back," JR called from the hall.

Abruptly, Killion stopped, leaving me breathless as he stepped back. His eyes were deep pools of lust.

He raked a hand through his hair, making it spike. Spinning around, he shook his head, voice so quiet, I almost didn't hear him. "Well, that was...uncalled for."

Uncalled for? It took several tries to get enough oxygen into my lungs. Peeling myself off the wall, legs trembling, I felt like a junkie who'd been denied her fix. I touched my tingling lips. He had more willpower than I did. "What is going on with you?" I could barely get the words out. "With us?"

Continuing to face away from me, he put his hands on his hips and stared at the floor once more. "I didn't..." He huffed out a sigh. "I hate the way he looked at you. The way he assumed he could embrace you in such a way. He *sniffed* your hair."

"You're protective of me. I get it."

"It is far more than that."

The tingling spread from my lips down my body. I touched his broad back. "Because of my blood. Your reaction is due to that. Totally normal, right?"

He stilled under my hand, head still bowed. "Nothing about this is normal, and as I said, my reaction is due to... I can't... It is more than being protective of you. I was—*am* —jealous."

"Good." I tried to lighten the moment by poking his side. It was like hitting a steel wall. "It's hard to deny the CFE."

A pause. "Sorry?"

"The Chloe Frost Effect. Surely, you've heard of it?"

My usual snark sounded a lot like Death's.

Killion shifted, his serious gaze flicking to me. "You've made it clear you have boundaries. I overstepped."

"You sure did." I moved to face him fully. "And I sure hope you do it again."

NINE

I grinned, and he narrowed his eyes. In the next instant, he tugged me to him and I emitted a tiny squeak. His eyes bored into mine. "This pleases you?"

Anticipation raced through me. "Shut up and kiss me."

He carried me to the wall and pinned me there. My pulse skyrocketed. With his hard body pressing into mine, I wound my arms around his neck, lifting my lips to tease his this time.

Down, down, down, I fell into his intoxicating scent, his hands, his body. He braced my hips in place, and I happily wrapped my legs around his waist.

His kiss was hard and unrelenting. Held suspended, I stopped thinking and let myself drown in his possessiveness, his strength, his magic.

I licked my tongue over his bottom lip, brushed it across the tips of his fangs. He growled low and deep again and the electricity between us crackled in the air. An insistent ache set up between my legs.

From some distant place, I heard the door open, hinges

squeaking. "I can clean up the office—Oh, whoops. Sorry" It was JR. "I didn't realize—"

Killion reached over and slammed the door in his face.

Unfortunately, the air went out of our stolen moment. The vampire released me slowly, setting me on my feet. Heat scorched my cheeks—not at being caught, but by the realization I'd just crossed a precarious line and there was no going back.

I felt exhilarated. "Well, that was...um, amazing." I fiddled with my shirt, then his. "I should probably go talk to him, right?"

Smugness covered his face. "It's your clinic."

I smoothed down my hair. "Right. Looks like I may need to hire someone else, though."

He raked his gaze over me and my body screamed for him. "I believe I have marked you sufficiently. If you wish to hire him, there will be no issues."

Something behind his eyes had changed. I'd seen that look before in supernatural alphas—both male and female. "Marked me?" He had, and there was no denying it. My skin, my body, my blood—I burned for him, and only him.

What had I gotten myself into? I pointed a finger at his nose. "Stay here, fang boy."

He snickered. "I promise to behave."

Out in the lobby, JR played with Ghost. Seeing me, he rubbed the back of his neck and looked contrite, and was smart enough not to bring up what he'd witnessed. "The place looks great. Your parents would be proud."

I tossed the end of my braid over my shoulder. "Thanks. I'll review your resume with our head vet and let you know about the position in the next few days."

He would be a great addition to my staff, and if I kept him close, I might be able to figure out why he was going to die. If I let him go, he'd still be in town but I wouldn't be able to keep a close eye on him.

Pointless. I had a deal with Death. I couldn't interfere.

He went to hug me, then seemed to think better of it. He turned for the door. "It could be like old times," he said, that sadness in his eyes again. Sunlight shone on his wheat-colored hair. "The two of us saving animals."

All I could do was nod. Once the door closed behind him, I locked it, and blew out the breath I'd been holding. Ghost jumped into the display window, watching him walk to his truck. She whined and wagged her tail, glancing at me with a question in her brown eyes.

"Don't fall in love with him," I scolded. "He's going to die this year."

She whined again and I left her there, needing to clear my head. JR. Killion. My deal with Death. Last night's murder. All of it swirled in my mind. I retreated to the one place I hadn't touched yet—my parents' shared office.

The distraction soothed me. As I opened the door and peeked in, the scent of old books and metal file cabinets teased my nose. The single window across the room let in a beam of peach light and I wandered to their matching desks which faced each other.

The computers were gone, but mom's spot had a pile of papers and a picture of me. Dad's had a ceramic dog I'd painted for him in fourth grade art class. A layer of dust clung to all of it and I traced my fingers along the back of his chair, remembering the times he'd set me in it and wheeled me around the place after hours.

A row of black file cabinets sat undisturbed, and my parents' diplomas and certificates hung on the paneled walls. It was like stepping back in time and I brushed at the wetness that burned in my eyes.

Killion found me sitting on the striped couch Dad had napped on when he stayed overnight to watch patients. I had the pillow to my nose, the hint of his aftershave making me tear up all over again. "I know I have to tackle this room, but I need a minute to remember them before I change anything."

He sat in the dilapidated striped chair next to the sofa. "Take all the time you need."

"We were happy," I mused. "*They* were happy. Both of them worked too much, but it was their passion. Sometimes, I felt jealous of how much they loved it here, but a part of me knew I was the same. Saving animals is what I do."

"Not only animals, as I recall you once stating quite emphatically." The corner of his mouth quirked. "There was something about nectar of the gods?"

After the intensity of the make out session, it was good to simply be friends again. I always claimed coffee saved lives, and my work at The Bean was important. In all honesty, there *was* the fact I'd given Vera more years on her contract and convinced Death to bring Megan O'Leary back to life. I'd prevented her father's death, as well.

I'd even saved the vampire. I slid the pillow to cover my face, peeking at Killion over the edge. *Bite the bullet, not the vampire,* I told myself.

As if he read where my thoughts were going, he said, "About earlier."

"I don't want to be a vampire," I blurted.

The laugh started low, then built into great guffaws. At first I smiled at the rareness of it, the sound warm and infusing me with joy. When it didn't stop, I sat up straighter. "What's so funny?"

He wiped his eyes and bent forward, as though catching

his breath. Being half human, he did breathe at times. "You would *suck* at being one."

I hit him with the pillow. "Did you just make a pun?"

That started him laughing all over again. I jumped up and began pummeling him. "Why would I be bad at it?" *Smack.* "Is it my lack of fashion sense?" *Smack.* "My clumsiness?"

He grabbed my wrists to halt the attack, and gently tugged me down into his lap. I didn't resist, now laughing, too. He brushed strands of hair from my eyes. "You're squeamish about blood. I can't imagine you consuming it."

I made a face. I truly couldn't stand the idea.

"And the Undead are not in the habit of saving humans."

True. I sighed deeply. "I can't save JR."

He cupped my chin. "Sure you can."

"How?"

"You're quite skilled at manipulating Death. It's why I'm still here. You can do it again."

I kissed the end of his nose, his brow soft under my finger as I stroked it. "Not if it means losing you." Conflicted about where we were headed, I still meant what I said. "I will not jeopardize your Undead life. Which means, we have to deal with this...relationship thing. If Death or SMG find out..."

His hands rested lightly on my hips. "I cannot express how grateful I am for your sacrifice. It's been many years since I've found something— some*one*—worth living for. We'll work it out. It will serve no good purpose for Death or SMG to call in my contract. There's no other master vampire in this area who will do the work they need, and they will have an uprising on their hands if they do so."

"I'll be leading that revolt." A lump formed in my throat

and my heart squeezed. I loved my aunt and uncle, my friends, but I hadn't felt this type of intensity for anyone since my parents had died.

And that scared the reaper out of me.

I kissed him, slowly, gently, enjoying the feel of him under me. His magic surged and mine met it, the intertwining of silver and gold threading around us.

There was no urgency like before, and I felt almost shy as I probed his mouth with my tongue. He let me lead and it was heady, tantalizing. How often did a master vampire set aside his alpha dominance and allow a human to tease him into submission? "About that marking thing," I said on a breathy exhale.

His fingers twined in my hair, massaging my scalp. He slowly drew my head back, exposing my neck. He kissed down the vulnerable skin of my throat. "I'm only getting started. Everyone will know—"

The back door banged open. "Chloe? Killion? Are you here?"

Killion's grip loosened and we both let out audible sighs. "We need to find privacy," he grumbled.

Dr. O'Leary strolled past the open doorway and I jumped off Killion's lap, once more straightening my shirt and smoothing my hair.

The doctor reversed and came back. "There you are." He carried a box. "I wanted to drop off a few of my things."

Killion came to my side. "I didn't realize you'd be stopping in, it being a holiday and all."

"Hope you don't mind." He viewed the room. "I need to set up my desk."

My heart gave a tug when his attention landed on the two spots in the center. It was difficult to imagine anyone else sitting at either of them. Killion slipped his hand in mind and gave a squeeze.

My parents seemed to hover around me, and I imagined them giving me the go-ahead. It was time to move on, to help animals again in this place. "Take your pick," I choked out. I swept my arm over the desks, doing a decent Vanna White impression.

O'Leary gravitated to my father's, setting the box on the corner. Dust particles glittered in the sunbeam. "Perhaps I should clean it first."

"I'll get you a cloth." Killion disappeared.

O'Leary lowered his voice as he smiled at me. "I know this is a big step for you. If you'd rather I used a different room..."

I shook my head. "I can't think of anyone I'd rather see here resuming the role of veterinarian. Outside of me, of course."

He nodded. "We'll make them proud."

The sting of fresh tears warned me to escape. "Let me know if you need anything."

I bolted as Killion returned with furniture spray and a cloth. O'Leary thanked him. "Did you hire Jackson?"

I did an about-face, wiping away the tears. "Not yet."

He frowned. "Is there an issue with his credentials? References?"

"I'm sure they're fine. I simply want to consider all the options."

He glanced at Killion. "I was under the impression he was our only applicant."

Was that true? A nod from Killion confirmed it. Okay, then. "I'll contact his references this week and let you know."

"I don't mean to pressure you, but we *are* opening in six

days. I lecture Mondays, Wednesdays, and Fridays. We'll need him to cover those times."

Killion interceded. "Perhaps a probationary period? Offer him a thirty-day contract and we'll see how things work out."

A weight lifted off my shoulders. The vampire was a business mogul. He had all the experience handling these types of things, where I had none. "Yes, let's do that."

"Great." O'Leary began cleaning the desktop.

"We'll let you unpack." Killion led me to the door. "If you have any questions, please speak to me. I'll be happy to assist."

Ghost was asleep in the front window. A mother with two children had stopped to watch her. When she saw me rousing the dog, she tapped on the glass to get my attention. "Is she for sale?" she called.

Ha. I held the five pounds of magical canine up and peered into her sleepy eyes. Would I get to keep her when my grim contract was up? Thinking about a life where I finished school, passed my exams, and ran the vet clinic should have made me happy. It should have been enough.

It no longer seemed to. "No." I shook my head, sorry to see the kids' disappointment. "We'll have a few for adoption soon, though."

The three moved on and Ghost yawned. When I turned around, Killion stood in the background with a Cheshire grin on his face.

"What? I can't let the demon dog loose into the world."

"That's the only reason?'

I grunted. He knew I'd fallen for her, even if she was chaos wrapped in fur. *Just like I have for you.*

His grin didn't diminish and I hugged Ghost. "What

happens when I'm ninety, and you're still...like this?" I waved a hand at his body.

"I will cherish you even more."

"Liar."

"Why would I not?"

"Because I'll be old and wrinkly. I won't remember my name, much less be a grim with magic anymore. I'll probably be cranky and you may have to spoon-feed me."

He gave a mock bow. "I'm at your service. Every moment will be an honor."

"You're weird, you know that, right?"

He purposely stared at my lips. "You seem to like it. Or am I wrong?"

Touché. "You're not," I admitted.

And holy reapers, was I in trouble.

TEN

That evening, my training consisted of self-defense combat with Katarina. After she beat me up several times, and Killion doled out endless suggestions of how to defeat her—none of which worked—I begged for an end to it.

He dismissed her, asking her to fetch the "package" he'd sent her out for earlier. I didn't ask what that might be, fearing it was something dead. He fed me while she was gone, and encouraged me to drink several bottles of water.

She returned wheeling a cart of dead houseplants into the room. The five shelves were crammed full, and she gave him a curious glance.

So did I. "What is this?"

"Remove the amulet," he instructed. I did, laying it on my backpack. He guided me to stand in front of the plants and I felt a tug in the center of my chest. "Life-giving, remember? You are afraid to resurrect humans, and don't want more pets. Bring these to life."

Katarina nodded with understanding, and once I thought about it, it wasn't a bad idea.

"I have a black thumb. Ask Nita. I can't even keep a cactus alive."

His fingers traced over my palm. "Your fear causes you to hold back. The necromancy is part of your magic—magic you've been denying. You don't have to hold back any of it with these."

"They don't have souls." And neither did the grass or bushes I'd seen come out of dormancy at my presence. I'd even had the amulet on. "It's not the same."

"Science has proven that trees and plants have sentient abilities. They are living things. Your magic offers you many gifts and it's time you explored them. Now, close your eyes."

The dead things were already calling to me, tickling my magic with their longing to live again. I took a breath and did as he instructed. Even with my lids shut, I could see them, not as they were now, but as they had been—alive and growing.

"Relax and let go," he cajoled. I tried, his voice melting my resistance. "Allow yourself to send a finger of magic—"

A burst of heat flowed out of my chest.

"Whoa," Katarina said, and there was so much surprise in it, I opened my eyes.

"Whoa is right." The plants hadn't simply revived, they were growing at an astronomical rate. Vines curled and reached for me. Roots burst through the bottoms of containers, splitting them open. Flowers bloomed.

Killion chuckled. "Very good."

The jungle continued to expand. I had to step back from an ivy winding itself around my ankle. "Great. Now how do I stop it?"

"That's the key to releasing your fear," he said, completely calm. He still held my hand. "Simply close the connection."

"Close it how?" My screech echoed in the chamber.

"Like a faucet," Katarina interjected, climbing onto a pew to get away from a trailing vine with heart-shaped leaves. "Turn it off!"

I slammed my eyes shut and imagined turning a tap handle. "Enough. Stop," I murmured urgently.

"That's it." Killion's voice was once more soothing me into peace.

Ahhh... The houseplants sighed.

I peeked an eye open. The growth had slowed, but not stopped. I opened the other and glared at them. "Cease. Halt. *Please!*"

Everything came to a standstill. When I faced my mentor, one side of his mouth was quirked into a smile. "See?"

"See what? I created monster plants!"

"You controlled your magic."

I pointed. "You call that control?"

"Practice. It will come with time."

Katarina hopped down. "What do we do with all of them?" She sounded slightly disgusted. "I interrogate enemies, not run a greenhouse."

"Leave them outside the community garden tonight." Killion eyed a peace lily, its white blooms brilliant in the shadowy room. "And see that Moss takes that one to the penthouse."

We both shot him inquisitive looks. "You like houseplants, master?" she asked.

He smiled at me. "I do now."

"It would be nice to have a few at the clinic," I added. I would put them in the office to keep pets from snacking on their leaves. They would remind me of my mom. She'd loved to garden and always had plants in our home.

After Katarina left with the jungle, Killion guided me through a visualization, making me sit cross-legged on the raised dais.

Usually, I struggled to stay still and not fidget, but listening to him sent me instantly into that calm state. Using my skill had left me with a blissful edge—it had felt good to revive those plants, give them a second life.

As he wrapped me in his energy, my tired body and overworked mind gave in. On the back of my lids, I saw a light show of colors. Then without warning, I was transported to Shepherd's Rest, once more on the corpse road.

The air shimmered like heat waves rising from asphalt on a summer's day. Earthbound spirits loitered, but none seemed to notice me. In the distance, the glow of magic called to me, as if I were a magnet drawn to steel. I was suddenly there, staring at the headstones of Eliza and Marius. I didn't even have to think about it, I simply moved, rippling from the original spot to that one like the air around me.

The jasmine was in full bloom, the only vibrant thing in the cemetery. The scent of it carried on the breeze. As I watched, it flowered, then died, then became green once more.

"You shouldn't be here," a female spirit said, hovering behind the stone marker. She wore a high-necked dress and short jacket. "You are not deserving of him."

As if I'd conjured the male in question, I felt my blood heat. I turned my head and Killion shimmered into view. He sucked in a breath, focus glued on the tombstone, and then *bam*. We were both thrown out of the vision and dumped back in the church's nave.

He gripped the back of a pew, seeming stunned.

"What just happened?" I asked.

"Astral projection. I knew you'd left your body and I needed to make sure you were okay."

I'd undergone different types of out-of-body experiences. It came with being a 'tweener'—walking between the worlds. "You can do that at will?"

A nod.

Silence.

Heavy, guilt-filled silence.

There was no ignoring it. "She was beautiful."

He flinched, eyes snapping to mine. "My wife? You saw her?"

He hadn't. Back in the fall, I'd found his family ring and his wife's locket, both of which had been lost. "She looked like the woman in the locket."

A hand went to his chest. "She was my...everything. Is she an earthbound soul?"

My heart clenched and my stomach cramped. *You don't deserve him.* He would know if I lied. "I don't know."

I untangled my legs, brushed off my pants, and found my backpack, Ghost sleeping next to it. I didn't hurry, giving Killion time to work through the shock of what had happened, the remorse and grief he still carried.

He offered to drive me home, but Ghost needed exercise, he needed space, and I needed to clear my head.

The shadows were long and fleeting when the dog and I walked out of the church, Death's amulet around my neck once more. Night came early this time of year, but I found the darkness soothing. I wanted to be as invisible as a spirit and nurse my wounds in peace.

My mind whirled and I overanalyzed everything, while Ghost sniffed at trees and bushes, marked at least every other one, and sniffed some more.

Would the nightmares about Killion stop now? Would there be more witch killings? Would JR die at the clinic?

Did I deserve Killion?

Was he right about Death and SMG? Would they look the other way about our relationship?

I couldn't jeopardize his life, but I couldn't stay away from him either.

I felt itchy inside my own skin. Leading Ghost the long way home, I stopped at The Bean. Nita was working, along with a newer employee, Piedmont Johnson.

The coffee shop was open every day, since according to Wade, the owner, people needed coffee three hundred and sixty-five days a year. I didn't disagree.

Apparently, our customers concurred. Although it was New Year's, the place was busy. Not hectic—but a cozy gathering of some of our regulars. Ignoring the "No Pets" sign, I tucked Ghost into my bag and got in line behind a pair of thirty-somethings discussing their trainwreck Christmases. When I made it to the counter, Nita brightened and hugged me across the expanse. She smelled of lavender and patchouli. "Happy New Year, girl. Did you have an amazing night with tall, rich, and sexy?"

She was my best friend and I wanted to tell her everything. Since she didn't know he was a vampire, nor that I was a grim whose blood he craved, it was a moot point. I certainly couldn't tell her what we'd really done last night. "Great time," was all I said.

Her high ponytail swung forward as she peered over the counter, searching out my left hand. "No proposals?"

"Do you really think I would have waited until now to tell you?"

She sighed dramatically, returning to her side, her pink glossed lips curving in a knowing smile. "You would be on my doorstep, shouting the news, but... A girl can dream. I thought maybe he was keeping you busy today in the best way possible."

Her wink brought a grin to my lips, yet the crushing weight of my situation hung heavy on my heart. "Have you seriously been here all day? Did you bombard Killion with questions when he picked up my drink earlier?"

There were circles under her eyes she'd covered with extra makeup. "Double shift, and no, I kept our pact about limiting my harassment of your perfect boyfriend to a minimum."

"Thank you. Has it been busy?"

She shrugged. "Good tips. Do you need another fix?"

The caffeine would get me through the coming hours. I needed sleep, and to forget about Eliza, but I had to review Aurora's notes.

And steer clear of Stormfinger.

I hadn't mentioned the sorcerer to Killion because I didn't want him worried about the guy, or worse, taking Death's side and insisting I train with him. Reopening the clinic and solving the case were equally important, and as O'Leary had reminded me—classes started next week. My dance card was full. "Make it a double," I told Nita. "I'm going to need it."

"Dogs are not permitted," a male voice on my right said.

Ghost bared her teeth, her head sticking out of the top of the bag. I glanced over and my stomach fell. The sorcerer, minus his hat, sat at a table near the wall.

"She's a therapy dog," Nita retorted. Under her breath, she mumbled, "Why can't people mind their own business?"

While I embraced the sentiment, I ignored him and ·

adjusted my strap, my pulse picking up speed at his presence. "I should go."

"I'm off in a few minutes. How about dinner at Noodle Bowl?"

"I'd love to, but I have tons to do. Paperwork and contracts for the clinic. I haven't even hired an office manager yet."

"Megan's looking for a part-time job."

Shifting aside to let another customer get to the counter, I asked, "O'Leary's daughter?"

Nita nodded and took the woman's order. She bagged the muffin, accepted the payment, and sent her on her way. "She came in last week and wanted to know if we were hiring. She can only work Saturdays, though. Wade turned her down."

I would still need a full-time manager for weekdays, but Megan might be an option, *if* she could get along with her father. "I'll reach out to her. Thanks."

"Of course. I've got a handful of ideal candidates with admin backgrounds." She began making my drink. "I'll bring their employment apps to the Noodle and go through them with you."

She always seemed to have a sixth sense about reliable workers. Wade had put her in charge of pre-screening hires. He had final say, but she interviewed the potentials before he signed off on them. "I trust your intuition, but are you taking them from The Bean's cache?"

"Wade didn't hire them. They're fair game."

We agreed to meet at the restaurant after I dropped Ghost at my place. I was in a pickle to hire someone quickly, but mostly I simply wanted to spend time with my best friend. Hanging out with her made me feel normal.

Walking to my place, I pressed pause on the looming

issues swirling around my head and played with Ghost. She loved hide and seek, so I hid behind a tree, she found me and barked her glee. We wrestled gently, and then she sunk her teeth into the hem of my pants, using the material to initiate a tug of war.

While I was indulging her, the sorcerer emerged from behind a massive oak and gave the dog a dismissive glance as he stepped into my path. "I wish to speak with you."

I picked her up and stepped around him. "Not now."

Ghost kept a wary eye on him when he began walking beside me. "Your reluctance to learn how to control your skill is a ticking time bomb."

"I'm controlling it." I glanced around to make sure no one was near. "I don't need your lessons."

"The witch has only succeeded in helping you suppress it. Her tea is little more than a placebo lulling you into believing you're controlling it." Under the streetlight, he studied my neck. "The amulet is what's doing it, but do you really want to wear that all the time? Like a dam, you are holding back. The pressure will become too much, and it will break."

Aurora and Killion had both insisted the only way to control it was to use it. Sounded like a horror movie to me. Unfortunately, I knew they were right.

The first time my mom and dad took me skiing in Colorado, my initial lesson was on how to fall properly to avoid injury. My necromancy was comparable—I needed to be comfortable with the feel and use of it, so I didn't end up raising the dead—supernatural, human, or animal—accidentally. "I've found a new way to practice. I don't need you."

As the words left my mouth, the palm of my hand warmed and tingled. *Kill*, my scythe said in my head. Even when it wasn't with me, I could hear it. Feel it.

"We must begin your lessons immediately."

Death knew how to pick 'em. This guy wasn't taking no for an answer. "Not gonna happen today. Give me your number and I'll be touch."

Stepping in my way once more, he held out a hand as a stop sign. "Death will kill me if you don't cooperate."

My palm seemed to agree, itching like mad for the death blade. The man's face gave no indication he was lying, or even stretching the truth. No ticks or twitches. He held my gaze, a bit of pleading in his eyes.

I rubbed my palm on my pants. "My boss doesn't know how to ask nicely, does he? Only demands."

His lips rested into a softer line and he blew out a breath. "You understand the position I'm in?"

No one wants to die. "Trust me, if you're the best teacher he's got for this, he won't kill you." Especially since I was a challenge and he knew it. "Let's set a date for my first lesson. That will get him off your back for now."

"He stated we must start today."

Of course he had. "My witch friend believes you're bad news. Why should I agree to train with you?"

"She may be wise, but she is also paranoid. Hurting you in any manner would result in Death's fury. Why would I risk that?"

Sounded reasonable, although I suspected the big guy might not be all that upset if something happened to me. "I'll give you twenty minutes after dinner. Then I'll decide if we go further." I handed him my cell. "Enter your number. I'll text you when I'm available."

His relief seemed genuine. "Twenty minutes is hardly enough time for in-depth education."

My palm cooled and stopped itching. That was a good

sign. He gave the phone back and I pocketed it, edging around him. "This will be a get-to-know-you meeting."

"But—"

"No buts. And if you try any funny business with me, you won't need to worry about Death." I turned so I was walking backward while still facing him. "I'll kill you myself."

ELEVEN

W ith so much yet to do that evening, I called Noodle Bowl and ordered Nita's favorite, along with mine, and messaged her to pick up the order and come to my place. She arrived bearing white bags, a bottle of wine, and three potential candidates for the clinic position.

Corvus fluttered about, trying to snatch the shiny watch from her wrist, as well as sections of her spicy tuna poke bowl. Good thing she loved him.

We decided on Patty Parsons, a middle-aged woman looking for a full-time day job, as our top applicant. She hadn't been employed since her thirties, but she had managed the old Tuckerman's Drug Store prior to having her second child and becoming a stay-at-home mom. Before marriage, she'd been a hairdresser, and still had clientele who visited her home for cuts, perms, and colors.

I called her, fingers crossed, and explained who I was and that I needed an office manager. She remembered my parents, as well as me, although I had no recollection of her. The barking dogs in the background cemented the fact she was an animal lover.

We agreed to meet the next day for an official interview and I planned to have a copy of Killion's contract ready for her.

Satisfied that my multitasking was working, I decided to do more. Nita attempted to seduce me to go with her to her favorite karaoke bar, but my friend was dead on her feet. She hadn't even finished her single glass of wine, and I sent her home with the leftovers and promised we'd hit the bar soon.

Ignoring my own tiredness, I texted Killion and then the sorcerer. I had an idea. I downed a glass of Aurora's tea, and made sure the amulet was in place. Vera offered her car again, and soon Ghost, Corvus, and I were headed to Shepherd's Rest.

THE SORCERER WAS WAITING when I got there, sitting inside a sad looking Chevy that had to be older than I was.

"Please tell me your name isn't actually Neymar Stormfinger," I said when he finally vacated his vehicle and came to meet me. "That's a stage name, right? Your real one must be something awful if you went with that. What is it? Fred? Ralph? Barry?"

The night air was crisp but foggy. I leaned against a tree trunk next to the church road. Although it wasn't New Year's Eve, and still several hours from midnight, I had no desire to repeat the previous night's events. I was hoping my posture would convey confidence and a relaxed disposition. I was anything but. My fingers twitched, wanting to hold the scythe, regardless there was no active threat or target in sight.

Hat in place and wool coat buttoned, he carried a

leather satchel and affected the same disinterested stare he'd worn earlier. "Would you like to see my birth certificate?"

Ghost barked. Sounded like a "yes" to me. Corvus bounced on a tree branch. "Kill!" he squawked.

The sorcerer glanced at each, then back to me. "Your familiars, I assume?"

"I'm no witch."

Killion and Moss rolled up in the limo, interrupting further conversation. Moss got out to open his master's door and crossed himself at the sight of Stormfinger. The vampire exited and raised a curious brow.

Once Killion joined us under the tree, the chauffeur skedaddled back into the vehicle, and I made introductions.

"I'm aware who he is," Killion said. He stood close to me, Ghost coming to sit at his feet. "Why is he here?"

The man tugged at his lapel. "I was hoping to learn the same regarding you."

I pointed at Stormfinger. "He's tasked by Death to help me with my necromancy." I swung the finger to Killion. "He's my partner." Back to the sorcerer. "You believe I'm woefully beneath you when it comes to my grim work." I glanced around, wondering where the ghosts from the previous night were. "I'm more than a reaper, and Killion and I are on the trail of grave robbers. Possibly witch hunters, too. I want you to see me in action, investigating with Killion, and crossing earthbound spirits. He and I need to work, and you can answer my questions about the necromancy training while I do. Two birds, one grim."

I smiled, but both men seemed unimpressed with my word play or perhaps with my plan in general. Hard to tell.

Corvus cackled. At least he got it.

Disbelief was clear on Killion's face as he studied the sorcerer. "Why would Death entrust her to *your* keeping?"

Stormfinger drew himself up a haughty notch. "I have successfully taught nineteen necromancers how to control their gifts."

Killion's energy pulsed around me, protective. "And you used one of them to amplify your own."

"What?" I frowned at Stormfinger. "Is that true? Used him how?"

The man was already pale, but in the foggy night, his face looked positively ghostly. A cloud of chilled breath encircled him when he exhaled loudly. "There were extenuating circumstances."

"The mage ended up dead," Killion told me, "and couldn't be resurrected, if I recall. He mishandled the situation."

So that's why Aurora had warned me about him. "Seems you have a bad reputation."

Stormfinger looked toward the Montague mausoleum. "I mishandled nothing. Death trusts me and so should you."

I couldn't help it—I burst out laughing. Death played both sides of every situation. While I had no doubt the sorcerer could handle his assignment, I would never blindly step into anything simply because Death put his stamp of approval on it. "Let's get something straight." I unsheathed the scythe and Ghost perked up. "You touch my power—my *gift*, as you call it—and like I mentioned before, I'll end you. I'm not your average necromancer, nor grim. All I want to do is find the kill-switch for it. SparkNotes version, if you please. I have work to do and a murderer to apprehend."

"Spark notes?" Killion echoed.

"Study guides, like Cliff Notes."

"Ah." He nodded. "Those I've heard of."

I glanced around. Where were those ghosts? I could feel the buried dead nearby becoming aware of my presence.

The amulet on my collarbone warmed. I needed to get on with this.

"Kill-switch?" Stormfinger appeared mortified. "The gift of necromancy is to be honored and—"

"Save it." I twirled the blade. "I don't want to bring animals, or anything else, back." Although I did like the plant option. "Just tell me how to flip the switch to off. Permanently."

"There's no switch," he groused through gritted teeth, "and it takes months, if not years, to learn how to use it properly."

I stopped twirling the blade. "I don't want to *use* it!" A soft brush of Killion's hand over the back of mine made me realize I was shouting. Digging for patience, I lowered my voice, as well as the scythe. "I have a life—a busy one—and I can't keep drinking potions and wearing magical amulets to stop me from raising humans."

"This amulet," Stormfinger said. "Are you wearing it now?"

Due to my agitation, I again sensed the nearby dead trying to wake. It was a strange sensation, as if they were opening their eyes, moving their stiff fingers. I yanked the pendant out, feeling it pulse and warm, ready to send out a bubble to protect them. "Please," I added. "I don't want to depend on tools to keep it in check. I just want to turn it off."

When Stormfinger took a step closer to look at the necklace, Killion moved in front of me, cutting him off. "Your magic is part of you, like your blood, your arm, your hair." He rubbed my wrist with his thumb, slowing my rapid pulse. "It's intangible, but you need to accept it's there in every cell, in your very DNA. You've only recently discovered your abilities. It will take time to learn how to work with them. We've discussed this, Chloe. Instead of fearing your magic, embrace it. Let yourself be powerful. Like you were earlier at the church."

I scrubbed my face. "That was pretty cool, I have to admit. But they were plants."

"When you want to lift your arm, you just do it, correct? You don't think about the physiology involved. How the muscles must contract, the tendons engage, or the nerves respond?"

I tucked the amulet away. "Of course not."

"And if you don't wish to raise it, you don't have to force it to remain still. That's how your magic should be. Effortless. You trust your arm will move when you so will it. You believe your blood will continue to pump and your hair will grow, without any conscious direction from you. Once you view your magic in that way, it will respond to your wishes, just like your arm when you need to, say, lift a cup of coffee."

Sounded easy, but it wasn't. "I don't know how to do that."

"I'll show you, like with the plants. Not just the necromancy, but *all* of your magic."

Ghost danced and Corvus made sounds of approval. Behind Killion, Stormfinger snorted. "Don't be ridiculous. *You* can't teach her anything."

The hand holding the scythe came up so fast, Killion almost wasn't quick enough to stop me. He did, catching my wrist. A delicious smile curved his lips. "While I would enjoy his demise, remember you're on probation."

Stormfinger's Adam's apple bobbed and he stepped back. "Death will hear about this."

I didn't want to, but I broke free from Killion and followed the sorcerer as he marched to his car. "I thought you needed this gig to be successful or Death would kill you?"

He pulled up short, keeping his back to me. I sensed the wheels turning in his brain.

"I have a solution for both of us," I offered.

Silence. Then, "I'm listening."

I was surprised. "Let me practice with Killion and I'll assure Death that you're doing as instructed to help me. If I can't handle it, I'll"—I made a face at his back—"train with you."

After a long, drawn out minute, he pivoted. "I want your commitment in writing."

"Thirty days," I countered. "I want that much time to work on my own with Killion, under the guise that you're mentoring me."

Seconds passed. Ghost sniffed at an iron stake in the gate, bored.

"Fine," he relented.

"Draw it up and I'll sign it." I turned and scanned the area, marching back to the master vampire. "Now, let's get to work."

"What are you looking for?" he asked.

I stopped at the tree. There wasn't the slightest bit of otherworldly anything. Not even a hint of magic, that roiling fog, *nothing*.

A crawling sensation went down my spine. This was all kinds of wrong. I bit my bottom lip. "Where are all the ghosts?"

TWELVE

Killion sidled up next to me and gave the area his own perusal. He seemed reluctant to journey into the graveyard. Big surprise. "Perhaps you've frightened them off. You did send six to the afterlife last night."

"Technically, seven. Ghost delivered one on her own."

Stormfinger was at his car, door opened, but apparently eavesdropping. "You allowed the dog to reap a soul?"

We both glanced at him. He didn't deserve an answer, but I gave one anyway. "She was protecting me. I thought you were leaving."

He huffed and tossed his briefcase into the vehicle. "Why do you care so much about ghosts? You reap the living."

No way was I explaining my plan to him. I suspected that if the spirits were AWOL, it had more to do with him than me, although I couldn't quite put my finger on it. "This is part of my grim duties as a tweener. Earthbound spirits need to move on. You're welcome to stay and watch."

I didn't actually want him to, but it had been part of my earlier speech.

"There are no spirits here, no suspect humans, either. You're wasting time."

The death blade warmed and my palm itched. "I know," I murmured to it, "I want to behead him, too."

He apparently had incredible hearing, or maybe I'd said it louder than intended. Oops. He shook with anger, snatching his hat off and creasing it with a tight grip. "You are the saddest excuse I've ever seen for a reaper."

Corvus dive-bombed him from the branch, screeching. Stormfinger hollered and scrambled into the sanctuary of his car. The bird landed on the hood, pecking at the driver's window.

The man's yelling came through the glass, cursing the bird, and I wanted to kill him all over again. His tires kicked up rocks as he jetted off, Corvus flying over to land at my feet.

Killion and I exchanged a look. "Death hates me," I groused. "That's why he's saddled me with this idiot."

A chuckle from the master vampire cut through my irritation. "You are such an unusual grim. A good one, mind you, but you mustn't allow others to get under your skin."

He stuck his hands in his coat pockets and I threaded an arm through his. "Thanks for backing me up. Things are getting out of control, and I don't just mean with my plant buddies."

We glanced at the nearby graves before we began walking, him steering me away from the path that would lead to the plot with his wife and child. "You have a lot on your plate. If you wish me to stop flirting with you, I shall."

You don't deserve him.

I opened my mouth, but didn't know what to say. He was giving me an out. Or one for himself.

The thought of not being able to touch him, kiss him, laugh with him, made me sick to my stomach. "I need you."

His magic flowed around me like a hug. "And I will always be here for you." His gaze traveled toward the invisible double markers on the other side of the hill. "What's the real reason we're in this place?"

"I wanted to interrogate a ghost or two and see if they could tell me about that fog that produced JR. Aurora said it was a timeline fracture, which I don't know anything about, but something's off now, and it's not simply that they fear I'll reap them."

"I sense it as well." He switched his focus to the giant Banks' mausoleum rising in the distance. "When you inserted your scythe into the void, perhaps it did something to them."

"There were several still hanging around after it happened."

He faced the road behind us, Stormfinger long gone. "Do you wish to stay? Wait to see if any appear?"

Participants of that night's ghost tour were arriving. It was a different guide tonight, and she hailed a family exiting their car with EMF scanners and wearing headlamps. The mother, father, and two teens had their phones out and were already scanning the grounds as if there were ghosts lined up waiting for them.

Did the earthbound souls get sick of such stuff? Killion led me past a weeping angel statue and back toward the road. "Actually, I'd like to visit St. Joseph's," I told him. "Check out the grave where the woman was found. Maybe I can rouse her ghost. She wasn't hanging out at the autopsy. You game?"

He walked me toward Vera's car, the limo idling behind

it. Several of the tour attendees glanced in our direction, inquisitive, but seemed too excited to care.

"Good idea." He opened the driver's door for me, but held my arm. "We'll have to be on guard for thrill seekers. Everything is a tourist attraction these days, including murder."

While his words were straightforward and normal, there was a distractedness in his tone. His light grip on my arm conveyed more than a simple touch.

Grief, sadness, longing. If my therapist, Dr. Maxwell, were here, she'd tell me to talk about my feelings. To validate Killion's concerning his wife and child. That's what mature adults did.

The bird and dog hopped inside, and I chickened out. I could only imagine how difficult it would be for him to talk about Eliza to me.

Maybe I *wasn't* a mature adult. Maybe I *didn't* deserve him. I blew out a long, slow breath. Talking about feelings could help, but focusing on work could, too. "This can't be a coincidence, all this happening in the past twenty-four hours. Even JR showing up in town seems weird after I saw his spirit. And the witch being murdered at midnight, the same time his future ghost appeared? There has to be a connection."

The distracted look in his eyes faded. "Agreed." He helped me into the seat. "After we check St. Joseph's, we'll practice embracing your power."

"Do you truly believe you can teach me how to use my magic?"

He leaned down and caught my chin in his hand. "There are few things I have ever failed at."

"Lucky you."

He planted a kiss on my lips, and though it was brief, my toes curled inside my boots.

"Yes," he said, and the desire was back, his magic licking against my spine. "Lucky me."

THIRTEEN

On the off chance someone might be watching, we retraced our steps from our early morning visit. The place was dark and quiet, and leaving the bird and dog with Moss, we eased over the stone fence on the east side and slipped in.

My pulse kicked up as Killion took my hand and his magic merged with mine. *We should use extra precaution,* he said telepathically.

We became invisible, except for our glowing auras, and stuck to the edges of the grounds until we were positive neither humans nor supernaturals were hanging around.

There were no ghosts either.

Hand still in mine, he led me past the crypt with the owls. *I don't sense any spirits, do you?*

None. Seemed there was little reason to keep up the mental communication, but I rather enjoyed it. *What are the odds all the ghosts are gone here, as well?*

He paused, allowing us to become visible again. "Death would have mentioned a mass crossing of souls, and since you are currently the only reaper in this area who could perform such a thing, it seems unlikely two graveyards are empty."

Play time was over. "Should I message him and ask?" It almost felt abnormal to speak out loud again. "Is a mass crossing common?"

"Hardly, and it would require a grim, but what other reason could there be?"

The frosty air stung my nose. It wasn't as bad as the previous night, but I still shivered inside my coat. Dried grass and sticks crunched under my boots. "I have no idea. This is all new to me." So many supernatural things were. "I wonder what the tie is between the dead witch and JR? Maybe they were friends." Or something more. I couldn't exactly text him with the autopsy photo and ask. "I wish we knew her identity."

A breeze rustled dry leaves on a nearby tree, the brown stragglers refusing to fall off. Killion glanced toward the taped-off grave. "Aurora hasn't heard of any missing witches?"

"No, and she didn't recognize our victim from the autopsy photo, but she put out the word to the local covens to be vigilant. Whatever is going on, I have to stop it. I can't let anyone else die."

Yellow crime scene tape fluttered from stakes, warning us away. "*We* must stop it," he reiterated. "You don't have to do this alone, and I want to remind you that life-giving is part of your natural being. You wish to save everyone, and there's nothing wrong with that. That *is* your magic, Chloe."

I squeezed his fingers, grateful for him. "Thank you."

The shadows wrapped around us like a blanket. His energy engulfed me. Even with all of this going on, I felt happy.

When I'd told Dr. Maxwell I was having nightmares, she'd asked me to describe them. I kept Killion's name out of it, and certainly didn't mention anything about vampires, but I did explain that there was a monster attacking me. She'd listened and nodded, and asked me to journal the details.

She'd then suggested that the monster in my dreams was actually me. My subconscious, rising up out of the murky depths of fear, guilt, and grief to make me question this next step of opening the clinic.

Obviously, she didn't know about the actual monster I'd faced in St. Anne's, or the fact I seemed to be reliving that encounter as nightmares, but I wondered if what she claimed was also true. Was I transferring my fears onto a physical entity, my subconscious attempting to sabotage my relationship with Killion?

The ghost of his wife seemed to hover over my shoulder. Not actually, but her presence was in the back of my mind. My therapist always insisted that helping others with their grief would help me handle mine. I knew if she were here, she'd encourage me to have an "open conversation," even though it felt vulnerable to do so.

If I followed her formula, I'd ask him a question about the deceased and validate any feelings he brought up regarding her death. Dr. Maxwell often did this with me, encouraging me to remember something about my mom or dad, then delving into the importance of those memories.

I was no therapist, and I lacked the ease of social graces others found simple. Half the time, I struggled to put feelings into words or pinpoint the correct term or phrase to express myself.

But the memory of Eliza would not leave me alone.

I cleared my tight throat. "I've always loved the scent of

jasmine." If I was going to jump into the deep end of this dark pool, I was doing it my way. "My grandmother had a bush that wound up a trellis outside the guest bedroom window. When I spent nights there in the spring, she would open it and the smell would flood the room. I miss that. Miss her."

There was a lengthy pause, and then he said, "It is one of my favorite perfumes as well."

"I think my necromancy simply thinned the veil so she could come through and speak to me." I didn't need to say her name. He knew. "I don't believe her spirit is stuck here."

"She spoke to you?" His face brightened. "What did she say?"

I held my tongue, debating whether to tell him the truth or make up something more palpable. That she loved him, missed him, was proud of him. Nita often made me watch a famous medium on TV and that's what she always said to folks.

"Chloe?" Killion's tone held an edge. The excitement in his features disappeared. "We have promised to be honest with each other. What did Eliza say?"

Eliza. Such a beautiful shortening of an already lovely name. He was right—I wouldn't lie to him. Honestly, I couldn't anyway. He would know. "She told me I didn't belong there, and that I don't...deserve you."

He blinked, seemingly baffled. "Perhaps you misunderstood. That doesn't sound like my Eliza."

My Eliza. "It was her."

"And my son? Did he come through, as well?"

"I'm sorry, no. Just her."

He took my hand and drew it through the crook of his arm. He led me to a concrete bench, our magics mingling. All was quiet, the only sounds penetrating the grounds were those of nocturnal creatures and far off car engines. I could smell pine and the smoke from someone's hearth fire.

"Your grave sight grows stronger," he said. "You will continue to walk 'between the worlds' with greater and greater efficiency."

"I'm not sure that's a good thing."

He patted my hand. "Good or bad isn't the question. It's pure power. You decide how to use it and what you will accomplish with it."

The air dropped several degrees and suddenly had a crystalline edge to it. He tensed, and I did, too.

"What is it?" I whispered.

He answered telepathically, making us invisible once more. *Someone approaches.*

I wished I was an owl and could spin my head around. I did the best I could to glance in all directions. Nothing.

Use your magic, Chloe. Tap into it, like you did earlier.

Slowing my breathing, I nodded and closed my eyes. I wasn't sure tapping into it like I had at the church was the best idea, but I trusted his advice. I wore the amulet and I had no intention of raising corpses.

I envisioned feelers leaving my body to reach out and find the intruder. My aura hummed and began to do just that, tiny golden vines stretching out in all directions.

Unfortunately, the dead responded, reaching back for me.

I shut it down. "Bad idea," I accidentally said out loud.

His thumb rubbed over my pulse. *Lower the wattage and try again.*

He pushed the image of a dial into my head, one that could adjust an indicator needle from zero to ten.

Drawing in a deep breath, I imagined channeling magic into moving it gently. The needle rose to one.

I nearly broke our handhold and clapped. *I did it!*

Of course, you did. Give it more.

I swallowed and nodded, teeth beginning to chatter from the deepening frost in the air.

One.

Two.

Three...the needle moved deliberately as I allowed a steady *dripdripdrip* of my power.

The corpses all around us stayed silent, unmoving.

The rush of relief buoyed me. Maybe I *could* do this. I gave another gentle push, raising it to four.

On the very outskirts of the stone walls, I sensed a presence. *Human.* I let my awareness probe along with the golden vines to track what was there.

A cloaked figure. He's running around the mausoleums.

Which way? Killion asked.

Toward the—

A howl went up, lifting the small hairs on the back of my neck. My inner vision cleared and I blinked.

My gaze landed on the marker in front of me. The information carved in stone was partially covered by mud and debris, but the part of the name I could make out registered.

"Oh, my god." I dropped Killion's hand and ducked under the yellow tape. Aurora had claimed this was her grandmother's grave, but it wasn't. *How did I miss this?*

"Chloe," he hissed in warning.

Avoiding the bloodstained ground, I wiped my hand across the debris, exposing the name.

Killion peered over my shoulder. "What is it?"

I blinked, trying to clear my vision, as well as my disbelief. It couldn't be. "Jackson Rawlings Banks," I uttered, not bothering to lower my voice.

My friend was buried at my feet.

FOURTEEN

Killion eyed the marker. "What are you talking about?"

Another howl rent the night, this time closer. A pale shadow darted through the trees, snagging my attention—a ghost.

Shaking off my shock, I pointed. "There."

The sharp crack of a downed limb and the crunch of frozen leaves told me our visitor was running after the apparition. Killion moved to keep him in sight. Straightening, I followed, closing the distance.

While my speed and strength continued to increase the longer I was a grim, the vampire was far my superior. The predator in him gave him innate balance and grace, which I sorely lacked, leaving me panting and managing to clip several tombs, stones, and statues as we gave pursuit.

A giant wolf joined us, his gold eyes flashing, along with his curved canines. Andy.

The three of us formed a serpentine chain, Killion at the head, me struggling to bring up the rear.

The distance between us became too much and my

body turned fully visible, but I knew Killion and the shifter had a bead on the ghost and whoever was chasing it.

Sleet began to fall, stinging my face as we crossed the center of the rolling grounds. I hopped over corners of raised beds and dodged an assortment of holiday grave decorations.

On a hill, a towering mausoleum anchored the center of the cemetery, a giant statue of a skeletal grim reaper sitting on the roof. A fence with various symbols on the tops of the iron railings enclosed it.

The reaper held a true-to-size scythe that pointed up toward the sky, even as he turned his macabre smile and empty eye sockets toward those buried below.

While the lawn and Christmas bouquets throughout the graveyard were already dead or dying, here the garland outlining the entrance, as well as two wreaths that hung on the double doors and were the size of Vera's Prius, were green and thriving. Seemingly in defiance of the death symbol staring from his lofty perch, even the grass was alive and vibrant.

The ghost had vanished, and the hooded figure stood inside the boundary, his back to us. Killion leaped the railing with the grace of a stag, and as his feet landed on the lawn surrounding the building, a swirling mass of fog appeared a few feet from our cloaked figure.

Seeing that void, bigger but similar to the one JR had emerged from, made my skin prickle. "Watch out," I called.

The hooded man stepped into it. Killion covered the space between them in a heartbeat and reached for him.

"Don't!" The word ripped from my throat, but it was too late.

The swirling fog flashed, causing Andy and I to flinch back. There was a sizzling "pop" and it all disappeared.

"No!" My scream echoed against the mausoleum's walls and back to me.

In the chilled silence that fell, my heart shivered. I clamored over the fence, catching my boot on one of the iron symbols and landing on my hands and knees. The edge of a palm smacked the rough edge of the raised platform the burial chamber sat on, abrading my skin. Blood dripped down my finger, the mossy grass soaking it up. Instantly, the green turned brown.

"Come back." I patted the air where the two men had disappeared.

Andy became human, bare-chested, but otherwise clothed. "Where did they go?"

The scythe made a soft "zing" as I withdrew it from its holder. "I don't know."

"How do we get him back?" The shifter shook his head, his long curls sliding over his shoulders. "What am I saying? I should be glad he's gone. He's my enemy. Man, I've been hanging around you too much."

"Shut up and help me." I waved the blade through the air, ignoring my stinging hand. "It's a portal. There has to be a way in."

He sniffed the air and shrugged. "Not my area of expertise. Want me to call Aurora?"

"All the places you've broken into and robbed and you can't help me with this? You're good at discovering hidden entrances, right?"

"To buildings, sure. Not to...whatever that was. That's some sci-fi spectral stuff."

I stomped around the space, and hacked at a group of flowers now blooming at my feet. Where had they come from? My hand flew to the amulet, but it wasn't even warm. No corpses inside the structure called to me. "This can't be happening. How could I have lost him to the void?"

But lost him I had. Andy and I tried everything to make the fog reappear, but to no avail. Even a spell Aurora provided via phone didn't work.

No magic, no Killion, no ghosts. Slumping onto the cold ground, I let out a roar of frustration and sunk my blade deep into the earth.

A ghost sprang from it as if my action had summoned her. She shoved her rotting teeth and stringy hair into my face. "Get out," she screeched. "He'll be back for you and your soul!"

FIFTEEN

I yelped, jerking the weapon from the ground and swinging it at her.

The metal gleamed but went right through her with no effect. She was dressed in a threadbare gown with "Dante Springs Sanctum" stamped on the left upper chest area.

The mental hospital. No longer in service, but everyone who lived here knew the stories about that place.

She's just a lost soul, I told myself. "Are you the spirit the cloaked man was chasing?"

Her head whipped from side to side and she shuddered, a dry, moldy odor emanating from her. "He's coming. Run!"

"Who?" Across the expanse, the fog appeared, spinning in its center. Andy and I both retreated several steps and I kept the scythe at the ready. "Who's coming?"

The specter vanished as fast as she had appeared, only her cloying scent lingering.

A growl came from the fog. The layers began to part in the center. Bracing my feet, I lifted the blade higher. "Get behind me," I ordered Andy.

He shifted. The crack of bones and stretching of muscles

filled my ears. It looked and sounded painful, but in seconds, a giant wolf stood next to me, the gleam of magic in his eyes.

A pale and gnarly claw emerged from the mass. Then an arm, a chest, a leg. Inch by inch, a naked creature formed, dripping a grayish slime. By the time the features appeared, I was reared back and about to swing.

Andy charged. At the same time, the face turned my way and recognition dawned. "Wait!"

The shifter was on him before I could finish, his powerful jaws clamping onto the thing's thigh.

Killion roared in pain and raked the snarling wolf with one of his deadly claws. Andy yelped, but hung on. The two fell to the ground and rolled, all fangs and nails, their combined supernatural abilities on full display.

"Andy, stop!" I stepped into the fray, my own magic jetting out of me and slapping them. "*Stop!*"

My voice had an odd timbre to it, and the wolf and vampire flew apart with such speed, it was as if I'd snapped a taut rubber band with my command.

Andy's muzzle was covered by the gray slime, and it pooled at Killion's feet, both of them heaving from their efforts. Blood seeped from Killion's leg, and his violet eyes, wild with anger, locked on mine.

"It's okay." I lowered the scythe and my voice, trying to slow my erratic heart. My magic coiled back into my chest, but felt on edge, ready to protect me if necessary.

When the master vampire fully vamped out, it was a horror-movie result. No wonder I had nightmares. Regardless of the cool, sexy human exterior he projected most of the time, this was the predator that lay underneath.

"You're back," I said. "I'm sorry we attacked. We didn't know it was you. You're safe."

Witnessing Andy shift was uncomfortable. Watching Killion wrangle control of his inner beast made me want to turn away and give him privacy. He rarely lost control and allowed the true form inside him to surface.

I'd once asked Andy where his clothes and shoes went when he shifted, and he'd claimed they were suspended in an in-between dimension where the laws of time and physics didn't exist. Aurora had confirmed the same about hers when she transfigured from human into panther. As I watched in fascinated amazement, Killion morphed into his normal self—quite nude for a heartbeat—before his attire was restored.

And wow. He was a beast in more ways than one.

The thing that didn't change was the viscous liquid coating his hair, face, and hands.

Shucking my coat, I dropped it to the ground, and laid the scythe on top of it. I quickly removed my shirt. Shivering in my tank top, I held out the cotton garment, warm from my body. "Are you okay? What is that?" I motioned at the slime.

Andy returned to human, too. "Sorry about that," he muttered.

Killion wiped his face, features drawn, and paused to examine the now sticky cotton. "Ectoplasm from The Ghost Lands—the portal took me there."

Andy peered closer. "Ectoplasm as in, '*Who ya gonna call? Ghostbusters?*'"

I touched it. It was oily, sticky, and sent revulsion through me. "What are The Ghost Lands?"

"An interdimensional wasteland of sorts." Killion rubbed some of the plasm between his forefinger and thumb. "The subject was covered in your grim manual."

"Souls trapped there are lost," Andy said quietly. "Miserable existence, that's for sure."

My psychopomp ate my first manual. I had a replacement, and I had skimmed it once or twice, but I couldn't recall reading anything about a lost soul dimension. "How do you guys keep all this trivia in your heads?"

Killion discarded the ruined shirt and helped me into my coat. "More importantly, how did you bring me out of it?"

"I didn't." I picked up the scythe. Blades of grass, green as everything else in this plot, stuck to the metal. I wiped them off.

He eyed the blade, his gaze flicking to the ground where I'd marked the earth with it. "There's no coming back from that place, unless Death himself intervenes." His eyes rose and he sniffed the air, his nose turning toward the raised corner of stone nearby. He gripped my arm. "Did you make a blood contract with him?"

"Death was never here. All we saw was a ghost. I think it was the one the robed guy was chasing. She told me to run, that he was coming and he would take my soul."

Killion raised my hand, examining the dried blood on my palm. The wound had healed. "But your blood has been spilled."

"I tripped and fell." I pointed in that direction. The lawn was browning at a quick rate now, as if death were seeping into all the roots underground.

"Uh oh," Andy said. "This can't be good."

Killion pulled me to him and hugged me. Not in a "hey, I'm glad you're okay" manner, but something that made my hair stand on end.

"What?" I asked, afraid of the answer.

He set me back, face tense. "This tomb must be a

gateway to The Ghost Lands. It is being used to capture spirits and hold them—for what purpose, I'm unsure. I did not see the hooded figure in them, but there is something very wrong with this."

"Why is my blood killing the lawn?"

"A sacrifice has been made." He rubbed my arm. "The magic granted you your deepest desire—to return me to you."

Andy glanced around as if the shadows were about to come alive. "In exchange for what, though?"

Killion glanced away. He sighed audibly and I felt it in my bones. "Her soul," he said quietly. "The Ghost Lands have claimed Chloe's soul."

SIXTEEN

At two a.m., I was in my apartment with Killion and Death. Aurora and Andy were present as well, entertaining Ghost and Corvus.

Death placed a soundproof bubble around us to keep Vera from hearing.

His intense stare burned a hole in me. "You blew off Neymar to tramp around the cemetery."

Still slightly numb in order not to freak the hell out, I glared back. "I worked out a deal with him and I was following up on the grave-robbing case." I motioned between me and Killion. "A case, I'll remind you, SMG gave us."

"And to which you've made no progress."

Killion didn't so much as twitch a brow, but I felt his hackles rise. I was right there with him. Death hated vampires on principle, since they'd defied him and the laws of nature to extend their lives. He despised the master even more, because I'd given him my blood, violating one of the hundreds of statutes SMG had laid down. "You can't demand we investigate, then reprimand us for doing so."

Death puffed out his chest, ready to argue when I held up a hand. "In the past twenty-four hours, I have seen the ghost of a friend who *isn't* dead, assisted with a gruesome autopsy for an innocent woman who was brutalized, and now I have a blood contract with The Ghost Lands, a place I was unaware existed. Save the snarky comebacks and reprimands."

Tense silence enveloped the room. The others, with the exception of Killion, seemed fairly shocked by my audacity. Death, especially so.

The aura around him crackled and he pursed his lips, licking his teeth behind them. For a brief heartbeat, I could see all the things he planned to do to me when he didn't need me anymore. The Ghost Lands might be a spa day in comparison.

He sank into my desk chair, and I feared it might fragment from his weight. He had to be pushing six-seven, and easily two hundred-eighty pounds. As if this were boring him, he crossed his ankles and rocked. "I was making an observation and stating a fact. You deny it?"

Don't let him goad you, Killion warned.

Too late. "Not everything is black and white, O'Mighty Death, and I know you blackmailed Stormfinger into training me, so don't act holier-than-thou. I've had enough of your attitude."

Both his brows shot up and he stopped rocking.

Whoops.

Killion stepped slightly in front of me, acting like a shield. "Perhaps we should discuss the sorcerer who was chasing the ghost, and how you can unlink Chloe's soul from The Ghost Lands."

Death ignored the vampire, staring at me over his

shoulder with the same future threats of harm in his eyes. "Another situation you need me to clean up."

My retort was cut short when I realized he was, in fact, correct. "I never intentionally mean to screw-up, and you know it. SMG should have supplied me with all the facts coming into this reaper job, and if they had, I might have handled things differently." Before he could comment, I raised a finger in another *I'm not done* gesture. "Just an observation. However, fate or destiny, or simply my expedience trying to save my partner, combined with my klutziness, has resulted in a situation I don't understand, and I'm in need of your immense wisdom and guidance. If you don't assist me, I will inadvertently land in more hot water. Do you want to take that chance?"

He frowned, yet I saw how the appeal to his enormous ego—or perhaps the implied threat of causing more chaos—did the trick. "The Ghost Lands are a phenomenon created by magic users attempting to harness souls for their own means."

Aurora joined the conversation, petting Corvus on his shiny black head. "They want the ultimate power."

Didn't everyone? "That's why the sorcerer was chasing that ghost? To trap her?"

She nodded. "The man you saw must have been an archimagus. They're the ones who seek that kind of control."

Andy perked up. "You mean like in Minecraft?"

She gave him an admonishing glance. "I mean the high priest, a top mage, of an exclusive magic order. The last one I encountered, Theodore Methuselah, was head of the Order of Alexandria here in town. There aren't many around these days, and they tend to stay under the radar, but their power is immense, especially if they're charging it with souls."

"Power to do what?" I asked.

Death explained. "Souls amplify rituals and give the users the ability to act as alchemists, changing matter into other forms and even manipulate time."

Aurora continued. "But binding souls and using their energy is dark stuff, and it's a rare user who has the skills to control it, much less contain earthbound souls to begin with."

Killion faced her. "Manipulate time? How so?"

The raven decided to add his two cents. "Magic, magic, magic," he chanted.

Death gave the bird a look I'd labeled the 'Death glare.' "Using quantum energy to jump timelines. It grants them a way to step in and out of their current one and access forbidden knowledge. They can, at least theoretically, change situations and outcomes in the present."

Fascinated, I had to ask, "Like a time turner?"

All eyes landed on me, yet nobody seemed to get the reference, except Andy, who pointed a finger at me and nodded. "I've always wanted one of those."

For the others, I clarified, "In Harry Potter, Hermione had a device so she could go back in time, and..."

Death gritted his teeth. "For reaper's sake."

Aurora leaned on the back of the couch. "The archives recount a few who've tried, and even less who've succeeded. It takes an enormous quantity of souls, and a clear under-standing of moving between dimensional time shifts to pull it off. But that might explain the time fracture on the corpse road."

"JR's soul is caught up in all this?" I asked.

"Possibly, although I'm not sure how. Users can only step into their own past, since the future has not been technically created. To change even one thing then, however, can affect their current life, making them more powerful. Change history, change the present, and that, in turn, creates a new future."

The chair squeaked under Death's resumed rocking. "A few have committed soul stealing to dodge me."

"Can hardly blame them," Killion muttered.

The squeaking stopped. "They should have taken the easy way out and become a vampire."

Here we go again. These two were going to kill me. "So the ghosts power the time turner and that transports the sorcerer back in time so he can change the present."

"There is no *time turner*," Death corrected. "Whatever the blazes that is."

"Cut me some slack. I'm trying to wrap my mind around this. Don't tell me you haven't seen the films."

"Sure," Death said, putting his hands behind his head and leaning back. My chair groaned, poor thing. "We have movie night once a month at SMG."

I almost wished my chair would break and dump him on his backside. "Bottom line, this archimagus is attempting to change his past in order to control the present, and by extension, the future. He's messing with earthbound spirits and time." I glanced at Aurora and she nodded. "Could he be behind the grave robberies, as well?"

Ghost pawed at Aurora's leg and she scooped up the dog and began scratching under her chin. "To collect earthbound souls, he could use an item like their personal property to lure them to him. A piece of jewelry, a medallion, even a letter they wrote. Better yet, he could collect their

DNA, perform a spell, and like a moth drawn to a flame, they'd be magnetized to their genetic material. He'd be able to trap and hold them in The Ghost Lands until he had enough souls for this alchemy."

Killion crossed his arms. "He must have the ability to see them, so he's a medium or necromancer, then? Someone with grave sight, like Chloe?"

That gave me an idea. "Earthbound spirits are usually still here because they died violently or tragically. The graves that have been disturbed—do they belong to people who've died that way?" I had the photos of the three grave markers on my phone. I grabbed it and scanned them, calling out the owners' names. "Herbert Longrove, George McBroom II, and Thomas Bingham Anderson."

Death was nodding when I glanced up. "The first was shot on his way home from work, the second poisoned at his daughter's wedding, and the last, I believe, was trapped in a well."

"Are you kidding me?" I made a face. "How awful."

"That's the connection," Killion said. "The graves belong to earthbound souls."

"He needs more than three," Aurora added. "How many did you see when you were in The Ghost Lands?"

Killion shook his head. "My time there was brief. I saw nothing but mist."

Something finally made sense to me. "Three or a hundred, how do we stop this jerk and set those poor souls free?"

Death came to his feet slowly, as if he was weary of this. Of everything. "You're not going to like it." The words were directed at Killion, rather than me.

The master vampire stilled in that preternatural way

that made goosebumps race down my spine. "There must be an alternative."

"'Fraid not." Death strolled to my back door.

"What?" I cut my attention between them. "Tell me."

Death paused. "You, Chloe. We stop the archimagus and free the souls by sending you into The Ghost Lands."

SEVENTEEN

A cacophony of "Noes" rang out. Ghost barked and Corvus squawked, "Kill!"

Killion's magic wrapped around me and although he didn't move, I sensed he wanted to shield me again. "That would be ineffective and potentially fatal." The air crackled with his energy, raising my arm hairs like soldiers snapping to attention. "She is untrained, and as she mentioned, unschooled when it comes to all of this. No one in this room, in fact, has knowledge of that place and its horrors, and I've even been in it."

"Actually,"—Aurora raised her hand—"I do, but my magic is earth based and may be null on that plane."

Andy touched her shoulder. "None of us can handle it."

"I can." I kept my focus on Death, the stares of the others weighing on me. "I'm Grim Zero. I can see and harvest ghosts, and I can do the same to the archimagus if he tries to stop me. I've faced far worse and succeeded." The memory of my run-in with a group of ancient shiftlings made me shiver.

Death pointed at me and winked. "That's my girl."

"*Not a girl.* Jeez, you have to stop using that phrase."

Killion's magic, and the mental argument he was filling my head with, felt as if he was about to explode. *You cannot do this. It's far too dangerous and you don't know what you'll encounter. I can't protect you—*

Tamping down my shaky nerves, I faced him and forced myself to appear calm and confident. "I don't need protection. I can handle it."

"Chloe..." Aurora's tone was chastising. "We all know how powerful you are, but storming in unprepared will create the chaos you just threatened to bring about."

"I realize that. What I need is all the info you've got on what I can expect when I go in there. All the options I have when it comes to dealing with the spirits and this archimagus dude." My gaze swung back to Killion. "And I need more hand-to-hand combat training. I need to be faster, stronger, and less clumsy."

Jaw tight, he shook his head and voiced his fears. "It's far too perilous for you alone." He wanted to reach for me and it took all his willpower not to. "No matter how much I teach you."

Death rocked on his heels. "As much as I hate to admit it, he's right. It's going to take someone with high-level necromancy *and* grim skills, as well as someone knowledgeable about the Order and magic. Someone who won't die from normal physical injuries and can even survive those caused by a supernatural creature."

I checked those boxes. On a good day. With some help. "That's me."

He barked a laugh, giving me a 'get real' face. "The shifter said it—individually, none of you can handle this assignment, but together?" He made a see-sawing motion with his hand. "Fifty-fifty odds."

"When you say, 'together,' you don't mean…" Andy sounded as though he didn't want Death to actually answer. He eyed my bed as if he might crawl under it to hide.

"That's exactly what I mean, mate." Death's Aussie accent came out when he was being 'friendly' and wanted to downplay his scary presence or outrageous demands. "Chloe needs help, and each of you has at least one skill she can use."

Corvus flew to me, digging his talons into my skin and making me wince. "Too me, too me."

"Sure, why not?" Death shrugged. "The bird, too."

My heart beat a jerky rhythm against my ribs. "You can't be serious. They could all die."

"So could you," Killion shot back. He inched closer and touched my arm. "With us, you have a fighting chance."

"Neymar will also join you." Death opened the door as Andy, Aurora, and myself gaped at him. "Be in the cemetery ready to enter the portal at dusk. See you then."

Without a backward glance, he evaporated through the opening, much like one of the ghosts haunting the night.

Removing the raven, I set him on his perch and rubbed my shoulder. "Well." I searched for a bright spot in this new development. "Guess the Scooby Gang rides again."

The others stared at me with worried expressions. As expected, they all blurted out their misgivings and doubts, and I had the feeling, while I kept quiet and let them vent, they secretly wished they'd steered clear of this whole mess.

I couldn't fix it. I had caused my soul to be linked to the horrible place, and I had to free those trapped there and myself at the same time. I didn't disagree with their arguments, so I nodded and validated all of their concerns, like a mature adult. Go me!

Meanwhile, as they talked, paced, and deliberated how to get out of this predicament, I formed my own plan.

EIGHTEEN

K illion and I drove Aurora and Andy to her place, the three of them talking nonstop still. I listened with a sinking heart as they brainstormed idea after idea of how we could succeed, and tore each apart with equal fanaticism.

Stopping this archimagus was truly a perilous adventure. Having to worry about my friends on top of not getting myself killed weighed me down like cement blocks.

My dad had a favorite saying about the unexpected, his time as a veterinarian convincing him that he couldn't predict what kind or how many emergencies he and mom might encounter in any given day. *"You can never be ready for everything,"* he would say, *"but you can be prepared."*

With the clinic only days from opening, I needed to prepare if things went sideways. Continuing to listen to the others formulate our best course of action, I opened an app on my phone and started a list of to-dos I needed to complete. It was short, but several were biggies.

I emailed the employment contract to JR with a note explaining my hiring procedure included the thirty-day probation clause and asking him to attend a staff meeting Sunday night to finalize our plans for Monday's opening.

When we arrived at Aurora's, she told us to wait. She had books she wanted to give me so I could cram the limited, but important, info she had archived regarding the Order.

As the limo purred, and she and Andy disappeared into the shadows, Killion said, "You are abnormally quiet."

I created a new note and declared it my last will and testimony. *I am of sound mind,* I typed.

Questionable, but I'd never done one of these before and it was how my mom and dad's wills had begun. Now that I was close to my dream of reopening the clinic, I had to be sure it did, indeed, open—with or without me. "I'm organizing a few things for next week. I have a lot to plan for." It was true. I made Killion my executor, stating the clinic would go to him in the event of my death. "Can you ask Mason to cover my morning shift at The Bean?"

The only illumination inside the car was from the tiny floor lights and the glowing controls in the doors. Shadows clung to both of us, yet I could see his concerned expression.

His silver aura pulsed, his magic soothing against my heart. The deeper my emotions for him became, the more in-tune with his energy I was. The clip-clop of my pulse and the tingling in my blood weren't only from my attraction to him—his fear for my life had his normally calm, cool self highly agitated.

"Of course." He glanced at my cell, and I kept it angled so he couldn't read the screen. "Do not agonize over this. I will speak to SMG and advise them what Death is up to. There are better ways to handle the situation and I am certain they'll have concerns regarding his plan."

Nita could have my personal stuff. I added that, then I

pocketed the phone, not sure what else to put in it. I had so little. All I needed to be sure of was that the clinic was in good hands. It already was, thanks to the Undead master next to me. "The archimagus is violating the rules. He has to be stopped and brought to justice. I can deal with him and the ghosts. You're the one who shouldn't worry."

He scanned my face and I kept my expression open and neutral. I was rewarded when his hyper-protectiveness relaxed slightly. "You have proven yourself to be more than competent in handling unusual situations. You're correct in that you can take care of this one as well—especially with our assistance."

The door opened and Aurora stuck her head in. A heap of old, dusty leather-bound volumes dropped into my lap. "I've marked the important passages."

Bright pink sticky notes poked out from the edges in stark contrast to the yellowed and stained pages. "Thank you," I told her. "For everything."

Her hand grasped mine and she squeezed. "Get some sleep. I'll call you in the morning to go over two counter-spells we can use in case he tries to hex you, okay?"

I nodded, and she left. As we drove to the hotel, Killion contacted Mason. While he spoke to the young man, I finished the will and sent a copy to Death with a note. *Hang onto this for me.*

Hip-hop music greeted us when we entered the pent-house. Pennyworth was twerking while he dusted and jumped when we surprised him. The song immediately cut out and he bowed deeply. If he could have blushed, I believe he would have been red as a tomato. "Master. Ms. Frost. What can I get you?"

"Are you hungry?" Killion asked me, carrying Aurora's books to the coffee table.

Ghost greeted the butler, who made a fuss over her. I set my bag in its usual spot near the door. "Coffee would be appreciated. Strong and black. I have a lot of reading to do."

The butler gave another bow. "Coming right up."

Despite the caffeine, an hour later I was falling asleep at the dining room table. My head continually crashed into the open books, sunrise creeping in through the windows. Pennyworth pulled the blinds and heavy drapes, plunging the rooms back into shadows.

I needed a training session with Katarina, but I couldn't lift a pencil at this point, much less block an attack. My body needed rest.

I tried to power through, but eventually succumbed. I woke a few hours later under the heavy comforter on Killion's bed. After a quick shower, I answered texts from Nita and my uncle, and assured Dr. O'Leary I had hired JR. It was nearly time for the interview with Patty. After that, I had two more items to complete before my trek into The Ghost Lands at dusk.

After thinking it over, I dropped Death's amulet in a vase of blood red roses sitting on an oversized antique dresser. Then I went out to enjoy what might be my last breakfast.

Patty beat me to the clinic, her generous frame wrapped in a puffy white coat that set off her silver dreadlocks and glittery eyeshadow.

She smiled as I exited the limo and extended her hand. "Hi, Chloe. Gosh, you look just like your pretty momma, rest her soul."

The compliment caught me off guard. While I saw my mom's eyes when I stared into the mirror these days, no one had ever said I resembled her. A warm sensation rooted in my chest and I returned Patty's smile as I shook her hand. "Thank you for coming."

I'd assured Killion I would handle this on my own. He had house business to attend to with his new lieutenant, Mason's vampire mother, Harlow. He and Moss drove away as I unlocked the door.

Inside, we shed our coats and I gave her a quick tour. "Nothing fancy. I've kept things like my parents had it."

She studied the back where we now stood. "My first rescue was a crow." The corners of her chocolate brown eyes crinkled with mischief. "He was injured on the side of the road when I was on my way home from work. That sad, little thing! His wing was broken and he was barely breathing. I brought him here. The clinic was closed and I had to use the emergency number posted on the front door. Your dad came right over, and even though wild birds weren't his specialty, he had Gordy fixed up in no time. I took him home, trained him to use a litter box, and never had a bit of trouble with him—outside of the fact he was always stealing my favorite pair of hoop earrings." Her eyes crinkled with a teary smile. "He even learned a few words, and he always got along with my dogs. I loved that little guy. If your father hadn't answered my call that night, I don't think Gordy would have lived."

The warmth in my chest expanded. "That was Dad." I fought not to tear up myself. My relationship with Corvus wasn't quite so loving, but he'd grown on me. "I have a raven. He hangs out here some days, and I consider him our mascot. Are you okay with that?"

Her eyes lit up. "I'd love it. Have you taught him any words? They are quick learners and can mimic human speech."

Refraining from telling her his favorite expression was "kill" seemed prudent. She hadn't accepted the job yet and I didn't want to scare her off. "He knows a few phrases, mostly from his previous owner, and he watches movies with my landlady. That's broadened his vocabulary, but not always in the best way."

She chuckled. "Gordy taught my eldest son how to take the Lord's name in vain, and at the ripe age of four, no less. Jeffrey dropped that bomb right in front of my father-in-law! He was stacking blocks and they fell over, and...out of the mouth of babes, you know. At least he used the swear in an appropriate manner."

We laughed, and I motioned her to follow me to the front desk. I liked her and that she remembered my folks. She was open to pets of all types, and I had the feeling she could keep Corvus in line.

From the drawer I withdrew a printed version of Killion's contract. "Can you start Monday?"

She accepted the paper and snatched a pen from the holder, a mug shaped like a cat face. "Consider me starting right now."

Once she'd signed and dated it, I gave her the phone numbers of all the employees, along with Nita and Aurora's. "Our first staff meeting is Sunday evening at five. I know it's short notice, but I need you there. I'll order pizza and we'll go over Monday's schedule for the grand opening. Later in the week, the Chamber of Commerce wants to have an official ribbon cutting."

"Wonderful. My first request is for cheese pizza. I'm vegetarian."

Cheese pizza had always been my favorite. "You got it."

She rubbed her hands like a child in front of a stack of Christmas gifts, ready to tear into them. "I have a few ideas for scheduling."

"I'd love to hear them."

"It would be effective for the doctors, as well as the rest of us, if we reserve one day a week to batch elective surgeries, dental procedures, new patient visits, and the like. Also, the homeless shelter residents have dogs and assorted other pets who never receive veterinary care. Those poor animals aren't getting proper nutrition either. Perhaps once a quarter, we can offer a free spay/neuter clinic, and get them vaccinated. The youth group I work with can help and we can place a basket up here to accept food and toy donations."

Her energy was infectious. "Bring all those ideas to the meeting and we'll create a timeline for when we can begin instituting them."

Her smile made me feel as if everything was going to be okay. I hoped it was. "I'll contact the paper and the radio station," she continued. "Get us some publicity."

I definitely liked this woman. "If by chance I can't make it Sunday night, I need you to do me a favor."

The radiance fell from her face. "Can't make it?"

"I know it sounds weird, but I have something serious to take care of and it may interfere with me being here. My partner and the others will be, though, and I need you to be sure they all agree to my stipulations, even if they don't want to."

"I can't guarantee they'll listen to me, but I can try."

No pushy questions. A relief. "No matter what, this needs to open. I want you to make sure it does, even if something should happen to me. I know it's asking a lot of you, but even if you have to stand up to my business partner, Killion, I'm asking you to see my dream through."

She placed a kind hand on my arm. "Aw, sweetie. Nothing bad's gonna happen to you. Your mama and daddy are watching over you from heaven."

Once more, her comment took me off guard. Tears pushed at the backs of my eyeballs. She hugged me before she left, and once I closed the door behind her, I let myself cry.

I sure hoped she was right.

TWENTY

St. Joseph's was gloomy even in the light of day. No sneaking in this time, I strolled through the open gates, Ghost trotting beside me, wagging her tail.

It felt odd to be here without anyone, yet it was necessary. Killion had questioned me earlier about my claim that JR's grave had been the one the victim had been left on. He'd argued that Aurora was right—it was her grandmother's. I needed to see it with my own eyes.

I stared at the stone marker from outside the still-present crime scene tape. *Constance Ciara McCormick.* The woman's name, birth and death dates did not match what I'd previously seen. I shook my head and blinked several times. Nothing changed.

Envisioning my internal dial, I channeled my magic up to a four and let my grave sight slide into place. I scanned the area for Jane Doe's ghost, or any others, including the lady with the stringy hair.

None appeared, but I felt Esmeralda's long-dead corpse respond to my necromantic energy.

I shut down the grave sight and cut the power, dropping

to zero once more. I'd taken the chance of leaving the amulet behind because I couldn't risk Death discovering I was about to defy him, and I prayed Aurora's tea, and my new way of handling my power, would allow me to control it.

I thought about what Stormfinger had said—that the beverage was a placebo. I knew it was more than that, but I *had* placed enormous faith in it.

I would continue to do so. No waking the dead today. "I'm sorry you were disturbed," I said to the corpse at my feet, then whistled for Ghost.

She appeared from behind a tree and the two of us set off for the central mausoleum.

Thankfully, the place was devoid of visitors. The dog ran ahead on the interconnected paths, stopping here and there to sniff dead flowers and faded decorations. Like in the church, I felt a tug in my chest—the dead, lawn, flowers, and bodies, all wanting me to restore their lives.

The skeletal grim on the roof smiled down at us as we approached. Weak blades of light streamed through the trees, dancing over his scythe and making his exposed ribs glow.

Or maybe it was magic. I sent my awareness out to see if I could sense any, but caught only a slight essence that felt vaguely familiar. As if we'd "met" before. No doubt because the ground had absorbed my blood and created a connection.

"Why would anyone want such a grotesque and—dare I say it?—*grim* statue on the top of their final resting place?" I asked the inanimate object. "Normal people choose comforting images, like angels or animals."

In my gut, I knew there had to be a reason for this representation of, well, *me*, and the fact the portal had appeared here.

Ghost barked cheerily in response.

The grass where I'd spilled blood was still dead. My skin prickled when I drew close to it.

Walking around the exterior of the raised plot with its ornamental iron fence, I scanned for swirling mists. Ghost, head up, mimicked me, tail wagging again.

No such thing appeared.

"Well," I said to the dog. "No time like the present."

The weight of my bag was heavy with the tools I'd brought. Staying outside the gate, I let it slide to the ground and began unpacking it.

Crystals went in the four corners, and I used a black marker to draw a circle in the lawn around the perimeter. The statue's hollow gaze followed me as I poured black salt on top of that, then sketched protection sigils I'd memorized from one of Aurora's books on the Order of Alexandria on the insides of both my wrists.

While my grim tattoo protected me when I was harvesting a soul, I figured extra defense wouldn't hurt.

Ghost had climbed into the open bag and made herself comfortable, watching me. I chased her out and withdrew my now dog hair-covered robes. They vibrated in anticipation.

While the intel on the Order was slim, it had given me confidence. The members were human, even if they *were* exceptional magic practitioners. No vampires, shifters, or grims. They needed spells and potions for alchemy, and that gave me a slight upper hand. I wasn't discounting the archimagus' power or abilities, but I was unique in the supernatural department. I wore the robes, had my trusty scythe, and I'd brought my psychopomp.

The death blade hummed when I slid it out of its leather sheath. I glanced around to ensure I was still alone, and outside of some chilly pigeons waddling around searching for food between gravestones, all was clear.

Scythe and dog at the ready, I loitered for a few heartbeats. Was I really going to do this?

I waited, secretly hoping the ghost from last time would appear so I could question her. Any ghost for that matter would do. I called on the grave sight and held my breath, calling softly to them. "I won't harvest you, I just want to talk."

Being in full grim fashion, holding my scythe, was probably unconvincing. I called again anyway.

It was simply unnatural not to see a single ghost. Eventually, I gave up, dreading the idea that they were all in The Ghost Lands.

Gray clouds scooted across the sky. The air was dry and crisp against my cheek. I glared back at the concrete version of me, daring him, as I secured my weapon in its carrier and placed it on my back. "Gotta say, I wear the robes better."

I swear, his grin widened.

"Come on, Ghost." I lifted her and we crossed the salt circle. The gate squeaked as I opened it.

My ears popped and the air went electric once we entered the container the circle created. I took a few seconds to adjust to the heightened energy. My grim tattoo heated and the sketched sigils on my wrists glowed.

The hem of the robes dragged along the grass as I walked the perimeter of the plot, once again searching for the portal. If it didn't appear, this was all for naught.

The fog that had appeared on the corpse road had been similar, perhaps a mirrored image or a type of "offspring," but these were meant for me. I felt it in my bones as a surety.

Even if I couldn't see it, I knew the "mother" portal was here. All I had to do was locate it and let myself in.

I didn't want to put Ghost on the ground, but she struggled determinedly, so I did. She sniffed the lawn, the bushes, the building itself. She thoroughly inspected everything, yet gave no indication she could sense the doorway to the other dimension.

I stared at the mausoleum itself, sending a probe of magic over it. A thin gray film existed around the arched entryway, but that appeared to be more of a security measure to keep entities out, rather than an invisible portal to suck them in.

I even considered the reaper statue, but his location was too hard to access, and when the previous portal had appeared, it was ground-level.

The family entombed here bore the surname Methuselah. I straightened. That was the name Aurora had mentioned—the archimagus who'd belonged to the Order of Alexandria.

The four original founders dated back to Mesopotamia. Men learned in science, astronomy, medicine, and engineering. They believed they could master everything in existence by breaking down its parts and reformulating them into what they wished to create. No magic involved.

Far ahead of their time, they lifted the veil of many mysteries and postulated theories later proven.

The one major area they couldn't create a provable formula for, or control, was death. The human body had far too many systems, quirks, and anomalies to fully grasp. Over and over, experimenting with their formulas, they attempted to create life outside the human body, and became obsessed with raising the dead.

What they succeeded at—besides driving themselves crazy—was a form of necromancy. They could stitch together the healthiest parts of corpses and infuse the body with a charge, much like the fictional Dr. Frankenstein and his monster. In fact, it was proposed by one of Aurora's histories on magic, that Mary Shelley had found such writings during her research on the supernatural and had been inspired to compose her epic tome.

The essence of the soul, however, did not inhabit their creations, no matter what scientific manner they employed.

Refusing to believe in magic, and determined to succeed, they added scholars, priests, and other scientists to their group. Over generations, they also became tied to royalty, as well as those with deep pockets who'd funded experiments and paid officials to look the other way when they raided burial grounds or committed murder themselves in the name of science. In so doing, they could study the process of death and end up with a fresh corpse to work on.

Legends and myths about the Order were abundant, but true facts were scarce by the time descendants of the original group ventured to the United States. The Order's goals and rules had morphed considerably by then, as well, and the men of science became more of a secret society for rich, pompous egomaniacs. They yearned for money, power, and control.

While I wasn't excited about taking on one of them, from all accounts, our local archimagus was working alone. There was no indication he had cohorts or accomplices. My plan was to slip in, get the lay of The Ghost Lands, and be out before he knew I was there. Then the gang and I could mount a full attack based on facts, rather than theories. Less dangerous for them.

As I worked at finding the entry point, I kept an eye out for ghosts, the archimagus, and any innocent visitors who might venture by. I also considered the idea that my new buddy, Neymar, was the sorcerer collecting ghosts for his own purposes.

Twenty minutes later, it was still just me, Ghost, and the pigeons. "Come on," I complained to the giant reaper watching me, "throw me a bone here."

My psychopomp sat down on her haunches, eyeing me with anticipation. I suspected the word "bone" was the reason. The long hair on her ears fluttered in the light breeze and her dark eyes glittered. She barked twice.

"I know. You're bored. I should have brought your toy. Or a snack." For both of us. I was building up a hunger. "Maybe this is a waste of time. Killion and Aurora will kill me if they find out I tried this on my own. Putting them in danger, though, makes me break out in hives. I just want to find out what we're up against and I don't want to risk the welfare of my friends until I do. The two of them mean well with their books and training, but I'm Grim Zero. I've handled worse than a bunch of guys playing with magic, right? And one thing I really need to know is how this ties in with JR's death."

She stood and gave another bark. Marching over to the dead lawn, she pawed it, then morphed into her psychopomp form.

Seeing her as a giant, slobbering beast was something I'd never get used to. Head larger than mine, fangs as big as my hands, and those eyes—she panted, and drool dripped to the ground.

"Wait." *Duh!* "You can cross dimensions. Can you take me to The Ghost Lands?"

One giant paw smacked the ground. It was the communication system Andy and I had created when he was stuck in his wolf form.

A single tap meant yes. Two, no.

I did a fist pump. "Yes!" I held out a hand to her. "Let's go."

Her fangs sank into my flesh and I swallowed my yelp. A breath later, I stood in a gloomy landscape devoid of life—and full of ghosts.

TWENTY-ONE

My stomach flipped over on itself and my head swam as I landed on my knees. Gravity here worked differently, my body now as light as cotton candy. When I stood, I couldn't feel my feet and tumbled sideways.

Ghost still had her teeth buried in my arm. That was the only thing that kept me upright.

My last meal threatened to come up. I commanded Ghost to release me and she did. A few drops of blood floated into the air, the tiny droplets suspended in space. I leaned on her side for support.

The mist teased my skin, tiny pricks assaulting me. A thicker mass gathered around my wound, the sensation of a dozen invisible razor blades tasting my blood.

I shook my hand, chasing the mass away, and fought the sick feeling, but the world spun again and my grave sight kicked in hard. I nearly tossed my cookies, choking down fear along with my stomach's contents.

I blinked to clear my vision and the landscape shimmered. While my body felt light as a feather, my head weighed more than usual. Thanks to the sight, I now made out a dozen spirits floating in a circle around us, their energy pressing into my skull.

The spirits' eyes had a white film over them, their lips drawn back from their gums in freakish grimaces. Some were dressed in modern clothes, others in styles not in fashion for a hundred years.

A low buzzing started, reminding me of a swarm of flies. It took me a second to realize it was coming from them. Ghost growled, and the noise gained volume, making me wish I could scratch my eardrums.

"Don't be scared," I said over the drone. As long as I had the group so close, it seemed a good time to put them out of their misery. "I can free you from this place."

I unsheathed the scythe and the din ratcheted up. The flies had become wasps—and they were angry.

"You've been trapped here by a powerful sorcerer," I told them. "I can break his hold on you, and you can move on. I'll set you free."

Two of them twitched and shook their heads. Others hissed.

"He wants to use you for his own purposes and you'll be trapped here forever if he succeeds."

They snarled and gnashed their teeth. I'd been around enough animals to understand that warning. They wanted me gone.

Ghost tensed and lowered her enormous head, ready for a fight. My whole body trembled from the bitter cold the spirits were exuding. Either they didn't understand, or they didn't want to get out of here.

This was about to go three shades of bad. "Why would you want to stay in this place? Surely you don't want to be trapped here, under a madman's control."

Reasoning with the dead never worked, no matter how

much I wanted it to. The scythe heated in my palm and I held it out like a peace offering. "Please." I had to try one more time. "This will be so much easier if you go willingly. The afterlife is beautiful. Peaceful. I promise."

As one, the group drew closer. For a second, I thought they might understand and were going to pass on without a fight.

Then one—a male in the suit he'd been buried in—reached for the blade. When his gnarled hand touched it, however, he did not cross over.

His bony fingers grasped the steel and his sneering mouth twisted into a misshaped smile. Every cell inside me cried a warning. This is what I'd felt on the corpse road—something trying to take it from me.

I jerked back, but he held tight.

How was that possible? He was a ghost, noncorporeal, yet he had a physicalness that allowed him to grasp things.

And he was still here.

The laws of physics don't apply in this realm.

Yet, surely a grim blade still commanded power over spirits.

A tug-of-war ensued. The other apparitions hovered, watching intently. My balance was still wonky, and I banged into Ghost, trying to remain planted as the male gave a hard yank.

I fell.

And kept falling.

The ground seemed too far away. When I finally landed, my knees sank into spongy soil. The odor of grave dirt and long-dead things clogged my nostrils.

Before I could get up, the scythe was ripped from my grasp. The raging spirits descended on me.

Icy fingers clawed at my limbs, my back. They

scratched my hands and face, but the robes protected the rest of me. I wrestled with the mob, retaking the weapon from Suit Man. Why he didn't move onto the afterlife was still a mystery, but I didn't have time to care.

Normally, I handled one or two spirits at a time. This was bedlam. The training I'd done with Katarina deserted me, and the fact gravity was not on my side didn't help. The ghosts were able to push me around, tug at my braid, bite me.

Always up for a good fight, Ghost joined the fray. She both assisted me and got in my way. A large fleshy man in tattered clothes landed a punch to my jaw. She lunged at another, but knocked into my side, sending me sprawling.

With three others forming a wall behind me, I didn't go far. The man's aura was a sickly yellow as he stomped forward to strike again. My psychopomp whirled, clamped onto his ragged shirt and he barked in pain before the two of them disappeared in a flash.

His transitioning soul gave me a shot of bliss, and like caffeine infused directly into my system, I felt instantly refreshed. "You all have the wrong idea," I gasped, facing those left. "I don't want to hurt you. I'm here to help!"

"You bound us here," a woman in a hoop skirt shouted at me. "I want to go home!"

Me? I held out the scythe. "Touch this and you will."

Her filmy gaze slid to the steel. "Lies! You are a demon!"

I've been called worse, but I still flinched. "I'm a grim reaper," I corrected, "but I can see where you might get the wrong idea with these ugly robes. The Ghost Lands are not my doing. An archimagus"—I stopped at her odd look. What term would she understand? "A wizard. A magic user who's evil. He caused this. Not me."

A gloved finger shot out to point at my nose. "You raised our spirits and trapped us here."

Jeez. Her IQ as a human might not have been all that high, but it seemed she'd lost points upon death. I leveled the blade at her and wondered what was taking Ghost so long to return. A shiver of panic raced over my skin. What if she couldn't?

Don't be ridiculous. She'd been my way in, of course she could.

The woman lunged, her hands forming claws. Her lips pulled even farther away from her teeth in a snarl.

I didn't have to move the scythe—she simply dove into it. Her weird eyes went wide and she exploded into thousands of sand particles.

That's not right. Her spirit should have vanished, even without Ghost to escort her to the afterlife. I should have felt another rush of bliss.

The sand showered over all of us, and I covered my face with my sleeve. The others scattered. They, too, protected their heads and faces with their hands.

An aging woman peeked out from between arthritic fingers. "What have you done?"

"Good question," I muttered. Was this a result of no psychopomp? "This place doesn't adhere to the laws of nature." I poked at the pile of sand. "Anyone have an idea why your friend turned into a beach?"

To make things even stranger, my death blade flashed a bright pink and sucked up the particles like a Hoover vacuum.

Okay, then.

The group backed away. I didn't blame them. Death was one thing; annihilation, a whole other ball of spirit.

My manual stated that souls could never be destroyed.

Once created, they were timeless. So what had just happened? It sure appeared I'd blitzed this one.

"Seriously." I pivoted, meeting the wacky white gazes of those left. "Anybody have an idea?"

Blank stares. At least they were no longer attacking me.

I shrugged. "I guess maybe I need to do some research—"

Blinding light burst all around us and Ghost reappeared.

Surprise!, her wagging tail seemed to say. She'd brought company.

TWENTY-TWO

"What in the…?" Killion stepped toward me, magic pouring off him as his gaze roamed over the group. "Have you lost your ability to think clearly?"

The remaining ghosts scrambled back, screeching and buzzing again. Aurora, hands raised as if she were about to fling magic at them, paused and tilted her head. "Oh my," she said. "How many are there? This is bad."

Andy tried to sidle up next to her, but his wolf paused and faltered, making him appear drunk.

At least I wasn't the only one struggling with the lack of gravity. I wondered why it didn't impact the other two. "What are you doing here?"

The ghosts faded into the gray essence, shimmering away like fog dissolving in the sun. "The question is," Killion said, "what are *you*? You were to wait for us and Death."

"I understand you're upset, but hear me out. Our archimagus seems to only work at night, right? Coming here then, when he might be present, is when it's truly dangerous. I wanted us to have intel about this place before we did, so Ghost and I came to scope it out."

Andy lifted his muzzle to sniff the air and the mere action caused him to list sideways. He clipped Aurora and knocked her off balance. "What is wrong with you?" she barked.

I pointed at the massive shifter, still struggling not to fall over. "He and I are reacting to the energy dynamics differently than you. If I hadn't already discovered that, I'd be struggling with it when we arrived to face our enemy." I nodded, encouraging them to concede my plan was a good one. "Why doesn't the odd gravity affect you? And how did you know I was here?"

The two of them exchanged a look, and Aurora grabbed Andy's scruff to hold him in place. "I don't feel any different."

"Nor I." Killion looked me over from head to toe. "A woman named Patty called me. She said you listed me as an emergency contact, and while she didn't know you well, she was concerned for your wellbeing after she met with you earlier. When she relayed what you'd said to her, I assumed you were attempting to take on the archimagus yourself."

I would have if he'd been present. My temples throbbed and ringing pierced my ears. I swayed, not from my gravity-induced drunkenness but lightheadedness. "I think it's time to go."

Killion grabbed my arm and pulled me into his embrace. "I warned you that you cannot stay in Death's domain. How long have you been here?"

Ghost whined. I brushed a strand from my face. A sickly heat crept up from my stomach. "Not long." My body was suddenly weak, as though I'd aged twenty years. "At least, I don't think so."

Killion motioned for the others to take hold of Ghost. Aurora placed a hand on her back, while Andy gently took one of her ears in his mouth. Killion guided my hand to her thick neck fur, entwining his in it as well. He continued to hold me around the waist with his other arm. "Take us home," he commanded.

Her psychopomp power was an electrical charge, pitching my already unsteady senses into a whirling cyclone. All I could do was focus on Killion's solid body, the presence of his fingers enfolding mine while I held my breath.

With a sudden shift, like a runaway train suddenly breaking to a dead stop, we landed in the graveyard. The impact left me sprawled on the ground near the Methuselah mausoleum, and I lay on my stomach for a long moment, absorbed in trying to breathe and not vomit.

I turned my head from side to side. "Killion?" I called, but it came out raspy. Closing my eyes, I willed my spinning head to slow and swallowed the bile in my throat. I tried again.

There was no answer. Forcing my eyes open, I staggered to my elbows. "Aurora? Andy?"

A shower of pain lanced down my spinal column. I gritted my teeth and kept going, pushing myself to my hands and knees. The scythe lay far away. My legs were tangled in my robes. Fear took hold of me, and I shouted now, ignoring how every movement sent a ripple effect through me. "Ghost! Somebody—*any*body—answer me!"

The cemetery was dead silent, the grave markers in shadows. Everything had a strange fluorescent glow, and I rubbed my eyes, willing them to see at least one of my companions.

Something large and heavy hit the ground behind me,

causing everything to reverberate. My bones quaked as if a dump truck had just landed on the grass. A frigid cold wrapped around me, and I told myself not to look. To get to my feet and run.

Move! Go!

Like in my nightmares, my body ignored the command. I couldn't help it. I swiveled and gasped.

The skeletal reaper had come to life and was bearing down on me.

He lifted his giant scythe over my head and swung.

TWENTY-THREE

His concrete scythe had to weigh as much as I did. Head still swimming, I dove out of the way as the mighty blade cleaved the air. It skimmed past my cheek, and I swear it sliced hairs from my scalp.

I screamed. The sound echoed around the gravestones and the impact when it hit rocked the ground. Dirt flew up into the air and rained down on me.

The skull face leered as he raised it again. A swampy green magical aura enveloped him. He had no skin or lips, yet I swear he was grinning with glee and embracing a focused determination to kill me.

"I'm one of you," I yelled, fighting with the robes. "Stop it!"

The gigantic blade sliced through the air once more, and I gulped as it landed between my ankles. It cut through the tangled fabric, freeing my legs.

The robes shuddered. My skin crawled.

"Chloe!" Killion's voice boomed through the air.

I'd never been so glad to hear it. "Here," I cried, and stumbled to my feet, as the reaper tugged his weapon free.

My own flew into my palm. The solid handle snugged itself in and my fingers wrapped around it. Could a steel blade take on a concrete one? I fled toward the closed iron gate, not sure I wanted to find out.

From the corner of my eye, I saw two things at once—a figure whose magical glow was like that of the giant reaper's writing sigils in the air, and Aurora and Andy emerging from behind a row of trees at the rear of the cemetery. While they were a dozen yards from me, her voice came through crisp and clear, as if she were by my side. "Take him out at the knees."

The figure ran in and around monuments, stopping to glance my way as he continued drawing. The marks flared red and dissipated one after the other. Every time he drew one, the grim moved closer to me.

It seemed as if it all happened in a fraction of a second, time seeming to have slowed. My attacker swung the mighty scythe and, with an ease I'd never experienced before, I sidestepped the blow.

Maybe the sessions with Katarina were paying off after all.

In the next drawn out tick of the clock, Killion tore a marble tombstone from its base. "Get down!"

I ducked and the slab of stone sailed over my head. It collided with the reaper's hips, knocking him sideways. I straightened and aimed my weapon at his knees.

The glow of a red sigil teased my peripheral vision, the slab breaking in half before it fell to the ground. My blade, built for slicing through skin and bone, couldn't possibly do any damage. Yet, I braced for the impact and watched in amazement as it cut through the knobby patella of my concrete nemesis.

The skeletal grim listed to one side, his lower left leg no

longer attached. The assault was too much for his physical structure, regardless of the magician's power controlling him.

"The archimagus," I yelled, pointing to his hiding place. "Get him!"

Aurora ran in that direction, and the shadowed figure sent his glowing magic through the air toward her. She flipped a hand and it exploded into fireworks. Her next gesture sent the man to the ground.

Andy, close to me now, jumped the iron fence and braced all four paws behind the staggering grim. Ghost also appeared, standing on top of the roof of the mausoleum, teeth bared as she snarled.

Time seemed to snap back to normal and Killion reached my side. The reaper attempted another swing, using the scythe like a hammer. The vampire pushed me out of the way.

His overwhelming strength, paired with his need to protect me, was no laughing matter. I sailed out of the gated burial plot and landed face down on a freshly dug grave.

The headstone had not been erected yet, and only a metal marker signified who was buried there. My mind glitched when I read the name. Behind me, I heard the blade strike, felt the earthquake it caused.

Regardless of his limp, and the fact his master was now out of commission, the stupid thing refused to quit.

Heart hammering, I leaped to my feet. The reaper dislodged his blade once more, raised it above his head, and brought it down.

My breath caught as the scythe cleaved the master vampire in two.

TWENTY-FOUR

A scream tore from my throat and detonated the stone grim, uprooted trees and shattered headstones.

My vision flashed electric blue, but not before I glimpsed Aurora and Andy cowering with hands over their heads.

My legs went numb and I dropped to my knees in shock. Then I fell face-down onto the ground, sobbing. My ears rang, guts twisting, my heart ripped in half.

The smell of the grass suffocated me, my face buried in the cold ground. Grief racked my body in waves.

My robes pressed against my skin, and my voice became raw, the pounding of my pulse filling my ears.

After a minute, I sensed Aurora kneeling next to me. She placed a hand on my arm. "Chloe, what is it? What's wrong?"

Her voice was a background noise to the all-consuming sorrow raging through me. I heard more voices, both the living and the dead.

Death. I sunk my fingers into the grave soil and longed for it. Those buried nearby responded, their spirits dancing at the edge of my awareness, begging to be reunited with their bodies.

My magic roared out of me, a tsunami. The dead lawn under me sprang to life. I heard the dead sigh in relief.

Warm hands gripped my shoulders and rolled me over, forcing my face up. I kept my eyes shut and shoved at Aurora. "Leave me be," I commanded, and the words came out cold, hard.

Packed with power.

A matching pulse of magic came back at me. The grip on my shoulders tightened. "I will not. Open your eyes."

Not Aurora. The command was from a ghost. Nevertheless, I felt the thrum of it—of him—in my blood.

Emptied of all feeling, I had no energy to disobey. I cracked open one lid, then the other. My heart leaped, my voice caught. "But you're...*dead.*"

Looking confused—a totally unusual state for him—Killion stared at me. "I thought we had thoroughly covered my Undead status to your satisfaction." He cocked his head as he stared into my eyes. "What has brought on this hysteria?"

Hysteria? I stuttered, fumbling for words. This had to be a dream—a delusion. I glanced past him—there was no body split in two inside the iron fence.

"Call back your magic, Chloe. Do not wake the dead."

They twitched and squirmed in the caskets, wanting out. Speechless, I grabbed hold of his arms, squeezed hard, and hiccupped a breath when he felt solid under my hands.

"Rest," I murmured and turned the faucet off on my magic.

They did.

The others watched as he assisted me to sit up. On the other side of the expanse, the magician was bound to a tree.

Andy, now in human form, tugged on an ear as if to clear his hearing. "And I thought Aurora could yell. Those are some pipes you've got there, Chloe."

"You're not..." I touched Killion's face. He shifted his lips to kiss my palm. "I saw you get cut in half."

As one, we all glanced at the spot where the concrete blade lay. While my scream had shattered the handle into dozens of shards, the point of the blade remained buried in the lawn.

"I assure you, I am well." He looked at me once more and ran a hand over the back of my skull. "Did you hit your head when I shoved you out of the way?"

Had I?

"She's hallucinating," the robed man called from across the way. "A result of suppressing her magic."

"Wait," I said. I knew that voice. I gained my feet and slowly walked past the others. "You."

Neymar Stormfinger stared at me. "I've seen it before—necromancers who refuse to learn the proper way of handling their power. Told you the dam would burst."

I wanted to punch him. "You sent that statue after me! That was no hallucination."

"You are correct on the latter, but not about me animating the grim. Death asked me to keep an eye on you. He knew you would ditch his tracking device at some point, and he instructed me to follow you. I was attempting to control that rogue statue once it came to life, but it was not my magic that activated it."

Aurora joined us. "Then whose was it?"

"I have no idea, but I can speculate." He flicked his gaze to Killion as the vampire came to stand next to me, then refocused on me. "Yours. You did it."

"*Me?*" My voice echoed through the shadows. "I saw

you waving your hands and writing sigils in the air. I know it was you."

He chuckled dryly and shook his head. "You've suppressed your magic and it's causing a ripple effect. The Ghost Lands, mis-channeling of your power, these hallucinations—there will be more."

Andy arrived, glancing back at the destruction. "Can you do that all the time? Make things, you know..." He made an explosion noise and mimicked one using his hands.

I ignored him, grabbing Stormfinger by his collar. "It was you we saw chasing that ghost last night. She told me you were coming for me next. I don't believe for a minute that *I* created The Ghost Lands. You did that by trapping those poor spirits to ramp up your magic."

"I don't need spirits to do anything," he retorted. "Can't you see how warped your perspective on all of this has skewed you off course?"

Aurora placed a hand on my forearm. "I hate to say it, but he may be right."

"What?" I shoved her away. "You can't be serious."

"How do you explain the hallucinations?" Stormfinger asked. "The things you've seen that aren't real?"

The memory of the name on the metal grave marker I'd just seen flashed through my mind. "Wait." I glanced over my shoulder toward it. "You're dead."

His mustache twitched. "Is that so? Like your boyfriend here?"

Releasing him, I stomped through the debris to the place I'd landed. The marker was still there, but my scream had uprooted it. It was face down on the ground and I picked it up. The name was covered with soil. Wiping that away, I caught my breath.

The name I'd seen moments ago but hadn't had time to

process had been Stormfinger's. Like the one belonging to Aurora's grandmother, that I'd seen as JR's, this one now read differently. *Sally Comber.*

Tossing it down, I rubbed my eyes. Had I imagined it? Was I hallucinating all of this?

I hurried to the path leading from the mausoleum and followed it to the grave I had originally misread—Aurora's grandmother's.

Ghost, in her puppy form and ready for an adventure, caught up with me and we angled off the path and picked our way through the graves. I knew what name would be there, but I needed to be sure. Killion and Aurora called after me, and I heard their footsteps racing to catch up.

This area had avoided the brunt of my destruction and the plots were deep in shadows. I fumbled in the robes to pull out my phone and shine the flashlight on the engraving.

Constance Ciara McCormick. I hung my head. This couldn't be happening.

The cemetery was large and sprawling, and all the raised beds looked similar. Using the beam, I ran to the nearby raised plots. Reading each aged marble and granite headstone, I searched frantically. Not one listed Jackson Rawlings Banks.

Which was indeed a relief, but also juiced my panic. The sorcerer was correct. I'd lost my freaking mind.

What about Eliza? Had I imagined her?

Had I done the same with JR's ghost?

I sat down hard with a huff on the corner of one of the plots. "It's official," I said to my audience when they reached me. "I've gone insane."

TWENTY-FIVE

Killion took my hand and led me back to the Methuselah monument, but a few feet away from it, he pulled up short.

Death stood on the top of the crypt in the place where the stone grim had formerly been. "Started the party without me, did you?" He glowed more brightly to my eyes, and for the briefest moment, I thought I saw the outline of wings. Some were white, others gray, and still more at the bottom, black. I blinked, and they were gone.

He hopped down, as graceful as a spider on a silk thread, eyeing the destruction I'd caused. "Care to explain?"

I didn't have it in me, and while I opened my mouth to reply, nothing came out.

Killion started to, but Stormfinger cut in. "As you suspected, she's breaking the rules and going off on her own. I've emphasized the importance of training, yet she refuses to make time for it. Suppressing her necromancy has caused a dimensional pocket to form and has trapped a considerable amount of souls in it. She is also hallucinating, and cannot go on much longer before she suffers a total break with reality."

Death gave me a disappointed, but not surprised, appraisal. "Looks like it already has."

Stormfinger appeared gratified. "This is the tip of the iceberg, and I prefer not to be on the Titanic when it sinks."

That's when I saw her—the ghost from the previous night. She peeked out from behind a pillar and stared at Stormfinger.

I stepped toward her and her focus snapped to me. I knew she was about to dart away, and I was running before I could think. "Wait! I want to—*oof*!"

I was jerked off my feet and yanked through the air. I ended up inside the fenced mausoleum facing Death. He grabbed my wrist. "Sorry, Chloe."

The next thing I knew, we were flying.

The air was sucked from my lungs, and when we landed, I tumbled apple cart over reaper robes into a ghost.

I went right through the spirit, feeling the ice cold chills of his spectral form, before the momentum sent me skating to a stop a few feet away. Coughing and swearing as I gained my feet, my heart sank. A familiar gray mist hung in the air, and the ghost I'd plowed through wasn't alone. Several more floated nearby, all of them with accusatory, white-filmed eyes.

"Holy grim," I mumbled, my legs wobbling as I tried to steady myself.

"Grim 281," a woman said.

A hologram flickered in and out in front of me, showing a petite gal with a severe bob and bangs sitting at a modern steel and glass desk. She wore glasses with thick, round orange frames perched on her tiny nose, the single splash of color in her black designer attire.

I glanced at Death. He appeared to have no issues with the lack of gravity in The Ghost Lands. His demeanor was as serious as I'd ever seen. "Chloe, meet Mei Han, my boss," he said.

She withdrew a sheaf of paper from a stack and perused it. "Probationary hearing, SMG committee and Chloe Frost, Grim 281." She read the list of offenses I'd committed and statutes I'd violated.

"We're doing this now?" I was dumbfounded. "Here?"

The head of Soul Management Group didn't glance up. "I'm sure your time is more valuable than mine, but yes, we're doing this now. Don't worry, you'll have plenty of free time when we're finished."

I went still, glad my lack of balance didn't make me topple. Death always made me wary, and sometimes downright frightened me, but this woman, in her demure black suit and harsh hairdo, was a level of scary I'd never encountered. I tried to find my voice, only to discover I had no ability to speak. Something—or someone—had hit my mute button.

It had also grounded me in place. I couldn't move my legs.

She tapped the end of her pen on the paper as she continued. "Along with the aforementioned violations, due to your refusal to train with Mage Stormfinger, your suppressed magic is creating havoc with earthbound souls." Finally, she glanced up, yet avoided my eyes, instead scanning the gray scenery surrounding us. The handful of ghosts watching the interaction scattered. "This will not go on. You are in breach of your grim reaper contract, and extenuating circumstances aside, I have to say, I am extremely disappointed."

Of all the things I had anticipated might come out of

her mouth, that wasn't one of them. I responded, my lips moving but my voice still silenced.

Anger roared through me, hot and vicious. How dare she criticize me and put me on trial, yet not allow me to defend myself. I couldn't even offer to make things right with the ghosts.

The fiery emotion bubbled up into my throat and I started forward, but being as I was unable to move my feet, I stayed put. Snapping my fingers, I pointed at my mouth.

Death grabbed my arm to stop me and I fought his iron-clad grip. I yelled expletives, yet they emerged a whisper.

Not exactly the intended outcome, but even a whisper was better than nothing. At the scuffle, Han frowned and looked directly at me. Both of her narrow brows rose under her short bangs. "It would be in your best interest to not speak, Ms. Frost."

There had been a time when I never wanted to speak again. Yet now, my life and future depended on getting out the right words to defuse this.

A wave of her energy raked over me, along with her intense gaze. Anger continued to blister under my skin, but I knew I had to concede and gain her trust. She was one of, if not *the*, commander and chief of the entire soul world.

It took all my willpower to force my limbs to relax. I channeled Killion's cool detachment and dipped my head in acquiescence, hiding my rage.

Death released his grip. "She has been a valuable asset to my team as I've noted in my reports." I tried not to show my shock at his compliment. "With the proper training, I believe she can and will rise to the top of our squad and be an example for the other reapers. She is the most qualified of them, due to her original status, and I'm willing to personally make sure she embraces her nature and potential."

Han's flat stare conveyed that she knew he was gassing her. When her attention switched back to me, I held my breath.

An eon passed while she studied me. Her magic was invasive, fingers of smoke flowing into my mind and wrapping it in a hazy vapor. Next, it slithered downward, infiltrating my chest, and the sensation of her peering into my heart felt as if she were filleting it open. I might as well have been a corpse on Uncle Morty's table, my insides on full display to her.

I locked my knees, gritted my teeth, and held still, refusing to look away or squirm. I would not kowtow to her, or show one bit of fear.

She tapped her pen again. "Against my better judgment, I will offer one concession," she finally told us. "You train her, and have her in line and performing her duties to the letter of the law in two weeks. I will review her progress at that time. If she fails, her status will be revoked, her memory wiped." She glanced at me as if I were no more than a bug. "Get yourself back on track, follow the rules, and do your job."

Poof. Just like that she and her desk disappeared and the magic suffocating me vanished along with her. I'd been fighting so hard against it, I toppled from its sudden absence.

I could speak again and yelled at the top of my lungs, "*I am Grim Zero.* You can't do that to me."

Death lifted me up from the ground. "Better than both of us getting the ax, I guess."

Like I was worried about him? "They can't fire you," I

seethed. "Wipe your memories." At his look, I checked myself. "Can they?"

He gave a brittle laugh. "Everyone is expendable. *Everyone.*"

He meant Killion. SMG could wipe my memory, kill him and Aurora, dispose of Ghost, all because of me. "That's not fair."

"You're so...human, thinking everything should be fair. SMG doesn't care about that. They care about—"

"Universal balance." I brushed at my tattered robes. They'd taken a beating today. "I know."

"A boss is only as good as his employees, and you, Chloe Frost, are the worst reaper I've ever had."

I didn't feel bad about the rules I'd broken. I did feel a smidge guilty for causing Death so much grief. While I hadn't willingly signed up for this position, he hadn't expected to have someone like me in his ranks either. Right now, shock that it was, he seemed to be on my side.

I glanced at the depressing terrain. There were no ghosts in sight, but the gray energy of them was everywhere. "Do you really think I've caused this?"

He still held my arm, and I felt his magic engulf me. It felt...protective. Another shock. "You don't think so?"

"It's Stormfinger."

"Hmm. Seems that way to me, too." He flicked those wicked eyes at me and grinned, all traces of worry gone. "You game for a little fun?"

Before I could reply, we were once more in the cemetery.

TWENTY-SIX

I was exhausted. The past couple days, along with the threat from Mei Han, combined to leave me feeling out of sorts, even though I was on terra firma once more.

Killion and Aurora rushed us, Andy standing guard over Stormfinger. "What happened? Where have you been?" Aurora asked, her voice screechy.

Killion grabbed me by the shoulders, scanning me from head to toe, although his question was directed at Death. "What have you done to her?"

"She's fine," my boss said. He rubbed his hands together. "Her Smudgy hearing went great, and she's under my, how should I say it, *direct supervision* now."

A chill rippled through me. Killion's already creased brow pinched tighter. "You mean, her *probationary* hearing? They held it now?"

I could barely nod. "Not they. Mei Han." If I didn't do exactly what Death wanted and SMG expected, I'd revert to being just Chloe, my mind wiped, my new friends and all my knowledge of magic gone. "I'm in serious trouble."

"Nah." Death seemed almost gleeful. "You simply have

to rein in that wild side of yours." He pointed at Killion. "Your hearing will be soon, bloodsucker. You best run along and prep for it. Mei is in no mood for worthless excuses, so be ready for severe discipline."

I tore my gaze from Killion's worried expression. Ghost scratched at my leg but I didn't pick her up. "It isn't fair."

"What's not?" Killion and Aurora chorused.

"Again with the fairness?" Death rocked back on his heels and shook his head. "You're still alive and a grim, after all the trouble you've caused. Smudgy isn't in the business of being fair. They don't even care about justice. All they deem important is the fulfillment of contracts and universal balance."

"Would one of you explain what is going on?" Killion released me and faced death. "SMG is taking disciplinary action?"

"You didn't think she'd get off scot-free, did you?"

"Can someone please release me?" Stormfinger whined.

The night air closed in on me. Not even an ounce of breeze was present to rattle the lingering leaves. I wanted to scream again, yet it was as if I was back with Mei Han and couldn't find my voice. I was suffocating.

Death snapped a finger, and the sorcerer was freed. "We won't be needing you," he told the vampire and witch. "Leave."

"Wait, what?" Aurora glanced at me. "I thought we were tackling The Ghost Lands together."

"Chloe?" Killion looked like he was ready to haul me over his shoulder and run. "What is going on?"

"I have to train," I told them. "And I can't work with you right now. I'm sorry."

Death clamped a hand on me, and the other on

Stormfinger. "The three of us will handle things from here. Time for some real training."

I saw the master vampire calculating his options in the time it took me to send him a pleading glance. The last thing I needed was for him to rock the boat. *I'll bring you up to speed later.*

"You'll need a secure place for this training," he told Death. "Chloe is already too drained from being in your realm, a public spot like this is unwise. Use my church. It's protected and guarded, and the cemetery has plenty of souls for her to practice on."

Strategic, logical. Never had I loved his brain more than in that moment.

Death was quiet, seeming to think it over. I wanted to add my vote, mention how perfect it was simply because it was familiar and Killion had access to it, but I knew better. I needed to get serious about staying away from him, or I could jeopardize his Undead life. Besides, Death would ditch the idea on principle if I voiced an opinion in favor of it. Maybe that was the key—pretend the church was the *last* place I wanted to practice.

"That's a terrible idea," I groused, not having to work too hard to sound truthful. "Katarina hates me, there isn't a decent seat in the house, and those cemetery creatures are horrifying."

Death grinned and spoke to Killion. "Perfect. Until further notice, the place is off-limits to you, and is now mine for the foreseeable future. If you try to interfere, even once, I'll force her to reap you. We clear?"

Killion's eyes pinned me. A warm energy covered me. *Do not fear. All will be well.* "I give my word."

Aurora threw her hands up. "This is crazy. You're trusting her care and training to Stormfinger over us?"

Death's grip tightened and his grin disappeared. I pretended to be depressed at the thought of all of it, but I knew from Killion's ongoing telepathic commentary in my head that everything *would* be okay.

He had a plan.

So did I. "Aurora, please." I put a touch of whine in my voice. "It's for the best. Take care of Ghost for me?"

With that, Death whisked me and the sorcerer once more through space. The three of us landed inside the church, where I not so gracefully crashed into one of the torture chairs. "I'm fine," I said, untangling my dirty robes from the foot stirrup.

With an eerie glow in his eyes, Death rubbed his hands together in anticipation. He faced the mage, who looked a little green. "Let's get started."

TWENTY-SEVEN

What sounded like a giant smoke detector going off made all of us flinch and cover our ears. Katarina burst into the nave, armed with a crossbow ready to fire. Her eyes were lit with retribution, glowing red as she pointed the weapon at Death.

I squeaked and ducked behind the chair.

"Hold your fire," he yelled over the noise. "And turn that blasted thing off."

Recognition registered and she lowered the weapon. The red irises dimmed, and she waved her ring-clad fingers to make the blaring cease. It created a hollow vacuum in my ears. "What are you doing here?"

Stormfinger had slipped behind Death's massive frame and now peeked out at her. Death crossed his arms. "This place is mine until I say otherwise. Keep out the riffraff and we'll get along just fine."

Katarina's gaze flicked to me and I shrugged. The plants I'd revived were absent, but I felt at least one, if not more, calling to me from nearby. They wanted my magic again. "We need a training place and this is it."

Her finger lingered on the trigger. "Not without the master's consent."

Death blustered, but I spoke before he could bite her head off. "We have it—his permission. In fact, he suggested we make use of the church. Reach out to him and he'll explain everything."

This was part of the plan—to utilize her as a messenger between us. We wouldn't be completely cut off from each other this way.

She studied us for a long moment. "Don't break anything." Her attention lit on me before she stalked out, the promise of retribution back in her eyes.

Stormfinger straightened his sleeves and stepped from his hiding place. "Nasty creatures."

"Do not disparage my friends," I warned.

"All right, kiddos." Death took a seat on the raised dais. "Enough bickering. I'm on a tight schedule. Get on with it."

"Give me the amulet," the mage said to me.

"I don't have it."

His face went lax. "What do you mean, you don't have it? I thought you wore it to control your power."

"I left it at home," I lied.

He rolled his eyes and looked like he wanted to bite my head off. For the next several hours, he fed me a history of necromancy and then we trudged out to the cemetery. He and Death watched as I tried to raise a corpse.

I could feel the dead in their graves, but I was terrified of actually resurrecting one, and I had no intention of doing so. I kept the brunt part of my magic locked down, only freeing a tiny trickle to make it look as if I was getting the hang of it. I reanimated a few long-dead toads, two birds, a goose, and a fox, along with turning the brown lawn and dormant trees a healthy green.

Stormfinger blustered his frustration, but Death just watched, expression inscrutable.

At one point, I tried a distraction. While Stormfinger paced the grounds, attempting to come up with another method, I pointed to Death's shoulder blades. "Are we going to talk about your...?"

His face contorted with surprise and he suddenly became overly interested in a piece of lint on his slacks. "Absolutely not," he said.

"Are you an angel?"

He grunted. "How about we talk about your Last Will and Testimony? I'm rather disappointed you didn't leave anything to me."

"Boundaries, dude. I shouldn't have sent that to you, and you definitely shouldn't have read it."

He mimicked me, pointing to his back. "Boundaries. Don't ask."

I grinned sagely, letting him know this was not the end of it. "Fine."

I strolled away, needing to regain my composure. Of course, he'd read the will—why had I assumed he wouldn't?

I was sweating, regardless the temperature was near freezing, my shirt sticking to my back and my hair plastered to my head. Not disappointed in the least that I hadn't raised a corpse, and hating the fact Death had returned all the resurrected animals to their former dead status, I leaned on a concrete cross as tall as I was and prayed he would end this ridiculous session soon. Sunrise was only moments away, and I was completely out of gas.

The sorcerer was tired, too. His inability to teach me his skills seemed to eat at him. He stomped back to us. "She doesn't want to raise the dead." Both his glare and his tone had lost their intensity. "Until she wants to embrace her magic, or has a strong enough reason to, this is pointless."

Death smiled at me with a new light in his eyes. "You're brilliant, Stormfinger. Let's give it a try."

Cold dread invaded my chest. "Pretty sure I don't want to know what you're about to do."

He leaned forward, elbows on his knees. "What made you shatter statues and headstones earlier?"

Careful, the voice in my head warned. He was baiting me—he already knew the answer. "I thought the grim had killed..."

"Killion." His smile was pure evil. "We'll start with him."

He flicked his hand and the master vampire appeared halfway between us. Killion, without his standard suit coat and tie, startled and glanced around, taking us in. "Did you need something?"

"Yeah, I need you to play dead."

Before I could scream a warning, Killion's beautiful violet eyes rolled up in his head and he dropped at my feet.

For the second time in a few hours, my heart stopped. "Bring him back," I yelled.

"You do it." The taunt was delivered with a smirk. "I know you want it bad enough."

The sum whole of my emotional turmoil cracked me open from the inside out. My magic roared like a wildfire over my skin and my aura went white hot. Dangerous. "How dare you use him as a pawn."

Stormfinger chuckled. "Nice one."

I stepped over Killion's lifeless body and punched the sorcerer. His nose shattered, and he cried out, losing his balance and tumbling to the ground.

Facing my boss, I shook out my hand and prepared to

hit him next. I blasted him with my magic, but he didn't even twitch. "Stop playing games!"

He rose from the bench, nearly seven feet of menace towering over me. "Channel that where it will do some good."

My bones shook from the command, his power over me a tight thing that made me quake. "What will happen if I do?"

Vampires didn't have souls per se, having forfeited them in exchange for potential immortality. The extreme rarity of Killion's vampire-human hybridization made it possible he still had his. He wasn't sure. We'd discussed it thoroughly one night in front of his fireplace. He longed to know the truth, but feared the answer.

"Try it and find out," Death said.

"What part of him will return? Will he no longer be a vampire if I raise his human side?"

Daring lit his eyes. "Guess you'll have to risk it and see. Would that be so bad? The two of you, human, riding off into the sunset together?"

The red haze of anger covered my eyes. Everything in me went still and brittle. "Bring him back," I ground out.

"Or what? You'll kill me?"

I was on him before he could blink, all of my rage and fear exploding out of me as I pummeled him.

We landed on the ground, him under me. My already sore knuckles delivered an uppercut to his jaw, pain lancing through my fist and up my arm. The skin split on several of the joints and blood flew.

He gripped my wrists to stop the assault. "Didn't know you had such violence in you, Grave Girl."

I hadn't either. When I'd been attacked, I had fought

back, but this... "I will find a way to make your existence a living hell," I snarled.

"You've checked that box already."

With my hands hostage, I couldn't hit him again, so I kneed him in the groin.

His grunt of pain and freeing of my hands thrilled me. The emotions inside me, and whatever I've been suppressing, screamed through me. My head fell back, the force of it tearing up my chest and throat, and my mouth opened.

No longer silent, my scream of absolute and total gut-wrenching agony shattered the universe.

TWENTY-EIGHT

Mild mannered, animal loving Chloe Frost was lost in that scream.

What emerged was Grim Zero.

A chasm of grief opened around me. A gulf of eternal suffering. I felt every soul I'd reaped since the beginning of time.

Not in the blissed-out version of soul transference. No, this was entirely the opposite.

Because regardless of contracts and incarnations, I had touched each of them. Been a channel to the afterlife. And every one had experienced regret at the death of their physical body. Nearly all of them had feared dying. Feared *me*.

I had taken that fear, their sorrow and their anger, into myself. I had tried to comfort them the only way I could. I'd held their precious souls in my hands and my heart.

After I'd harvested them, I'd wished I could bring each back. Nobody understood life and death the way I did. No one had ever experienced it like I had.

All of that, along with more I couldn't name, went into

my scream. I was caught in a matrix I could never leave; a fate I could never change.

Muscled arms wrapped around me. Behind my closed eyes, a million stars burst to life. I felt as though I were flying through the cosmos, my scream now muffled in my ears. Lost in space and time.

A total detached sensation I'd experienced once before seeped into my body. The overwhelming emotions slid into a background simmer. I was as cold and as distant from all of it as the insignificant galaxies swirling on the movie screen in my brain.

"Let it all out." The voice swam in my ears, echoed in my bones.

I cracked open my eyes. Silvery stardust coated my skin, my hair, my vision. The taste of it was on my tongue —*heaven*.

Death stared into my eyes, his arms around me. In his gaze was eternity. We were no longer in the graveyard, we weren't even on earth.

Galaxies and nebulae flashed past as we flew through the cosmos. The cold in my body deepened, yet I relaxed into his hold. There was a quickening inside my chest, a remembrance—this was how it had always been. Earth and its human inhabitants were a grain of sand in this endless time.

Life was ever flowing, changing. All times. Every dimension.

"I've got you," he said, and the words reverberated through me, deep and more ancient than any planet or star. His wings—beating with graceful ease—carried us higher and higher. I sighed with relief.

The weight of everything left my shoulders. I tucked my head against his shoulder as we continued our flight through immortality. The two of us existed beyond all that was and ever would be. To beings interwoven in a web of our own creation.

I don't know how long I rested there, held in his arms, carried by his wings. Eventually, he lifted my chin. "Stay with me, forever." His lips grazed mine gently. "I will always care for you."

I wanted to resist, but I was too far gone. There was nothing left in me. When he kissed me, I didn't react. My cells felt fluid, my brain feathery. I couldn't remember who I was anymore. The kiss was everything and nothing at once.

His essence spiraled down the back of my throat and into my chest. My breathing stopped—I no longer needed to draw any kind of air. I was floating, subatomic particles separating. There was an endless void, soft and dark…

Peace.

"*Chloooeee…*"

The voice echoed around inside me, like a wave, rising and crashing against my mind. The blood frozen in my veins tingled.

Who was Chloe? I didn't care. I was free. Free of pain. Free of responsibilities. Free of life.

"*Chloe!*" More insistent this time, a fly buzzing in my ears, prodding my awareness.

But my ears were dissolving, like the rest of me. I could no longer sense my hands or feet.

Yet, the voice sounded so familiar. So…part of me. My heart did a funny *thudthud* in my chest, pushing back against that coiling tendril of Death.

"*Grim Zero.*" This was a female, cutting through the bliss. "*We need you.*"

The two voices tugged at my heart. I tried to shut them

out, but some still-conscious part of me recognized the pain and fear in their intonation. I didn't want to go back to that —emotions, feelings. The ache to let go, leave them and all of that misery behind, lifted me higher. I reached for the spinning-out that was coming, the *un*becoming.

The male spoke again, demanding. "Chloe Frost, I command you to come back to me."

My blood turned to lava. My eyes snapped open and my skin prickled. Every part of me felt as if it were raging with fire.

I blinked into Death's face. His eyes were blitzed out, his lips a breath away. I shoved against his chest. "Stop."

The word was lost in the space between us.

"Stop!" I shoved harder.

We flew apart. Shock and surprise contorted his features.

And then I was falling. Falling through space, through time. Stardust and planets.

It went on forever, and yet, was over in an instant. My physical body landed hard on my back, my ribs cracking from the force. Air rushed into my lungs as I blinked up at a purple and hazy blue dawn. A circle of faces peered down at me.

Killion, Aurora, Andy, and Ghost. Corvus landed on my chest. "Kill!" he squawked.

Sucking in mouthful after mouthful of oxygen, I laughed, dry and ragged.

Kill indeed.

TWENTY-NINE

"Killion?" I blinked rapidly, convinced I was in a dream, or maybe that alternate universe. "You're dead."

Ghost licked me and he gently lifted the raven off my chest. "I am as alive as I ever was."

Aurora wiggled her ringed fingers. "Necromancy comes in handy."

"You brought him back?"

"Didn't appear you were going to, so yes. Seems Andy and I arrived just in time."

"But are you"—I touched Killion's face—"human? Like, *all* human?"

He kissed my hand and squeezed it, flicking his gaze to Aurora and back. "I assure you I am still me in the Undead department."

I was relieved, and a touch disappointed. What *would* life be like if he were no longer a vampire? Could we have a normal future together?

I wasn't sure what normal meant anymore, nor if I wanted it.

Aurora scanned my face and touched my braid. "What happened to you?"

Reality crashed back. I sat up too fast and the world tilted. They grabbed my arms and steadied me.

Past them, Death sprawled on the ground, unmoving, wings absent.

Stormfinger, holding the hem of his shirt to his broken nose, was complaining to Katarina, who stood over Death. The vampire was grinning.

I pushed to my feet, no longer needing support, and marched to her side. "Is he alive?"

Death's eyes blinked open and stared at the brightening sky. "Beautiful morning, isn't it?"

My palm heated. *Kill*, the scythe whispered in my head.

I straddled him, falling to my knees and raising my hand. The death blade sailed through the air into it. "You tried to kill me." I was deadly calm. "I will end you."

He shifted his gaze to mine, eyes sad. "Do it."

Someone grabbed my arm from behind. I jerked, trying to pull free. "Chloe," Killion said, "you're not a killer."

"She's an abomination," Stormfinger said.

"Shut it." Katarina flashed her fangs, making the sorcerer back up. "Did you really try to kill her?" she asked Death.

His gaze bored into mine. "I was only protect—"

Another war cry broke free of my lips. Against Killion's strength, and ignoring my throbbing ribs, I wrenched my arm from his grip and raised the blade high, ready to behead my boss.

"Chloe bear? Is that you?"

I froze.

JR came jogging up one of the paths. "I thought I heard your voice." He stopped and took in my hair and robes, the group, and then the busted gravestones. His attention landed on me again. "Are you okay?"

I dropped the scythe and scuttled off Death. The question bounced between my ears as I took in the leaves and dirt on my robes. Loose strands of hair hung in my eyes. The end of my braid caught my attention. No wonder Aurora had examined it so closely—one of the sections had turned silvery white.

The same color as the star systems I'd seen on my jaunt through the universe.

Maniacal laughter bubbled up from my throat. "No," I answered, staggering away. "I'll never be okay again."

He wore running clothes and, although his breath clouded the air, he looked as though he could easily go another ten miles. "What can I do to help?" His focus once more went to the others, the destruction of the grounds. "What happened here?"

"Sheer force winds," Andy said. "Freakiest storm I've seen. Here and gone in an instant."

"What exactly are you doing here?" JR examined Death a little closer. "Does he need medical attention?"

Killion cocked his head. "You can see him?"

He gave the vampire a curious stare. "Of course."

"We're LARPing." Andy spread his hands wide and smiled. "Can't you tell?"

Killion gave him a questioning glance, and Andy shrugged. Andy the Fixer was definitely quick on his feet when it came to making up excuses that sounded perfectly plausible.

"Role play?" JR seemed relieved. "Wow, that's cool. I didn't know you were into that," he said to me. "Didn't even realize anyone around here was."

Stormfinger held out a helping hand to Death, who

waved him off and sat up, resting his arms on his bent knees. He rubbed a hand over his face. "I bet there are a lot of things about Chloe you don't know."

I shot him a warning glare, but he only winked at me.

I wanted to kill him all over again.

"So is it a cosplay setup?" JR reached out to feel my robes. "Or are you writing your own storyline? I don't recognize your character."

Death rolled his eyes.

Killion's magic buzzed against my skin. Andy felt it, too. He put an arm around JR's shoulders and began strolling away. "It's a complete world built around Chloe's character as a grim reaper. Mind blowing stuff. Life and death, the human struggle to understand why we're here, why our lives matter. All the big existential questions, y'know."

It was Aurora's turn to roll her eyes. As Andy led JR away, she sidled up next to me and Killion and lowered her voice. "How is he here? I mean, I know the place exists on the earthly plane and humans can see it, but it's warded, right? Most would never venture onto the grounds because the wards chase them away. Plus, how can he see Death?"

"I wondered the same," Killion said under his breath. He glanced toward me. "Does your friend have supernatural capabilities? I haven't sensed any. In fact, outside of respectable intelligence, he seems rather dull."

"Don't be rude." I huffed out a breath to dislodge the hair in my eyes. My ribs were nearly healed and it didn't hurt as much. "As far as I know he doesn't." JR and Andy had stopped at the sidewalk. I studied their auras. Andy's danced in red and gold threads, weaving in and around him. In JR's, I caught the movement of the shadow worm, there and gone in an instant.

The human energy field tended to extend approximately a foot around the body. Certain types of photography could show the colors in the field, and psychics could sometimes see it. The church behind the two males had its own field that I'd been able to see since the first time Killion had brought me here. As I watched, that layer seemed to reach toward JR, tendrils of the pale magic teasing away from the structure and stretching for him.

Time to move him on. "I hate to break this up," I called, chasing after them, "but we need to wrap up our... role play. I have a big day ahead of me, and I know the others do, too."

Stopping a few feet from JR, I offered a weak smile, encouraging him with my eyes to leave. I sent a pulse of magic at the worm and it vanished. The church stopped reaching for him.

He took the hint. "Sure, sorry to interrupt. I should finish my run and get home, anyway. Mother will need her breakfast." He glanced over his shoulder. "Funny, all the years I've lived here, and all the times I've run this route, I don't remember this church." He shrugged good-naturedly. "Why don't you come by the house this afternoon? Mother would be delighted to have a visitor. She's been asking about you."

My brain was too fried to come up with an excuse, although I highly doubted Mrs. Banks would be as excited with my company as he claimed. "That sounds...lovely." *In the let me poke my eye out kind of way.*

"Great." He looked entirely too happy about the prospect, and I once again felt Killion's energy surround me and give him a push. "Four?"

I'd have to come up with a reason not to go and text him later. "See you then."

He began jogging in place, his smile as bright as the rising sun. "Don't be late. "As he took off, he offered a parting wave. "Maybe I can play with you sometime," he called to Andy.

"Absolutely," the shifter called back, giving him a sloppy salute.

Katarina waved and grinned at him, thankfully fang-free. She watched until he was out of sight. "He's cute."

Stormfinger spit on the ground. "Non-magicals. Annoying creatures."

I rounded on him, closing the distance and picking up my scythe on the way. "You find everyone annoying, yet you're the most annoying person I've ever met."

He backpedaled. "What are you doing?" His foot caught on a piece of busted concrete, and he flailed both hands in the air. He glanced frantically at Death. "What is she doing?"

Seemed pretty self-explanatory to me. The scythe whispered, *kill.*

"I'm practicing," I answered and reared back to take a swing. "I'll kill you and we'll see if I can bring you back."

"Grim Zero." Death's voice was low and controlled, but every bit as powerful as he was. "Put it down."

The words hit like a sledgehammer at the base of my skull. Frigid cold skipped down my spinal cord and froze me in place.

Stormfinger stopped moving as well, and stared at me, dumbfounded. "Grim Zero?" His head whipped around to look at Death. "You never told me she was the first soul eater."

My boss' sigh made my bones rattle. "It's none of your concern."

"But my methods for raising the dead weren't designed for Grim Zero. No wonder they didn't work. I have to revise everything."

"Soul eater?" At least I could shiver. "I hate that name."

The ring of a phone interrupted the conversation. Death withdrew his and read the screen. He turned his back on all of us and walked away, speaking in quiet tones as he answered.

Stormfinger bowed his head to me. "I apologize for my rudeness. I had no idea who you truly were. Are." His eyes now glittered with fascination, and he lowered his voice as he once more made eye contact. "I assure you, I *can* help. I don't know what he's playing at"—he jutted his chin toward Death—"but I offer my allegiance to you."

That was an odd thing to say. I still couldn't move, but I could speak. I didn't trust the sorcerer any more than I did my boss, but right now, I needed as many friends as I could get. He would never be one, but he could be a handy resource. "I don't know what game he's playing either. Meet me here at sundown."

"Bring the amulet," he said.

The call ended and Death strolled back to us. "Do you promise not to behead anyone?"

I gritted my teeth and considered my answer. "I make no promises, but I'll try to keep my scythe in my pants."

He liked to make puns so he laughed. "Not bad." He waved a hand through the air and my body relaxed. I lowered the blade and shook out my limbs.

"Go home," he told Stormfinger. "I'll be in touch."

The sorcerer dipped his chin and shot me a quick glance before he fled.

Death surveyed all of us. "Who's ready for breakfast?"

Aurora and I frowned. Killion glowered. Andy raised a hand. "Me. I'm ravenous."

"I hear The Smoking Bean has good coffee." Death headed for the sidewalk.

Unbelievable. "Well, I'm going home to take a long, hot shower," I announced. "Besides, The Bean isn't open for another hour."

"Come, Grim Zero." The command made my feet move against my will. Death motioned at the others. "You, too."

"What for?" Killion demanded.

Death faced us. "To figure out how to stop Stormfinger from taking my job."

THIRTY

After the night we'd had, none of us had the capacity to care about Death losing his position with SMG. Personally, I didn't believe he could, even though he claimed everyone was expendable.

While he sauntered off, Killion took my hand. "Are you well? You are paler than normal."

I narrowed my eyes. "You think I'm pale?"

He pressed his lips together, seeming to consider his response. "You are always beautiful."

"Nice recovery. I'm fine." At his raised brow, I took a deep breath and lessened the impatience in my voice. "I'm *not* fine, and you know it, but there's nothing I can do about it at the moment. Don't worry, I'll be okay. I just have to figure out a few things."

He inclined his head, deciding it was better not to argue. It wasn't only the stripe of silver in my hair that signified how I'd changed—it must have also shown in my manner. "The limo will take us to the shop."

Across the way, Moss waited in the parking lot, standing ready to open the back door. I retrieved my things from the lawn and shook my head. "Take Ghost and the others. I'll meet you there."

Killion stayed glued to the spot. "Where are you going?"

"I need to clear my head." I tended to walk most places, and Killion had, at times, accompanied me. "Alone," I added.

The master vampire didn't like being rebuffed. Aurora saved me from further interrogation. "Are you sure it's safe?"

Safe was relative. I chuckled dryly. "I just stopped Death himself from killing me. Who do you think could hurt me right now?"

She and Killion exchanged a worried glance. "We will discuss what happened in detail later," he said, and it was directed at me. "As you wish, we will meet you at the shop."

"Thank you." I shrugged off the robes to stash in my bag. Sparkling dust fell from them and I paused, tasting it, feeling the call of it. An odd ache rose from somewhere deep inside me.

"Is that...?" Aurora stood mesmerized.

I shook myself out of the siren song that filled my head, and tried a smile. They wouldn't understand its lure, or the bottomless wellspring it had opened inside me. "Let's get our breakfast to go," I said, "and have our meeting at the clinic." I didn't want to worry about our upcoming discussion being interrupted or overheard.

I placed Ghost in Killion's arms so she wouldn't try to follow and started walking. I was a block behind Death, keeping him in sight, when I felt Katarina's presence trailing me. My magic was so much stronger now. Not even a vampire could elude my awareness. I knew Killion had sent her, and I wasn't entirely surprised. I let it go—I had bigger fish to fry.

With each step, I replayed what had happened. Death always had a reason for what he did, and whether he actually believed Stormfinger was after him, this whole "training" initiative now smelled like a setup. Purposely putting me with the sorcerer allowed him to keep tabs on what the man was doing, and observe, like in the cemetery, what he was capable of.

This must be what he'd meant about having fun. It had hardly been that for me, but it had revealed much about Stormfinger. I wasn't sure why it was important, I only knew it was.

Was the Kiss of Death only for show? To shake up Stormfinger and get him to reveal something?

Like the fact he was obsessed over Death's amulet?

If he wasn't actually after Death's position, what *was* he after?

The memory of his wing feathers surfaced. Was my boss actually the Angel of Death? If so, perhaps the sorcerer was after his power, rather than his position. Certainly an angel would be the most powerful being around.

Angels. Wow, my world had become incredibly weird.

A bird chirped at me from high on a branch, singing to the morning. A raccoon peered at me from under someone's porch.

As if I saw all the elements and players on a chess board, I systematically shifted them around, trying new combinations and seeking motivations.

The bird followed my progress, continuing to trill in the chilly air. As I was about to turn the corner to head downtown, it landed on a nearby street sign.

A bluebird. My mother's favorite.

The memory of her brushed up against the ball of suppressed emotions and I staggered.

I'd almost lost everything. I'd seen Killion die. If I made a tiny mistake, Mei Han would wipe everything and everyone I cared about away.

Like I'd been sucker-punched, I doubled over, trying to catch my breath.

The fear rushed up like a volcano. Grim Zero should have been created without emotions, able to harvest souls with no remorse, no guilt. Yet, Chloe Frost, who wanted to save everybody, was as Stormfinger had said—the tip of a silent, deadly iceberg. In the waters of time, Grim Zero was the rest hidden under the surface.

That deep, never-ending piece of ice was shrouded from the world, yet she felt everything. Every soul who'd died since the beginning of humanity.

If I opened up to that...?

The force of it would kill me. I had to keep my emotions —*her* emotions—buckled down, and continue to hide them under the calm waters. I was the iceberg that could sink the Titanic, only, I was the Titanic as well.

If I didn't keep my feelings contained, if I allowed her to rise and take control, I would raise every single person who'd ever died.

Talk about world overpopulation.

Death suddenly appeared at my side. He said nothing for once. He simply stood close and scanned the street.

A car drove past, the driver glancing at us, and seeing my obvious distress, slowed. While she couldn't see Death, she was compelled to move on, when he raised a hand and sent a burst of magic at her.

The bluebird flew away, a single feather floating down to land at my feet. Picking it up, I breathed deeply and straightened. "I'm waiting for an apology."

"For what?"

It was a good thing I didn't have the energy to slug him. "You know what."

He continued to face the street, tense. "I would never kill you, Z."

The sincerity in his voice surprised me. So did the nickname. Some echo of our shared ancient past made me feel there was a time he'd used it frequently. "You lie."

"I've been known to fudge the truth, but I never outright lie. Not to you."

"Then what was that?"

"A demonstration." He leaned against a tree, sullen. "I hoped to trigger your memories and release the dam you've built against your powers. If you did, space was the safest place possible for the destruction that might ensue."

So reasonable. Such solid logic. I thought about the graveyards I'd decimated with my screams. "While that may be somewhat truthful, you're not telling me everything."

He stayed focused on the street. "There's a lot to tell. Pencil me in when you've got a couple hundred years to sit and talk."

Down the block, a man with two dogs jogged toward us. I felt Katarina's energy, but she was nowhere in sight. "That's an excuse, but fine. Let's start with something easy. What was that thing in JR's aura?"

"You saw that?" I waited without answering. He continued. "He's tied into black magic. That thing was similar to the leech you had on you before Christmas."

"Can you remove it?"

He shrugged, seeming not to care. "You need to figure out where he got it. Obviously, there's something unusual connected to him, and that may be why you saw his ghost."

"Why can he see you? Why did it seem the church's magic was reaching for him?"

"Same answer." His phone rang again, and he held up a finger to put my questions on hold. As he walked away to answer, the owner of the dogs passed, giving me a wide berth. Both of his pets attempted to sniff me, but he tugged on their leashes to keep them moving.

"Good morning to you, too," I grumbled. While I understood the fact most people would have the same reaction to a person who appeared to be talking to herself, it still annoyed me. "Good manners never killed anyone," I called after him.

Death returned. "Duty calls. I've got to run." He pocketed the cell. "I thought I might have another couple hours before I had to—well, no matter. Smudgy says jump, and I ask how high. Watch your back with Stormfinger, but get close to him. Investigate his movements and anyone he's hanging out with. If he shares anything with you about what he's doing, go along with it. Gain his confidence, okay?"

"He seems unusually interested in your amulet."

"Does he?" He rubbed his chin. "I see."

"Why?"

He shrugged. "Probably because he wants to be sure if he opens your necro flood gates, that he can also close them."

Or the jewelry held more power than that, which seemed more likely. Power the sorcerer was keen to get his hands on. "Why would anyone want your job?"

Mock surprise crossed his face. "Are you kidding? Best job ever."

It seemed those in power always had someone trying to dethrone them. "We *are* going to discuss your angel feathers, because again, I know you're not telling me everything."

"No, I'm not, and be glad I don't. When we talk about

my...accessories, we can also discuss your will, how about that?" He tugged my braid, examining the new strip of white. "Keep an eye on your friend. I took a look at his contract—he's not scheduled to die this year, but something's definitely amiss with him."

You think? "And Stormfinger is tied into it, isn't he?"

Death disappeared without answering—an answer in itself.

Katarina's hovering presence made my skin tingle. "I know you're following me," I said over my shoulder. With her enhanced hearing, I didn't have to raise my voice. "Why don't you just come out?"

She materialized from the shadows near a neighbor's garage. I hadn't noticed before, but she was wearing the hair comb I'd given her at Christmas.

"Did you get all that?" I asked. "Miss any details?"

Placing an arm around my shoulders, she nudged me to start walking. "The master is worried. Everyone is, even Moss. He was in church yesterday lighting a candle for you."

"I'm not dead." Her show of camaraderie was unexpected. "And I've proven I can handle myself. There's no need for all this concern."

"There's a lot at stake for all of us if you go light side."

"Light side?"

"Death wants to destroy the Undead. If he convinces you to take up his quest, you could turn on us."

No one was more vain or consumed with themselves than the Undead. Her motives for buddying up to me made more sense now. They also made my heart hurt at the thought Killion had put her up to this. Did he believe the same? That after all we'd been through, I would turn on him? "I would never..." My voice faltered. I'd been a reaper for a few months, and in that time, everything had changed. Who knew what I would do if I was forced to accept Grim Zero?

In my peripheral vision, I caught sight of a dangling spider that hung from her hair comb. It swung lazily as we walked, but the legs were moving on their own accord. When I paused to look at it straight on, the thing latched onto the top of her ear. Beady eyes stared back. "Did you animate the fake spider?"

She reached up and patted her lobe gently. "Didn't need to. This is Neville. Alice and Frank's baby."

"Neville Longbottom?"

She nodded. "Remember the spider you raised at the church? I named her after the Harry Potter character, Alice Longbottom, because like, you were right. Those books are cool. Anyway, she had babies and Neville is my pet."

Walking again, I spied the coffee shop sign a few blocks away. Nita and Piedmont were opening. Mason was still off after his run in with werewolves before Christmas. Killion said he was healed physically but had qualms about leaving his house after the trauma.

Poor kid.

Katarina put her arm through mine and tugged on my braid. "You're okay, Grave Girl. Now," her eyes sparkled, "tell me more about JR."

THIRTY-ONE

Katarina and I caught up with the others outside The Smoking Bean. Nita and Piedmont were prepping for the morning crowd that would soon descend on the place. At the moment, it was only Killion, Aurora, and Andy.

The limo was parked out front taking up several spaces, since Moss, who waved at me, had pulled parallel to the sidewalk. He was wearing the driving gloves I'd given him.

"Death bailed on us," I told the group. "He got an important call—I suspect SMG got wind of what he did to me and isn't happy. Before he left, however, he told me to get close to Stormfinger, get him to trust me."

"Maybe we should go to the clinic like you suggested," Aurora said. "You can tell us what happened at the church."

Killion sensed my exhaustion. He squeezed my arm. "She needs to rest and recharge. We can convene there this afternoon to decipher what is going on with Death, The Ghost Lands, and Stormfinger."

"Can I still get an espresso?" Andy asked. Aurora

smacked his arm and he flinched. "What? We're here, why not get a drink?"

Nita appeared, the bell over the door tinkling. "Hey, guys. What are you doing here so early?"

Andy clapped his hands. "Angling for a free cup of coffee."

Aurora punched his arm this time, and not in a playful way.

"Chloe?" Nita squinted at my messy strands. "Did you streak your hair?"

It was too late to dodge her. I fiddled with my braid, the soft music from the speakers filtering out to the sidewalk. "It was a spur of the moment thing. To mark the new year," I added.

"New year, new you?"

I accepted her hug and made a noncommittal response. "Do you like it?"

She released me and examined it more closely, picking leaves from the strands. "It's certainly dramatic."

I laughed. After my night, a strip of white hair seemed the least dramatic thing that had occurred. "Come on, everyone." I waved the others inside. As usual, I was starving.

Nita held the door as my posse filed in. I introduced her to Aurora, Andy, and Katarina, then did a Vanna White impression at the bakery display case. "Pick your poison and place your order."

Piedmont was sliding a rectangular tray of muffins onto the top shelf. He was short and stocky, his bald head gleaming under the lights. The luscious scent of lemon and sugar hung in the air.

As I walked around the counter to wash my hands, he

pointed to the muffins. "Fresh from the oven. Lemon drop with my secret ingredient."

"I'll take two to go," I told him. I dried my hands and patted my trusty espresso machine that I had nicknamed Ambrosia. "Okay, who wants a drink?"

Piedmont worked alongside me to take everyone's orders. Nita chatted as she added napkins to bags and set the cups in carriers. When we were finished, I told them to put it all on my tab, but then noticed Killion slip Piedmont a bill. My caramel mocha latte was already kicking in and my mouth was full of lemon cake, so I said nothing.

I held the piece I hadn't snarfed down yet, balancing my paper bag and one of the carriers. "These are amazing," I told Piedmont.

He looked pleased and leaned forward, giving me a partial bow as Killion joined me, and Nita waved goodbye. A pendant dangled from a black cord around his neck. When he straightened and tucked it back under his polo, it reflected the exit light's red glow. "I learned everything I know from your aunt."

"You did?" This made me happy. "She's the best baker around."

He winked conspiratorially. "She's got some competition."

"Oh?"

"I'm taking what she taught me and going big. My girlfriend and I are going to have a food truck to take my delicious treats to the people. They won't have to go to Camille's—or come here—to get their caffeine and sugar fix."

Places like The Bean and my aunt's bakery skated by on a slim profit margin. It took selling hundreds of drinks everyday just to break even on expenses; the bakery goods were profit, and the difference between staying open and not.

The cupcake suddenly tasted like cardboard. "Way to stab her in the back after she trained you. Us, too."

Seeing the look I gave him, he stopped smiling. "Some friendly competition is good for all of us."

Friendly competition. Right.

Killion took the tray of coffees from my hand and guided me outside before my empty patience tank made me blow up again. As I sank into the back of the warm limo, Katarina handed Moss the espresso I'd made him and helped herself to my second muffin. "Want me to kill him?"

If I'd had my scythe in hand, I would have stroked the blade as I contemplated saying "Yes."

"Chloe." Aurora's voice was chastising. "We don't kill people over that kind of thing."

"Accidents happen."

Killion handed me my beverage. "You definitely need rest."

I caught Katarina's eye. Her lips twitched—she knew what I was thinking. To keep from grinning, she pressed her lips together, but when the others weren't looking, she gave me a wink that told me she wouldn't kill him just yet, but she was on standby if I needed her.

Maybe this friend thing was going to work out after all.

THIRTY-TWO

B y the time Killion dropped off the others and we arrived at my apartment, I was bone-tired. This wasn't the same level of exhaustion I'd had while cramming for finals, or picking up extra hours at The Bean. This was a weariness of life that not even mainlining a sugar-and-caffeine cocktail could overcome. I felt as old as Killion—older. I had a new respect for his reserved, often moody, countenance.

His silence usually grated on my nerves, but this morning, it was a relief. He assisted me and Ghost upstairs without Vera's awareness, and tucked me into bed once I'd showered.

I slept.

Ugly dreams tormented me, yet a handsome man with coal black hair and violet eyes kept showing up in them, wrapping me in his arms and chasing away my fears. Chasing away death, destruction, oblivion.

When I woke, it was afternoon and I was spooned against him. His arm was around me, his warm caramel and old libraries scent cocooning me.

For a long time, I simply lay there cradled and relaxed, relieved my nightmares hadn't been about him for once. Pale light danced along the edges of the window shade, and Ghost snored softly from her bed. Even Corvus was quiet and still, a rarity, as he perched on the bar in his cage. One black eye scrutinized me closely, waiting for some signal that it was time to rise.

"I'm not sure which is weirder—you or the bird watching me sleep," I mumbled.

Killion's finger stroked my arm. "You suffered a night terror. I suppressed your scream so your landlady would not be alarmed, but the only way I could calm you was to hold you."

I liked having him close. "I haven't had one of those since I was a girl." I shifted so we were face-to-face. His hair was mussed, a lock hanging across his forehead, and a five-o'clock shadow prominent on his chin. The semi-dark room felt like another place and time. We were safe and invisible to the rest of the world. "You were in my dreams."

Half-lidded eyes bore into mine. "Hopefully not as the source of your fear."

Not this time. I brushed the lock of hair off his brow. "The opposite, in fact. You kept showing up when I needed you most."

"Truly?" A tiny smile played over his lips. "You dreamed of me?"

There I lay with the master vampire in my bed. One who protected me, saved me from myself when needed, and had become one of my dearest friends. He was sexy, intelligent, and loyal. The smart thing would have been to rip off his clothes and kiss him until he promised to never leave me.

I wanted that—to forget my cares and responsibilities,

satiate my growing lust for him and take our relationship to the next level. But then Corvus croaked, "Kiss. Death."

A slight crease formed between Killion's brows and he glanced at my lips, then back into my eyes, somewhat forlornly. "He's right. Tell me what happened."

Thanks a lot, bird. I should have let the vampire kill you when he wanted to.

Sighing, I considered how to phrase the story so he didn't blow a fang, but there really wasn't a way to downplay what Death had done. Even as I related the brief tale, I could once more taste stardust on my tongue, see the glowing stars. Desire charged my bones. "It was beautiful and horrible at the same time. If not for you and Aurora calling me back, I might have surrendered to it."

My phone buzzed. I waited for Killion's response, but he stayed silent. I let the call go to voicemail and scrubbed my face. It was a lot to process, so I didn't push him. Honestly, I was still processing it myself.

Death was my boss, and also the only entity I knew who'd been there at the beginning with me. He held answers to my questions—answers I wasn't sure I wanted.

Yet. There would be a time when I would. First, I had to get a handle on my current situation that was quickly spinning out of control.

The raven squawked. "Go time. Go, go, go."

I ignored him, wanting to stay with Killion and pretend the rest of the world didn't need me. Ghost rose from her bed and shook herself, strands of long hair flying in a broken ray of sunlight. She then hopped on the bed, and eased the tension with puppy kisses for both of us.

My heart was raw, but the dog—as well as the vampire— had soothed it. I rolled over and climbed out of the blanket.

My phone beeped, alerting me to a message. I retrieved it and saw it was from an unknown number.

Killion stood and picked up Ghost. "I'll take her out to do her business while you dress."

"Thank you. Make sure Vera doesn't spot you."

"She left earlier with her reusable grocery sacks."

After he and Ghost disappeared outside, I listened to the voicemail. It was JR asking if I was still coming for tea, that his mom was really looking forward to it, *blah, blah, blah.*

Reapers keepers. I dropped my head back and stared at the off-white ceiling wishing the heavens might open up and swallow me. They didn't.

I had no other leads to follow for the grave robberies, and I had to get close to the sorcerer. A sudden change of heart might make him suspicious, though, so I needed to play my cards wisely. I wasn't exactly sure how to uncover whatever diabolical plan Death believed he had in mind, but I needed to at least appear to be following my boss' orders for now.

Maybe Stormfinger would prove useful after all—he certainly seemed more willing to work with me after discovering I was the original grim. Of course, I didn't trust him, but I needed to prove one way or another he was the culprit behind The Ghost Lands.

I texted him and he replied so quickly, it seemed he'd been anxiously awaiting my request. We set a time and place to meet that evening, and then I texted JR and told him I'd be at the house in fifteen minutes. His reply—instant as well—contained a smiley face and a high five emoji. Talk about two different worlds.

As promised, fifteen minutes later, Moss steered the limo down the tree-lined lane and to the grand Banks' mansion. Ghost stood in Killion's lap, her paws on the door while she peered at the passing scenery, wagging all the way.

The master vampire had been sneaking peeks at me since I'd emerged from the bathroom after cleaning myself up. "What?" I asked. I felt like a bug under a microscope.

"You look...lovely." His normal unemotional expression held a touch of wonder.

I owned a single pair of dress slacks in heather gray, which I'd paired with a raspberry sweater under a wool jacket that had threads of both colors. I'd hastily curled my lashes, added a coat of mascara, and slicked peach gloss on my lips. "Compared to how I *usually* look?"

Nonplussed, he hesitated. "You are a natural beauty." He touched the ends of my hair, running a strand of white between his finger and thumb. I'd braided it while it was still wet before I'd fallen asleep. Once I undid it, soft waves brushed my shoulders. "I simply mean you appear softer."

There was a compliment in there somewhere. I raised a brow.

He tried again. "More feminine."

Hmm. "I know what you're getting at. I look nice when I clean up. We'll leave it at that."

The limo came to a stop in front of the columned veranda. The double white doors opened and JR stepped out, waving. Ghost barked a happy greeting.

"I'll text the ride service when I'm done. You don't need to wait." I leaned over and kissed Killion's cheek. "I'm meeting Stormfinger at sundown at your church. I know you'll want to be there, but stay out of sight, okay? I need him to believe I'm really all in with this, and see if he'll talk to me. He's unlikely to admit to anything if you're hovering."

He stopped my hand to keep me from exiting, then slid the other over my cheek and around to the back of my neck. "Hovering?"

"You know what I mean."

He drew my face close to his and kissed me thoroughly. Every thought I had flew from my mind and desire coiled tight and low in my belly. "Dinner. Tonight. My place."

Panting, I nodded. He'd stated more than once that I talked too much, while I'd accused him repeatedly of not talking enough. We had multiple things to discuss, but from the look in his eyes, and the feel of his hands on me, I suspected that was the last thing we were going to do.

THIRTY-THREE

After I climbed out, I straightened my jacket and licked my lips—the gloss was long gone. I made a production of taking the tube from my purse and reapplying it as the car glided off into the late afternoon sun.

"How long have you two been dating?"

I turned to JR and made my way up the brick steps. "Not long."

"He seems...intense. Mother remembers his dad." He took my elbow and guided me through the doorway. "We've used Reveux Investment Services for years."

His Dad died a long time ago. Who Kitty remembered was Killion. Since he didn't age much, he had to 'reincarnate' himself over and over again so humans didn't get suspicious. "If I had money to invest, I'd certainly give it to him."

The foyer was elegant and airy, large windows overhead steeping us in pale yellows. "Of course, you'd say that," JR teased. His slacks were pressed and his trendy sports shirt was fitted. Expensive cologne teased my nose with notes of citrus and pine. "When he breaks your heart, you know where to find me."

I chuckled awkwardly as he took my jacket and hung it on the coat rack, then motioned for me to walk with him. He led me across the large vestibule and past the formal living and dining rooms to the west wing. Light music and chanting filtered out from the four-season porch.

Mrs. Rawlings was in a bright pink tank top and yoga pants, wiping the back of her neck with a towel. She looked thin. When she saw us, she smiled and shut off the music.

"Chloe, I'm so glad you made it." She tossed the towel on her yoga mat and air-kissed my cheeks. "I'm afraid I'm sweaty or I would give you a proper hug."

"It's good to see you." The room was filled with a variety of houseplants, a water feature, and crystals in various sizes, colors, and shapes. Window catchers caught the sun and reflected it around the room. Books on health and wellness, self-improvement, and Eastern philosophy, filled rows of custom bookshelves. "Thank you for having me."

JR helped her shrug on a nylon jacket. "Don't forget your necklace," he said, picking up a beautiful green stone pendant with dark swirls.

She held still as he looped it around her and hooked the clasp. "Do you see how he fusses over me?"

The smile in her voice said it all—she was thrilled he was home and taking care of her.

"I'll get the tea." He guided her toward a chair and motioned me to the nearby loveseat. "Be right back."

An assortment of prescription medications sat on a marble table next to her chair, along with bottles of vitamins, more crystals, and a bowl with dried flowers and herbs. She waved a hand over the collection. "This is all his doing. All this New Age stuff. I have to admit, he's done his homework. Some of these things have been used for centuries, in cultures all over the world." She fiddled with the stone, drawing my attention to it. "I figure, it can't hurt, right? My oncology team thinks it's nuts but has okayed most of it, and I would never quit my treatments. Maybe I'm looney to hope it might help, but when you face death, that can happen."

You're telling me.

There was a distinct symbol on the pendant. One I'd seen a few hours ago on Piedmont's. "What a lovely piece. What kind of stone is it?"

"Malachite. The woman Jackson got it from claimed to be a healer, and said this crystal strengthens the immune system and helps with cell regeneration." She glanced at the piece. "She claimed it was at least a hundred years old."

A bell went off in my head. "And the symbol? I know I've seen it somewhere, but I can't remember what it stands for."

She tucked a strand of her blond hair into her clip. "I have no idea. Jack believes in it, and for now, I'm humoring him. I don't know how long I have left, and I have to admit, the stone brings me comfort. I feel more energized when I wear it."

I didn't see any glow around it, but without thinking, I sent a pulse of my magic out to touch it. It felt cold, remote, and sparked when my magic swept over the symbol. I drew back, feeling like I'd stuck my finger in a light socket and gotten a shock.

"I'm sorry." She waved a hand in the air and seemed embarrassed. "You must think I'm a quack. And where are my manners? You didn't come here to talk about depressing things like cancer. How are you doing? I haven't seen you since the funeral."

Still a depressing subject. So much had happened since

then, I didn't know where to start. I fumbled for the right words to say. She might be facing her own funeral soon, and my heart felt heavy—for her and JR. "I've had a rough time, to be honest, but I'm lucky. The support of good friends has made a big difference."

"Jack is excited that you're reopening the clinic. I never imagined he would return to practice veterinary medicine, and I still wish he'd join the family business, but it's important that he follow his heart. We've argued too many times over his life path, but I've come to see that he isn't cut out for the banking industry."

Out of the corner of my eye, I noticed a Ficus tree starting to bloom. Uh oh. "You're very wise," I said, smiling and checking that my magic was reeled in. It seemed to be, but perhaps letting go of that one pulse had been enough to give the living plants a burst. I dared not turn my head to look at them. "He's lucky to have you."

"I feel guilty that he moved back to take care of me, but secretly I love it. It's so good to have him in the house again, to hear his voice every morning when I wake. I hug him every night before I go to bed. I feel truly blessed, and if I do get a reprieve, I know it's because of him, not anything the supplements, crystals, or treatments have done."

When I'd first walked in, she'd seemed rather pale, her eyes dim. Now they were bright with joy, and the wrinkles around her mouth had smoothed out. Had I given her a juice, too? Or was it the pendant? "It's good to have him home."

"What you said about having friends to support you—I hope you'll be there for him when it's my time. You've always been special to him."

Not enough for her to allow our friendship past the age

of eleven, but that was water under the bridge. They were in the "haves" category, while the Frosts had been in the "have-nots." We weren't poor by any means, but any extra money Mom and Dad made at the clinic went to help homeless animals. Kitty was a different woman than I remembered, though, and my mother had always insisted that everyone deserved a second chance. "I'll do whatever I can to help him."

JR returned with a silver tray containing a floral teapot and three matching cups with saucers. His mother made room on the table and he poured each of us some. He doctored hers with a sugar cube and a spot of cream from an elegant pitcher. He asked if I wanted anything added to mine and I shook my head. "Plain for me."

"I'm surprised," he said, winking. "You always had a notorious sweet tooth."

That I did, but after tasting stardust, I doubted anything would ever be able to compete. "Your mother was telling me about her pendant. It's so beautiful. Where did you get it?"

"You know the metaphysical shop downtown? The guru there, Livingston, put me in touch with a woman and she delivered it."

Mrs. Rawlings fingered the stone. "It should cure all my ailments, from the cost of it."

"I had the money, mother." JR looked out a floor-to-ceiling window, sipping his tea. "Your health is priceless."

She caught my eye and smiled, once again delighted by her son's caring. "Tell me, Chloe. Are you still going to therapy?"

JR turned on her. "Mother! That's none of our business."

She didn't appear the least bit apologetic. "I have a

vested interest in the answer. You're going to need grief counseling once I'm gone. I would like to know if Chloe recommends the doctor Camille told me she was seeing when we spoke at the funeral."

I held up a hand to ward off JR's anger. "Yes, I'm still seeing Dr. Maxwell. In fact, I have a session with her next week, and I have journal pages to send her. She's done me a world of good and I do recommend her."

"There. You see?" Mrs. Rawlings set down her cup. "You should reach out and make an appointment. See if you like her."

"Mother, I don't need grief counseling, and I won't for a long time. You're getting better every day."

"It will make me happy if you do as I ask." Her tone was laced with steel, and she gave him the hairy eyeball. "You do want me to be happy, don't you?"

JR rolled his eyes but smiled in concession. "Yes, of course." He shifted his gaze to me. "She knows the guilt card always works."

She winked at me. "Well, it's time for me to lie down for my afternoon nap." She stood and adjusted the zipper of her jacket before kissing JR's cheek. "You two enjoy the tea and conversation. It was good to see you, Chloe."

Neither of us said anything until she was gone, and then JR sighed heavily. "It's true—she's getting stronger every day. They caught it early and I think she's got a fighting chance of beating this."

"I do, too." It wasn't a platitude. Unfortunately, I believed it had a lot to do with the pendant, rather than the treatments. "I sure would like to get one of those necklaces for my friend, Nita. You remember her. She's into crystals and all that stuff." So much in fact, she'd had Livingston give me herbal supplements and a special tea at Halloween.

JR frowned. "You know, it's funny, the woman told me her name, but after she dropped off the necklace, I completely forgot what it was. Either I'm getting old, or I've been too focused on mother to remember it."

Or the gal purposely used magic to make him forget.

Yet another thing I needed to check on.

THIRTY-FOUR

I toyed with my cup. "I suppose I could ask Livingston. Can you tell me what she looked like so I can describe her?"

"Old. I mean, like seriously. She was probably in her nineties. Her hair was white and she had dull, gray eyes. Short, too." He offered to refill my tea, but I put a hand over the cup. "I'm sure he'll know who it is."

My phone buzzed with a familiar ringtone. "Sorry, I need to take this. It's Uncle Morty."

"Of course. Go ahead."

As I rose and paced to the far end of the room, JR began cleaning up. "Hey. What's up?"

"The autopsy is gone. Just...gone. I knew better than to let that numbskull, Jarvis, file the report. Detective Adams is breathing down my neck and now it's MIA. I need you to transcribe my notes and refile it. How soon can you get here to fix this mess?"

"The autopsy from the Jane Doe?"

"Yes! Jarvis claims he saved it and forwarded a copy to

the detective, but no one can find either. I'm going to kill him!"

"Don't do that. It will be okay." My uncle had a thing about providing the police with written results, rather than simply calling them with his assessment when it concerned a suspicious death or outright homicide. He always preferred they read his official report before they asked him any questions, so he could refer back to it. They were less likely to take things out of context or jump to conclusions about the victim or killer.

I checked the time. "I'll text the ride service now. I should be there in fifteen to twenty minutes."

"I can give you a ride," JR offered.

I shifted the phone from my mouth. "That's really not necessary."

He smiled. "You're not calling a service. I'm perfectly capable of taking you wherever you need to go."

His tone suggested arguing was a moot point. I conceded with a nod and told my uncle to expect me in ten to fifteen.

JR left the tray on the table and together we climbed into his SUV. It was a midnight blue number, with tons of gadgets and an adjustable lumbar pillow in the seat that was pretty amazing. I hadn't realized how tense I was until he showed me how to inflate it and I sank into the leather with a delightful sigh.

"Still at the morgue, huh?" He donned aviator sunglasses and grinned at me. "There must be some perk to hanging out with dead people, I just can't figure out what it is."

If he only knew. "They're quiet, and Uncle Morty brings me food from Aunt Camille every shift. I always have plenty of time to get my homework done, and I like the people I work with."

We cruised down the lane and onto the road. He adjusted the heat vents and the vehicle rumbled as he accelerated. "Soon, you won't need to be there or the coffee shop. Frosty Paws is going to be a huge success."

"From your lips to God's ears." My parents had done so many things at cost, there had been no profit. They had taken out a second mortgage on our home in order to keep the clinic running. I couldn't afford to do that, and I hoped Patty's ideas would bring in the funds we needed for free and low-cost programs.

"You don't think I'm weird, do you? Over the New Age stuff?" He slowed to make the turn into town. "I know it sounds crazy, but I have this odd sense it's not mother's time to go."

I didn't know her contract's expiration date, but Death had said it wasn't *JR's* time. "Our mind controls a lot. What we believe, we manifest." I'd heard Nita claim it a dozen times. She constantly wrote her dreams and intentions in journals, and repeated affirmations and mantras to train her brain to be optimistic. "If you and your mother believe it, it might work."

"It should be me," he said. "After all the wild things I've done in my life?" He shook his head.

I sat up, feeling weary again. "It doesn't work that way."

His attention was on the road, but behind the sunglasses he seemed a million miles away. "I've danced with the devil plenty. Took huge chances with my life. Plus, I haven't always been the nicest person." He flicked his gaze to me and back to the road. "I want you to know, Chloe, I'm sorry for the way I treated you in school."

I truly hoped he hadn't actually made any kind of

bargain with a witch or other supernatural. At least, I hadn't seen the shadow worm again. "That's the past, and from what I understand, being a good person doesn't extend your contract here on earth."

He glanced my way. "Contract?"

Oops. "My own theory." I rubbed my sweaty palms on my thighs. "I believe we all have a certain time we're supposed to be here, and when that's up, it's up."

"Did you learn that from your counselor?"

'Counselor' was a broad term I could apply to several entities in my life. "She's taught me a lot. If you want me to make an introduction, I'm glad to do so."

He was quiet, then nodded. "I don't plan to need her, but I guess it wouldn't hurt."

When he parked in the hospital lot, he turned in his seat to face me, resting an elbow on the back. "Were you and your friends really LARPing this morning?"

I'd been hoping he'd forget that. "It's a great stress reliever," I hedged.

He removed his glasses, giving me a lopsided grin. "I'd like to hear more about it. The invitation for dinner stands. Mother's care has taken most of my free time, but now that she's doing better, I feel like I need to get back into the swing of things."

There was nothing flirty about the invitation and I wondered if Killion's "marking" had worked. "I have plans tonight, but I bet Nita is available. She knows a lot more of the gossip and goings-on around town than I do. I'll give her your number."

The anticipation and expectancy in his face disappeared. He slid the shades back on. "Nah. That's okay. Enjoy your night."

His mother wasn't the only one who could lay on the

guilt. "Thank you for the tea. I'm glad your mom is doing better."

I bailed and watched him leave. Before entering the building, I typed a quick message to Aurora asking her to check into the pendant. I attempted to describe the symbol and asked her to research it, along with the woman who'd sold it to JR.

Detective Adams stepped out of the back door of the police station, which was connected to the hospital by a sidewalk that ran past the morgue. His thinning hair blew in the breeze and he used a hand to pat it down. "Got that report for me, Frost?"

Hastily, I pocketed the phone and headed for the single-story building on my left. "I'll have it to you shortly."

Just my luck, I found Death waiting for me.

THIRTY-FIVE

Dwayne, our security guard, was slumped at the front desk, reading his monthly issue of *National Geographic*. He glanced up, mumbled a greeting as I signed in, and then did a double-take, his fleshy jowls shaking. "You been to a funeral?"

"Contrary to popular belief, that isn't the only time I dress up."

Mary Lynn was in The Pit, where autopsies were performed, cleaning and organizing equipment. As I passed by with a wave, she, too, looked surprised at my attire.

Uncle Morty was nowhere in sight. When I entered the office, I jumped and put a hand to my heart, seeing Death behind the desk.

His feet were up, legs crossed at the ankles. He'd leaned so far back in the chair, his head touched the wall. "There you are." He scanned me with an approving nod. "You look nice. Got a date?"

I pulled the shade on the door's tiny window and lowered my voice. "What are you doing here? Whatever it is, I don't have time to talk right now. I need to get a report typed and sent to Detective Adams."

He made no motion to move. "I need to give you this." An envelope appeared in his open palm. When I simply quirked a brow, he waved it at me, lowering his feet to the floor. "Go on. Take it."

"What is it?"

"A formal apology."

I snatched it from his hand and yanked on his wrist. "Move."

Reluctantly, he did and I popped into the chair and grabbed the letter opener from the pencil jar. On the front of the thick envelope was my name in script. I ripped it open and drew out the folded sheet inside. A creamy linen document with more cursive writing. I scanned it and noted the signature at the bottom—bold and brazen, a complete contrast to the rest. "You nearly kill me,"—I glanced up at him—"and this is all I get?"

His jaw jutted out. "Smudgy insisted on an official, written expression of regret for my wrongdoing."

"That's it? They didn't put you on probation? Make threats about wiping your memory and your future career limitations?"

"Your sarcasm is charming."

"I'm not joking." I tossed the letter down and booted up the ancient computer. "Leave."

"Why are you dressed up?"

Ignoring him, I clicked on the form template to open it, and grabbed the paper file lying on the center of the desk. Our victim had not been identified and therefore had received a code made up of numbers and letters based on the hospital's system. I entered the combination and saved the file with the same identifier. "None of your business."

"You should talk to her shade." He pointed at the folder. "She could tell you who she is."

"Why don't you?" I typed the information from the initial on-scene report that I'd done, adding my uncle's notes concerning the suspected cause of death, approximate time, and details concerning the wounds on her body. The cuts were shallow, and although she had bled a lot, they were not responsible for her demise. "As you can see, I have work to do."

"Chloe, I know you're angry, but—"

The door flew open and Mary Lynn leaned on the thin frame. Her dark brown eyes were filled with mischief. "Hot date?"

I took a deep breath and forced my glare at Death into a more genial glance at my friend. "I do, in fact."

"I knew it. It's that yummy guy you're renting the clinic space from, isn't it?"

Death rolled his eyes at her description of Killion. I smiled broadly. "We're having dinner, just as soon as I redo the file on our Jane Doe."

She began unbuttoning her lab coat. "He seems like quite the catch."

"Well, at this point, we're only business partners." I pointedly looked at Death. While I assumed he knew what was going on between me and the master vampire, I wasn't giving him anything he could hold against me.

"Sure you are." She winked. "I'm really happy for you, Chloe."

"Thank you." I went back to the dictation. "I'm happy, too. It's been a while since I felt this good."

Her gaze dropped to the desk and the pages of the autopsy. "We have to live life to the fullest, don't we? You never know when death will come calling."

I glanced at the male embodiment of it, not two feet from her. "You have no idea."

"What was that?"

I'd said it softly, but didn't repeat it. "What was the cause of death?"

"Her heart stopped. Sad, isn't it? She was so young."

Sad and odd. Scanning the shared drive the hospital used, I noticed a file from the previous day that had all numbers as the name. I clicked on it, and bingo. The missing file opened. "Not lost after all."

"You found it?"

"Randy didn't use the Unknown Code system or file it in the right folder." I sighed my relief. On the form, I checked the necessary boxes, saved everything with an updated label, and sent copies to medical records, as well as the detective. I hit print and the ancient machine next to the desk groaned to life. "I'm going to take the paper copy to the police station."

"I'm off to get my own dinner. Have a good night."

The dinosaur printer finally finished and I added the report to the stack, aligning all of it with the official hospital form on top. I shut down the computer and grabbed my purse, skirting Death. "I'm off to see the wizard."

To my dismay, he followed. "Stormfinger? Are you training with him tonight?"

"Seriously, dude. It was just a reference to the *Wizard of Oz*, not an actual wizard." I went down the hallway, shifting my purse on my shoulder, and keeping an eye out in case our victim's shade was, indeed, hanging around. I didn't see her, and I knew one of the detectives at the scene had already lifted her fingerprints. If for some reason the police were not able to identify her, I'd come back and try to coax her spirit to talk to me. Or threaten Death to tell me.

Surely, he knew who she was. "I thought Stormfinger was a sorcerer—are they the same thing?"

"Not exactly, but similar in the ways they use magic."

I marched past Dwayne, pretending Death wasn't there. "Have a good night," I called.

"You interviewing for a new job?" He pointed a stubby finger at my getup. "Your uncle is sad you're leaving."

Apparently, while Mary Lynn had assumed I had a date, Dwayne actually knew me better. Under normal circumstances, it would never occur to him that I would find the time and energy to pursue a relationship. "I'm meeting with an investor."

He nodded approval. "For the vet clinic?"

"Yes."

"Knock 'em dead, kid."

We exchanged a smile. When you worked at the morgue, you had to keep a sense of humor, morbid or not. I gave him a thumbs up and headed out the door.

Death continued to dog me. "You left the letter on the desk."

"You better retrieve it if you don't want anyone to find it."

He blew a raspberry, but turned on his heel and went back inside. I glanced up at the sky and said thank you to whatever guardian angel might be looking over my shoulder. The sun had nearly set and clouds were moving in. The solar lights at the rear of the station had already come on and I saw the detective speaking to a man with a bald head, the outside light reflecting off it.

It was Piedmont. Maybe I really did have a guardian angel.

They stood close together, facing each other, voices lowered. "I think I know her," Piedmont said in a strained voice. He rubbed absently at his bare head. "Can I just see the body?"

"First, I want a statement."

"Detective?" I held up the folder. "I've got your print version and I've sent you the digital."

They both startled. Piedmont's face showed his confusion. "Chloe?"

"Hey. Sorry to interrupt."

He glanced at the folder and his face went tight. "Is that her?"

The detective had clear rules about us butting into police matters. I held my tongue.

"Waverley," Piedmont said. "My girlfriend. She hasn't been home since New Year's Eve, and I just heard about the cemetery murder." His eyes teared up. "I told her she was messing with the wrong people."

Detective Adams took the folder. "Come inside," he ordered. "I need to review this and then we'll proceed."

As Piedmont's shoulders shook with quiet sobs, the detective led him through the door and gave me a nod of appreciation. Piedmont glanced over his shoulder. "I'm sorry about earlier, I was just kidding about competing with your aunt."

I felt guilty about it now, considering the dead woman might be his partner. "Can you tell me who you got your necklace from?"

He stopped and his hand went to the pendant at his collarbone. "Waverly got it from her sister. She's..." He visibly shivered. "She's a witch. Like the real deal. She freaks me out, and I've tried to get Waverly away from her."

Another witch. "Does she make them? I have a friend who's sick, and I hear they work miracles."

The detective gave me an exasperated look. "Can you do this some other time?"

"She didn't make it, but it's definitely doing some good." He rubbed the stone. "I have a genetic blood disease that there's no cure for. It's been causing my heart to enlarge for years, and the experts told me I'd be dead before I got to fifty. That's why Waverley and I were going to use our combined savings to buy a food truck. It's now or never, you know? But she wiped out her half to buy this instead because her sister claimed it was magic. Seriously. Sounds completely whacked, but at my checkup last week, my doctor was shocked at how normal my heart and blood are. I think the damn thing is working."

His stone was a shiny gray, not malachite. The symbol seemed to glow when I sent a pulse of magic toward it, exactly like Kitty Banks' had done. "Do you know what kind of stone that is?"

The detective began flipping through the folder, impatient. Piedmont dropped the necklace and wiped his eyes. "Hematite. It's supposed to be good for the blood."

"What's Waverley's sister's name?"

Adam's head snapped up and he pinned me with a glacial stare. "Do not interfere with my case, Frost."

Before either of us could say another word, the detective hustled Piedmont inside and slammed the door.

First, I texted Uncle Morty to tell him all was well, then sent a message to Nita, asking if she knew Waverly's last name, and possibly her sister's. My phone rang as I was waiting for replies. It was Aurora. "What do you have?" I asked.

"I've identified the mark. How soon can you be here? I have a lot to tell you."

"I promised Stormfinger I'd meet at the church at

sundown, and I'm already running late. I'd blow him off, but I want to interrogate him about The Ghost Lands. After that, I'm seeing Killion for dinner. Definitely not blowing that off. Any chance you can send me the info?"

"I'll pick you up in five and take you to the church. We can talk on the way."

She hung up and I saw Death approaching, letter in hand. He walked right up and shoved it in my bag.

I smacked his hand away. "In review: boundaries include my home, my workplace, and my personal effects."

"Are you training in that?" He pointed to my clothes, managing to magically shove the letter in my bag without touching it. "I know you're meeting Stormfinger. I can zap you home, let you change into something more comfortable."

I pointed a finger at his face towering over me. "No zapping! Or anything else. Do not touch me or my things. Do not, under any circumstances, ever, and I mean *ever*, kiss me again."

He grinned, as though humored by my threat. "You gotta admit, it was stellar." He winked. "Get it? As in stars, the cosmos?"

"I keep asking myself what I did to deserve you."

The grin fell, but only slightly. "You don't like the pun? Come on."

I glanced up at the sky again. The guardian angel had to be laughing now. "Do you really think I created The Ghost Lands errantly, simply from suppressing my gift?"

He turned serious, pensive. "Possible, but not probable."

"I'm getting better with using it." I sent a pulse and the dormant grass along the sidewalk woke up and began to turn a bright lime shade. "Will that dimension vanish if I'm actively using my magic?"

He appeared mildly impressed, but shook his head. "Even if you didn't create that place, you're tied to it by blood. One way or another we'll have to clean it up and rescue those souls."

I drew my magic back and the grass stayed vivid but its growth slowed to a stop. "If I learn anything from Stormfinger, I'll be in touch."

"Want company?"

"No." I headed for the front and held up a hand. "Don't follow me. I can handle him."

For once, he listened. When I got to the sidewalk, Aurora was waiting, her tiny, white electric car idling.

I climbed in. "You got here fast."

She wove an invisible figure eight through the air with her purple fingernails and waggled her brows. "Magic," she said.

Her type I could handle. Although her homemade teas were hard to choke down, she would never try to kill me. "Speaking of, I have info on our dead witch."

She pulled away from the curb. "Then you better text that untrustworthy sorcerer and tell him to reschedule. We have a lot to do."

THIRTY-SIX

I got no reply from Stormfinger when I told him I had a hot new lead that I had to follow before I met him.

Not that I expected one. He was probably cursing me at that moment, since the sun had sunk below the horizon, and I'd once more blown him off. But if he wanted the amulet, or inside information on Death, I knew he'd eventually reach out.

I was starving and I instructed Aurora to stop at the coffee shop so I could pick up a snack. On the way there, she asked for details about Death kissing me, and I gave her the basics. I also told her he had wings.

"You kissed an angel. Huh." I couldn't tell if she was impressed or concerned. Maybe both.

"It wasn't sexual or even romantic. It was just...peace. Oblivion."

She flicked her gaze to me, back to the road. "You liked it."

"Eww, no. Not the kiss. But the nothingness wasn't so bad."

"To each his own, I guess."

"Do you think he's really an angel? Like as in heaven and all that?"

"Celestial beings aren't only found in Christian or non-pagan religions. They aren't all called angels, either, but most major belief systems include some form of sacred being who is an intermediary between humans and the Divine. Angels of Death—yes, there is believed to be a whole group of them, no matter the religion—watching over the transitions of life to death and vice versa. It makes sense that he's one of them."

My brain would explode one of these days, I was sure of it.

"Why doesn't he want to talk about it?" I mused as she found a parking spot.

"We all have our secrets."

She was hungry, too, so we grabbed a table in the back and helped ourselves to giant fudge muffins and iced caramel mocha lattes. Thankfully, Nita wasn't working. The twins, Shane and Keener, were.

"Omg, this is so good." Aurora licked whipped cream from the top of her drink and gobbled down more of the muffin. "Did your aunt make these?"

The jumbo size treats were her signature dessert. The Bean got a dozen every day, and we always sold out. "I told you she's an amazing baker."

Shane moseyed over, a towel in his hand from wiping down tables. The taller of the twins had a man bun, plugs in his earlobes, and a barbed wire tattoo circling his left bicep. He eyed the witch with a flirty smile, twisting the towel in his hands to cause his biceps to flex. "Can I get you a refill, gorgeous?"

Aurora slid her green eyes over to him. "No, thank you."

"Maybe I can get you something else?"

His method needed work, but I had to give him credit for trying. With anyone else, I might have jumped in and told him to get lost, but I knew she would eat him for lunch.

Her lips curved in a wicked smile. Never mess with a redheaded Irish witch. "You can't handle me, so run along before I turn you into a toad."

The poor guy was misguided, thinking she was flirting back. I grinned. "Sounds kinky."

Her face hardened. "I sleep with a wolf. Stop talking to me or I'll have him rip out your throat."

Shane's face turned startled. He started to say something, thought better of it, and walked away.

Smart man.

Aurora laughed. "Can you believe his audacity? He really thinks he can handle this?" She waved a hand through the air, pointing at herself. "Not to sound vain, but seriously, I'm so tired of being hit on everywhere I go by men who think they're my equal."

None of us were her equal, and I certainly questioned whether Andy was. "You can't blame them for trying. You *are* quite the catch." I sort of envied her. "No one but Randy from the hospital ever hits on me. What a douche."

She chuckled. "Death flirts with you all the time, and Killion is smitten. You've hit the jackpot with him. I believe you're the first to catch his interest in a very long time."

My cheeks heated. I couldn't talk about this stuff to my bestie, but I could with Aurora. It was a relief. "I met his wife...her ghost, anyway. She told me I'm not good enough for him."

Aurora about fell off her seat. "You called to her ghost and brought her here from the other side?"

"Not intentionally." I fiddled with my muffin. "I'm not even sure it was real. Maybe it was another hallucination."

"Did you tell Killion?"

"He was sort of there, although, he didn't see or hear her, and yes, I told him."

"You have an extremely complicated life, you know that?"

Ha! "I'm honestly nervous about our date later. We've definitely crossed a line and there's no going back."

One perfectly groomed brow rose. "I don't care for vampires, but he seems to be a good one. If there is such a thing. It's wise to consider where your relationship is going, but I believe you could do worse."

"Thanks for the vote of confidence."

We finished our food and then got down to work. "Epsilon," she said, tapping a mark in a book she'd brought along. It looked like an odd version of a lowercase e. "That's what's on those amulets. It's a Greek letter, but can also serve as a number. From my research, the last known owners of those pieces also belonged to The Order. There were five stones and they had healing properties."

"JR says his mother is better. Piedmont told me his genetic blood disorder seems to be reversing itself. Both mentioned how costly the pendants were. Whoever has them is milking people for money."

"Most will pay anything to extend their life."

"And Piedmont's girlfriend, Waverly, is the one who was killed at the cemetery, but I have no idea why. She got the necklace from her sister, who he mentioned is also a witch, but a *serious* one. I'm assuming not your happy, nature-loving Wicca brand. Maybe she was in to black magic? Ring any bells?"

"Without her name, it could be a handful or more." Her mouth turned down and she chewed her muffin in thought.

"According to what I read, the Epsilon members made a pact to be buried with their respective crystals."

"Did they think the stones could bring them back to life?"

She shook her head as I sipped my drink. "The last journal entry my grandmother made mentioned lore about them having a curse. She claimed they weren't safe to use, and that the group had taken them to their graves so no one else would be hurt."

"But somebody found out about them and dug them up." I remembered the description of the woman JR had given me. I told Aurora about her. "That old gal knows what they can do and is using them to prey on desperate people. Do you really think the stones are cursed? They seem to be helping."

"Both of the people you know have only been using them for a few weeks, correct?"

"Apparently so. Could it be too early to tell about the potential side effects?"

She shrugged. "I'm curious as to how this grave robber knew the names and locations of the five Order members. Even I couldn't find that in my histories."

"And if she's as old as JR says, how did she dig them up? It's January and the ground is hard as concrete. She must have had help."

She wiggled her fingers. "If she's a witch, she could have used magic."

"True." I pulled out my cell and opened my photos. "I never noticed any magical glow around the graves, or any obvious designation as part of the Epsilon group or The Order."

She took the phone and scrolled through the pictures,

zooming in on one and turning the screen to me. "Look at the e in 'died.'"

Now I saw it. The Greek version of a curved letter with a bar through the center in place of a normal e. "It's an epsilon."

We searched the other images, and sure enough, each had one, whether it was in their name, or something else written on the marker. Even the last I'd snapped on New Year's Eve.

"There was a guy staring at this one the other night." I showed her. "This must be another of the members."

"Why five?" She unfolded a paper map of our town that she used frequently to track magic users and find the nexus of where spells originated. "Wait." Using a pen, she circled the graveyards where the robberies had taken place. "Nope, I guess not."

"What?" I stared at the upside down map.

"The locations of these five cemeteries form a pentagram, but we only know of three robberies. If the fourth grave is also in Shepherd's Rest, the pentagram theory is a wash."

"Is there any other significance with the number five?"

"Earth, air, water, fire, and spirit. All witches use the elements to work magic. Some of The Order did as well."

Something tickled my brain. "The mausoleum with the grim statue. The family name was Methuselah."

"Yes, Theodore was part of The Order, but he hasn't been disturbed, except by you."

"He was an archimagus, just like the one who's created The Ghost Lands. Could our current day version and this old woman be working with each other? What if they could put all five necklaces together and use the trapped spirits to supercharge them? Could that override the curse and create...I don't know...immortality?"

Her eyes snapped to mine. "You're brilliant. If the archimagus has all five amulets and the energy of the trapped souls, not only could he time travel, he might be able to do just that—become immortal."

"Which means Death could be right about Stormfinger. He could be our guy."

"While I don't believe he's cunning or intelligent enough to do all this, it appears so. I told you not to trust him."

The names of the remaining Epsilon members were still a mystery. "We only know the location of a couple of the pendants, yet three graves have been disturbed," I said. "That leaves two still buried, so where is the fifth? And why is the woman blackmailing people for money, if the intent is to become immortal?"

"You can't live on magic alone and Stormfinger isn't immortal yet. He needs funds."

I thought about his crappy car. It made sense.

She rolled up the map and tucked it in her bag. "Have you heard any rumors around the hospital of patients having miraculous recoveries?"

I started to say no, then stopped. "Jimmy Haskell."

"Who's that?"

"A seven-year-old boy who has spent more of the past year in the children's wing than he has at home."

"What's wrong with him?"

"Brittle bone disease. It's a genetic abnormality that causes them to break extremely easily and can be severe. He had scoliosis and breathing issues due to it, and was going to end up in a wheelchair. His prognosis was poor, but right before Christmas, he got up from his hospital bed and disappeared. They found him three blocks from here at the park, playing on the equipment. His mother said it was a miracle, and it was on all the news stations."

She sat back and fiddled with her napkin. "That fits."

I brought up the local station's website and tapped on their human interest tab, scrolling through segments to reach the one they'd done on Jimmy. I let it play, putting it between us so we could watch.

"There." Aurora pointed to the screen and I paused the recording. "Do you see it?"

The boy was playing with his dog, looking like a typical kid, a grin on his face as his mother spoke to the reporter. A white stone with gray veins hung from a cord around the boy's neck and swayed when he threw the ball for the dog.

"That has to be it." We continued to watch, and Mrs. Haskell mentioned that they had no savings left, but having Jimmy home for the holiday was the best gift she could receive. A miracle.

A follow-up story was entered on Christmas Day, stating that a fund had been set up for the family, and donations had been pouring in. "What do you want to bet the reason she had no money was because she had to fork it over for that necklace?" I asked.

"Our three people could be in danger." She crumpled her napkin, sucked down the last of her drink, and gathered her bag. "We have to get those amulets. Plus, stop our mystery woman from digging up the others and capture Stormfinger."

"But..." I held up a finger. "We need to proceed with caution. Stormfinger is dangerous enough, and the woman is an unknown entity." A thought occurred to me. "Could she have been around when the previous grave robberies happened?"

"If she's a supernatural, absolutely."

I stacked our dishes. "You focus on the location of the other pendants."

As I rose, she got to her feet as well. "What are you going to do?"

"Find our mystery woman."

"How? We have nothing to go on."

I waved my hand at her, mimicking what she'd done earlier. "Magic, my witchy friend."

THIRTY-SEVEN

S tormfinger had, well, ghosted me.

After all his complaining, and his assurance he'd meet me, he was nowhere to be found.

It didn't make sense, unless he was guilty as I suspected. Or simply pissed that I was late.

Night had fallen and so had the temperature. Killion's church sat dark and quiet, a lone owl hooting from the bell tower high overhead. On the other side of the block, the rundown bar was hopping. Two very separate worlds.

Aurora was in her car on the phone, digging up contact information for the Haskells. I'd spoken to Livingston at the metaphysical shop, and like JR, he couldn't seem to remember the woman's name. He claimed he didn't have a number for her or know where she lived. He'd called her a nomad in a generic way, mentioning he believed she moved around a lot, but contradicted the idea that she was old. He pegged her at thirty, not a day over, and when I asked if he had any other pieces by her, he said he didn't.

I texted Stormfinger again and then called. Voicemail. The cemetery still looked like a tornado had struck, debris everywhere. I climbed the steps and used one of the iron knockers to raise Katarina. Her pets' muffled barks came through the wood.

After a minute, the slot in the section on my left slid back and a green iris, with an amazing eyeliner wing, stared back at me. "What?"

Our early camaraderie was as MIA as the sorcerer. "Have you seen Stormfinger?"

"No."

Short and direct, but not helpful. "You didn't eat him, did you?"

She opened the door and gave me a slow, evil grin. "He was delicious." She licked her lips for emphasis.

Okay, then. "In case you're joking, which I assume you are,"—often hard to tell with the Undead—"he could actually be gunning for Death's job, or some form of immortality, so if he's still running around, be wary."

"Do you really think I'd lower myself to feasting on a bottom sucker like him? Please. I have standards."

"Of course you do." Did that mean she ate higher caliber sorcerers? Pretty sure I didn't want to know, but I suspected she and Aurora would get along well. "Thanks for offering to help with Piedmont today, but don't bother him, okay? It appears his girlfriend is the graveyard victim from the other night."

"The witch that was sacrificed?"

"Did you know her?"

"She came around once with her stepsister, wanting to know if we were recruiting."

"Stepsister? The one who's into serious magic?"

She grunted. I took that as a yes.

The two dogs poked their heads out and wagged at me. I petted them. "Recruiting what? Blood donors?"

"No, vampires. *Duh.* She wanted to know if we would turn somebody for her."

Piedmont. "And Waverly knew to come here?"

"The stepsister did." She picked at a nail. "We're not a charity. We don't do that simply because they have a disease. The master would never allow such a thing."

I knew that to be true. "Any chance you know how I can get in contact with the stepsister?"

"Why would you want to? She's a freak."

I struggled not to laugh, considering who I was talking to. "In what way?"

"A fang-banger."

"A what?"

She flashed her incisors. "A vampire groupie, in it for the sex."

"So a blood donor with benefits?"

"How many witches do you know who want to be blood donors for vampires?"

None.

Manicure forgotten; she practically hissed her disdain. "I don't trust her. I could smell the blood magic she uses in rituals to power up her spells. Probably the only reason she leads ghost tours is to haunt the poor souls stuck here."

The things I continued to learn about the supernatural world. My memory called up the woman from New Year's Eve. "She leads tours?"

"Freakin' weirdo." She'd left her hair down and the spider peeked at me from behind her bangs. "She better hope I never meet her in a dark alley."

What were the chances this witch might be leading a ghost tour tonight? My dinner looked less and less likely to happen. I glanced around, still hopeful Stormfinger might show, so we could interrogate him. "Any chance you've seen headstones with this symbol on them?" I showed her a picture of the epsilon.

"Sure. It's an E." Her tone suggested I was purposely trying to piss her off. "One of the most common letters of the alphabet."

I zoomed in. "This version is Greek. I'm searching for gravestones that have it."

She shrugged after another glance and scanned what she could see of the graveyard. "If there was a headstone here with it, you'd be hard pressed to find it now."

Aurora left her car and rushed toward us. "It wasn't Jimmy's mom who bought the necklace. It was an aunt."

"Were you able to get a phone number?"

"There's no answer."

I faced Katarina. "If the sorcerer shows up, detain him for interrogation and call me."

"That I'm happy to do." The wicked smile was back. "What kind of necklace?"

I gave her a brief synopsis of what we'd sorted out, and what we were planning.

"Is JR in trouble?" She seemed sincerely concerned.

"I don't know." I noticed a black limo pulling into the parking lot. My blood warmed instantly and both Katarina and I turned toward it.

Killion emerged from the backseat and motioned me to join him. I saw the glow of his magic and felt a different kind of warmth flood my system.

Until he spoke. "There's been another murder. This time at Shepherd's Rest."

My stomach dropped. "Is it...JR?"

He shook his head.

"Stormfinger?" Aurora asked.

His slight pause told me he wondered why we would

jump to the conclusion either man was our victim, but then he motioned again. "A mundane female. Hurry."

Aurora and I exchanged a look of dread. Ten to one, the woman was Jimmy's aunt.

"I'm coming, too," Katarina said, locking the dogs inside.

"I need you to stay here and watch for Stormfinger."

She made a face and sauntered past. "I don't take orders from you, Grave Girl."

Killion gave me a questioning look but I waved off her defiance. "Fine, you can come, Undead nightmare."

She laughed and punched me in the arm.

On the way, I updated Killion. Our date was definitely postponed, and I was both disappointed and relieved.

Aurora filled him in about the symbol and the history of the necklaces.

"Do the recent grave robberies have any connection to those that occurred ninety-nine years ago?" Killion asked.

"Possibly." Aurora and Katarina sat across from us on the second leather bench seat. Aurora was frowning at the phone's screen. " I haven't had time to go through all of my resources, but I found a reference to two men, brothers, who claimed to be miracle workers back then. They were pastors who wore necklaces they declared came from God and were the source of their instantaneous healings."

"People were healed right away?" It sounded similar, but our recipients had each had their necklaces for weeks.

Aurora skimmed some more. "Apparently. People came from all over to have them lay the necklaces on them for everything from gout to baldness."

"I remember that," Moss interjected over the front seat. "Don't you, boss? The hotel was booked every night for weeks. The grave robberies took place right before those two announced they could cure folks, and then they fled town in the middle of the night a few weeks later, never to be heard from again."

Killion scanned his memory. "Within forty-eight hours of their leaving, the town was wracked by a plague."

"And the witch hunts started," Aurora added.

"These necklaces *are* cursed." I rubbed my temple. I now sort of wished I'd taken Death up on his offer—I desperately needed out of these dress clothes and into jeans and a hoodie. "So why would Stormfinger and his witch risk collecting them to create immortality?"

No one had an answer. Killion handed me Death's amulet. "Thought you might wish to have this back."

I accepted it, although I wondered if it was worth wearing. I stuck it in my purse.

Katarina eyed it. "How did the necklaces the preachers used end up reburied?"

Aurora shook her head. "No clue."

"*Were* they?" My eyes felt gritty from lack of sleep. I rubbed them and blinked away my tiredness. "Maybe that's why there's only been three robberies. Someone already had those two."

Aurora considered it. "That's feasible. My grandmother's journal doesn't mention much about them, only the witch hunts."

"How do we neutralize them once we do find them?" I'd been thinking about this since the coffee shop. Finding them was the first major hurdle, but like a Horcrux, what if they were nearly impossible to destroy? "Obviously, burying them to keep them out of the wrong hands hasn't worked."

"Perhaps they can't be destroyed," Killion stated, echoing my thoughts. "Burial is the next best thing."

Aurora sighed. "That's my guess, too."

We arrived at Shepherd's Rest, lights from a set of

police cars offering a spotlight view of the entrance. Staying in the shadows, the four of us snuck as close as we dared, Killion and Katarina using their magic to make us invisible.

Like Waverly, the dead woman was naked; her chocolate skin was bloody where it had been cut, no doubt carved with the word 'witch.'

My uncle was already examining her, his mouth tight. His voice drifted to us as he answered one of the officer's questions.

Mary Lynn was with him, taking notes. "She's still warm," she said, a note of sadness in her voice. "Hasn't been dead long."

Officer Loomis wrote in a small notebook. "Same MO?"

Uncle Morty laid a blanket over the corpse from her shoulders down before he felt the back of her head. "Can't say for sure until I get her to The Pit, but my guess is, yes."

Her head was turned, eyes frozen and vacant. They stared straight at me, and I had to look away.

That's when I caught movement near the road. A figure in a flowing robe. "Stormfinger," I murmured.

Aurora saw him as well. "That lousy piece of—"

"Leave him to me," Katarina said, and in the next sweep of police lights, her magical outline disappeared.

THIRTY-EIGHT

Only another vampire could keep up with her. Killion released the invisibility magic and gave chase, but he stayed within sight as Aurora and I followed.

Half a block east, we found Katarina standing over a prone Stormfinger, one booted foot planted on his chest. Killion reached them and jerked the sorcerer to his feet. The hood fell off.

It wasn't Stormfinger.

"Who are you?" I gasped, out of breath.

The man was short and carried an extra ten pounds in his belly that caused him to look pregnant. Male pattern baldness had not been kind, and he adjusted the dark framed glasses knocked sideways on his face. "Take your hands off me," he demanded.

The master vampire shook him. "Answer her."

"This is assault. I should report you to the police!"

"I was going to do the same to you," I told him. "Did you kill that woman back there?"

"What woman?"

Katarina smacked the back of his head. "The dead one who was cut up on that grave."

True alarm showed on his face. His nervous gaze flicked between us. "There's been another?"

Katarina sniffed him and the alarm grew. "There's no blood," she informed us. "If he carved up that female, I'd be able to tell."

"*What's your name?*" Killion growled. "And what were you doing in the cemetery?"

"Honus Sokoloff, Initiate Mage of The New Order of Alexandria. I was looking for my mentor. He's missing."

We all exchanged a look.

The man nodded urgently. "The last time we spoke, he mentioned he was training an important magic-user at a graveyard. He's not answering his phone, no one's at his house, and this is the third cemetery I've been to tonight."

Killion's protective magic shielded me. "You're friends with Neymar Stormfinger?"

Sokoloff's bushy brows climbed up his forehead. "You know the High Mage?"

We exchanged another round of silent glances. "Maybe he didn't stand me up after all," I said. "But then, where is he?"

"We need the shifter." Killion turned loose of Sokoloff's robes. "He can track the sorcerer's trail."

Aurora drew out her phone and shot off a message to Andy.

"Do you know anything about five necklaces that have an epsilon on them?" I asked.

He brushed at his garment, and ran a hand through the faded brown hair on the sides of his head. "I'm not to speak of them."

Katarina bared her teeth. "Talk or die."

He held out his hands like a shield. "Okay, jeez. He asked me to write incantations for them. That's all."

Aurora pocketed her phone. "Incantations? Why? To break their curse?"

Sokoloff paused, wary, lowering his hands. "To harness their healing powers. His girlfriend has health issues. He's trying to help her."

Girlfriend? Waverley's stepsister? "The witch?"

"Blair is an alchemy student." He puffed out his chest. "Like me."

Aurora snorted softly. "What kind of issue?"

"I'd rather not say."

Killion glared and I felt his magic take control of the man. "Tell us."

Against his will, he did. "Her magic's been off. She's psychic, sees spirits. She even gives ghost tours, because, like, she can actually interact with them. But she's sick from walking on that side of the tracks." When we all stared at him, he clarified. "The spirit world. She goes into it." He made walking motions with his fingers. "At first, she didn't notice anything wrong, but then she got into some pretty dark magic, trying to amplify her powers. Her hair started falling out, her teeth rotted. Her bones became brittle and she aged overnight."

"See," Katarina said to me. "Idiots messing with blood magic."

"Does she appear like she's ninety?" I asked the man.

His shoulders bunched. I took that for a shrug. "She's been using certain spells to compensate. Alchemy, you know. Some days, she looks and feels her age, others, not so much."

I squeezed the bridge of my nose. It answered a few questions, but created more. What were these two up to? If the amulets could heal, why sell them instead of using them?

Her health wasn't my most pressing concern, however. "Do you know anything about The Ghost Lands? Jumping timelines? Was she involved in that, or only Stormfinger?"

His face scrunched. "The what?"

His lack of knowledge about it didn't mean she wasn't involved. "We know where three of the necklaces are. Do you know if the others are still buried?"

"Neymar has all of them. They belonged to his great-grandfather, but their magic is quirky."

That was an understatement.

"He has all five?" Killion asked. "You're sure?"

"Yeah. I mean, I haven't seen them, but that's what he said. He's a powerful mage, my mentor."

Aurora chuckled. "A powerful snake in the grass."

"Wait." There was a wormy shadow floating behind his eyes. Tiny, quick. Not easy to spot, especially under the poor lighting. "You're lying. I saw you New Year's Eve here with the ghost tour, being led by the witch. You were looking at the crypt of an Epsilon Group member." I got in his face. I couldn't feel an ounce of magic that was native to him, only a scratchy kind that felt like multiple other users had layered theirs over him. "You're Stormfinger's scout. He doesn't have all the amulets, and you're helping him find them."

His jaw firmed as he straightened, indignant. "I don't know what you're talking about."

The truth of it vibrated inside of me. I didn't need his confirmation. I sent a finger of my magic into him, peeling through the layers of spells the witch had done on him. Dug through his thoughts, where there was little resistance, and read them as easily as a billboard. "Sure you do. It's part of your initiation. Find the amulets, dig them up, offer them to him. He promises to make you a member of The New Order."

"I *am* a member," he countered.

Aurora crossed her arms over her chest, and asked in a disgusted voice, "Who was his great-grandfather?"

He shuffled from foot to foot, flustered and I knew he was considering bolting. Another pulse of Killion's magic and he calmed. With a shaky finger, he pointed toward the center mausoleum. "Theodore Methuselah. He kept journals about everything, and was a founding father of the original Danté's Grove Order. Neymar freaked out when he saw how the family burial plot had been ruined. He was *furious*, but the power that the magic-user who did it possesses is off the charts, he said. He wants to recruit the guy for our group. That's what he was supposed to be doing."

The "guy" who happened to be me? Surely, Stormfinger didn't actually want to recruit me to join his nerdy magic group, did he?

Not me, per se, but Grim Zero. He'd realized I was the key to doing what The Order had wanted all along—control over life and death.

My head hurt from probing Sokoloff's thoughts. "Did Theodore create the amulets?"

"Nah, they're old. Came from Romania, or Russia, or someplace over there. I don't remember. They were brought by his grandfather when he came to America, but by the time Theodore joined The Order and inherited them, they didn't have much power anymore. He performed a ceremony to infuse them with new magic."

"And it backfired," I said. "Their magic started hurting people."

"No, no." He leaned in. "The spell didn't do anything. He didn't want the rest of the members to think he didn't know what he was doing, so he made a deal with a grim reaper."

My blood went cold, the pounding in my head now a bass drum. "What kind of deal?"

"A soul for a soul. For every person one of the necklaces saved from death, somebody in their family had to be sacrificed."

The universal balance had to be maintained. "Do you have the name of the grim?"

"You're joking, right? Soul eaters don't have names."

Name or not, the giant figure on Theodore's tomb had once been real.

"Stormfinger has the journal," Sokoloff added. "I haven't read it but it details a lot about The Order. The other founders discovered what he did and banished him. He tried to take revenge on them before he died, but well, they sort of…"

"Killed him," I finished.

He nodded, almost seeming embarrassed.

"What else aren't you telling us?" Killion asked.

"Nothing." He waved his hands and tried to step back. Katarina stopped him. "I swear."

A knife of pain tore through my head, but I scanned his thoughts again. "Neymar wants justice for his grandfather. He's hunting down descendants of the first Order who banished and killed Theodore."

The man pressed his lips together and gawked at me. "Are you reading my mind?"

I staggered a bit, holding my head, and let my connection to him dissolve.

Killion grabbed my arm. "Your skills are growing at an

impressive rate, but you need practice to build up your tolerance. Do not attempt any more, okay?"

I nodded and felt his wonderful energy sweep over and around me, taking the pain away. "Thank you," I said quietly.

"Is the journal where Stormfinger and his girlfriend got their spells?" Aurora asked.

Defeated, Sokoloff nodded petulantly. "It details how a necromancer with the right magic could use the necklaces to do great things."

Great things. *Sure.* I motioned Killion and Aurora to follow me a few feet away. "So Stormfinger is behind all of this, along with his girlfriend. I just can't figure out if he's doing it to save her or to gain immortality."

"It presents a mine field of possibilities," Killion said. "I suspect both."

Aurora tapped her chin. "Did the Epsilon Group figure out the amulets were wonky and attempt to nullify them?"

Killion's nod confirmed her theory. "That's why they had them interred along with their bodies at death. As we suspected, they aren't able to be destroyed. They were attempting to hide them."

Pieces of the puzzle fit more snuggly now. "Stormfinger has at least three, maybe all five, and has been using Theodore's burial plot as his entrance to The Ghost Lands, bringing everything together to heal his witch, or take over Death's job. Or both," I added.

"The two dead women are likely descendants of the men who banished Theodore from the Order," Aurora said. "But is *Neymar* making deals with a grim now?"

I grabbed my phone and sent a text to my favorite driver. I was going to need a ride. "Certainly not me, but that may explain why he changed his tune about me when he discovered I was Grim Zero."

Killion nodded. "And why he wishes to induct you into his New Order."

"It's a new order, all right. But I'm going to be its demise. Aurora, was there a Banks in the original group?"

"Sure was."

"Thought so." I messaged JR, and when I finished, I doled out instructions. "You two find Stormfinger. I need to make sure JR is safe."

"I should accompany you," Killion said. "To ensure *your* safety."

"The sorcerer isn't going to hurt me. The others are in danger. Regardless if he's selling the amulets to fund his lifestyle or to exact revenge, we have to get them away from the new owners and stop him from doling out the others."

Rafael, the driver I'd been using since Christmas, responded: *Veronica and I are taking the night off.*

Since Veronica was the name of his car, as well as the homeless cat I'd hooked him up with, I wasn't sure which he was referring to.

Me: *This is an emergency. I need you.*

Rafael: *Sorry, no can do.*

"I don't like this," Killion said.

Rafael never turned down money. Me: *I'll double your fee.*

Rafael: *Veronica needs a princess bed.*

Now we were discussing the cat.

"Me, either," Aurora commented.

Me: *Anything she wants. Please hurry. I'm at the corner of Fifth and Rosewood.*

Rafael: *The cemetery?*

Me: *Just out for a walk. Now get moving.*

His response was a rude emoji, followed by a cat and a crown.

A second text came in, this one from JR. He confirmed he was at home with his mother, and that everything was fine. He followed that with three question marks.

I explained I was on my way and wanted to discuss something with him. I hesitated to warn him to stay inside and keep the doors locked, because that sounded paranoid and weird, but weirdness was part of this gig.

Me: *They found another body in one of the cemeteries. There's a killer on the loose and you should take precautions. Be sure the doors and windows are locked and stay inside, okay?*

I held my breath until his response came back. JR: *Are you safe?*

Me: *Absolutely.*

JR: *Stay that way.*

I sent a thumbs up.

"This is not exactly how I planned for our evening to go." I stepped close to Killion and touched his cheek. "I'm going to pick up my robes and scythe, and then go to the Rawlings'. I need you and Aurora to locate the other amulets as well as Stormfinger. Until we do, we can't truly protect anyone."

Andy arrived and Aurora waved him over as she spoke to Killion. "She's right. We need you. I have powerful magic, but if he's been trapping ghosts and drawing on their souls for his purposes, he could be much stronger than I am."

"Maybe we'll get lucky," I joked, "and discover he tried to go back in time and got stuck."

No one smiled or laughed. Killion affected his thunderstorm expression. "Do not take chances. If anyone shows up, you call me and I will come handle them." He pointed at Katarina and Sokoloff. "Take him to the church and keep him there until I say he may leave."

The man started to bluster and Killion waved a hand in front of his face. "Sleep."

He dropped, eyes rolling up in his head. Katarina picked him up as if he weighed no more than a feather, and tossed him over her shoulder. "I could drop him off and then check on the grim and her friend."

I had a feeling she was mostly interested in my friend, but I'd take what I could get. "Great idea." Both vamps glanced at me, disbelief evident. I typically rejected offers of help, but I needed to keep JR and his mother safe. "Will Sokoloff be okay in the church with no one there?"

"Of course," Katarina said. "The dogs will guard him."

Dogs. "Is Ghost still at the penthouse?" I asked Killion.

He dipped his chin in confirmation. "Do you need her?"

It would be better if she was by my side, but I felt anxious to get to JR. I didn't want to take time to pick her up, too. "If I have the robes and the scythe, that will be enough. Katarina will join me, and you'll come if there are any problems." He was still holding my arm and I patted his hand. "Take Andy. Find the sorcerer. Then we'll regroup."

By the time I got to the street, Rafael was waiting. I climbed in and found Veronica the cat peering at me over the front seat. "She prefers pink with lots of bling," he said.

"Noted." Vera probably had a dozen like that in her stash. "How fast can you make this car go?"

THIRTY-NINE

J R called before we could stop at my apartment. "That woman is here demanding more money," he said, irritated. "I sent her away, but I don't believe she left. You don't think...?"

That she was our killer? "Is your mother safe?"

"I told you, the woman is ninety if she's a day. She's hardly a serial killer."

I wanted to smack my head against the window. I moved the phone away from my mouth and told Rafael to get to the Rawlings' mansion. "Double check all the entrances are secure. I'll be there in a few minutes."

"Should I call the cops? What if she attacks you?"

In the normal world, I would emphatically agree that he should. Since I didn't have my tools of the trade, I considered having him do it anyway.

But I needed to be sure it was Stormfinger's girlfriend, and that the two of them were connected to the murders before I alerted the authorities. I had no proof they'd done anything except extort money from innocent people, and I didn't want them to be turned loose and back on the streets if they were indeed killers.

"I'm armed," I told him. It wasn't a total lie—I had my pepper spray and my wits. There were those who would argue that wasn't much to go charging into the situation with, but I knew Katarina would soon be joining me. All I needed to do was get inside the house and wait for her to arrive and subdue the witch so we could get answers out of her. "I'm arriving in a brown Ford compact. Don't unlock or open the door until I give you the signal."

"Which is?"

"You've forgotten our old treehouse codeword?"

He chuckled. "Never. *Wingardium Leviosa.* See you in a few."

The spell from Harry Potter had been an obvious choice then. Hearing him say it brought back good memories, even at a time like this. "Be safe."

When Rafael and I arrived, I saw no signs of anyone lurking around. As the driver and cat waited for me to pay and exit, I considered the option of hustling JR and his mother into the car and taking them to The Beaumont. They'd be safe there, surrounded by Killion's nest members and employees.

Unfortunately, they were the bait I needed to flush out this couple. The way to do that was to keep them inside, so that Katarina and I could capture our witch and nab her wizard.

If that's who they were.

"Thanks," I said to Rafael, handing him the fee, along with an extra ten. Gently, I sent a pulse of magic around the perimeter of the house to see if I could pick up any lurkers. I felt nothing. "I appreciate your service and I will get that bed to you soon."

He accepted the money, while staring out his window. "Swanky place. Is that your boyfriend?"

I followed the direction of his gaze and saw JR in the open doorway, a shotgun in hand. "Why does he never listen to me?"

"You're not in any kind of trouble, are you?"

I laughed. "I'm always in trouble, but no, not from him. He thought he saw a stalker earlier, and that's why he's making a show of protecting the house."

"A stalker?" His dark brows pinched and he gathered up Veronica to hug her. "Do you think it's that killer that's on the loose?"

"You heard about that?"

"I listen to a police radio when I'm waiting on riders."

"You and Veronica better get home and lock your doors. No sense taking chances, okay?"

"How will you get home?"

"JR will drive me. Thanks again."

I scratched Veronica on her head before I got out, walking swiftly to the porch. "I thought you were going to wait for my knock," I chastised.

His eyes had an unusual tint courtesy of the sinking sun. "Let's get inside," he said.

"Is she still here? Did she try to break in?"

He grabbed my arm and yanked me through the door. I tripped over my feet and fell onto the shiny hardwood planks, my purse whacking into the coat rack.

Thanks to my slippery slacks, I slid past it and hit the side table. The vase of flowers toppled, the heavy porcelain whacking my shoulder while the water drenched me. The vase rolled away, unbroken, and I sucked in air, brushing blooms from my lap. "JR? What the devil are you doing?"

He slammed the door and turned to me, raising the

weapon and pointing it at my face. I now noticed a sickly glow around him. "Getting rid of a minor, but very annoying, inconvenience."

Everything went slow-motion like it had in the cemetery. His aura flashed, his lips firmed, and I saw him squeeze the trigger.

A split-second before the gun went off, I threw myself across the foyer, moving at lightning speed. *Boom!* The very floor vibrated and buckshot sprayed pellets into the wood.

My ears rang as I jumped to my feet. "Holy reapers!" I screamed, not only because I was being shot at, but because it was JR doing it. "Who are you?"

I was no vampire, but my quick movements and my question startled him. He hesitated before he brought the gun to bear on me again.

That tiny hesitation offered me a chance to see past the glamour my attacker wore. It was as if he were two people in one body, each fighting to be seen, almost like an old negative with a double exposure. The blur between the two faces happened so fast, I blinked, but I didn't have time to second guess what I'd witnessed.

The gun went off again.

My magic pulsed out in answer, but did nothing to stop him or the spraying pellets.

I ran. I'd been prepared to take on a handful of scenarios, but this was not one of them. My stun gun was in my bag, which was no longer in reach.

I needed a weapon, and I needed it quick.

FORTY

He chased me through the mansion, hot on my heels. Spent cartridges dropped to the floor as he reloaded, and the snap of the barrel made my blood freeze.

"I remember you," I called over my shoulder as I jetted towards the library. It had been years since I've been in this section, and I tried to remember the layout. "You were in The Ghost Lands." He was Suit Man with the mighty grip.

Boom. Another spray of pellets, these smacking into the wall not far from my head. Thank goodness he was a bad shot.

He laughed menacingly. "I'm certainly not JR Banks."

I scrambled into the kitchen, and realized my mistake. The only exit was the way in, and as I watched, the front of the gun appeared before the man followed. "What have you done to him? Why are you helping Stormfinger?"

The JR look-alike filled the opening, cocking his head to the side. A second followed the movement as if an apparition, prior to snapping into place. It made me feel drunk. His aura was fire engine red. The double barrels of the shotgun were black and terrifying as he stepped fully into the spacious room. "You know him?"

The counters were spotless and bare, save for the silver tray, now empty. I backed toward the huge stainless steel refrigerator. What I wouldn't give for my scythe or psychopomp. "I tried to save you in The Ghost Lands. Why are you doing this?"

"You're the grim. Didn't recognize you without your robes. You tried to cross me over."

I raised my hands in a surrender gesture. "My name is Chloe. Neymar Stormfinger is a person of interest in an investigation I'm working on."

An evil smile spread across the imposter's face. The man's true self showed in it, in those eyes that weren't JR's. "You here to reap me, Chloe?"

"Let my friend go, and I won't have to."

His aura became interspersed with yellow flecks, JR's features fading. "The Rawlings owe me. He's the payment."

"For what? You've already been paid handsomely for the necklace."

"That's Stormfinger's deal. Revenge on the family is mine. Kitty Belvedere Rawlings took mine from me. Now I'm going to take what she values most."

"You didn't tell me your name."

His aura faded to a dull orange. "It isn't important. Getting retribution on those who destroyed my family is."

Just like Neymar? "What does Kitty have to do with it?"

"Twenty-five years ago, I needed a healing amulet. My Carol Ann didn't have long to live." His body flickered and I blinked. "We were kids then, and I wasn't hurting nobody by digging up that old grave, but no, Kitty saw me and had to call the cops. Why do you think she was in that place to begin with? Getting herself knocked up with that brat of hers." Tears mixed with the vengeance burning in his eyes. "Carol Ann needed a miracle, but she died while I was waiting for my hearing. Three months later, they released me. You know what the irony was?"

I shook my head, feeling his pain, and also no small amount of shock that JR's mom had gotten pregnant in a cemetery.

He blew out a ragged breath. "As I walked out of jail, a free man with *nothing* left to live for, Kitty was marching down the aisle to marry Martin Banks, her future secure and bright."

"I'm so sorry." I truly was. I sent out a pulse of magic, but a sharp prick of pain exploded in my head. I'd overdone it at the cemetery, reading Sokoloff's mind. I gripped my temples, called telepathically for Killion, and then shut it down. The pain instantly faded and I could breathe again. "You knew about the healing stones?"

"My grandmother told stories about them. She was a girl when the preachers healed all them folks. They rejuvenated her father's ruined leg. He could work again at the lumberyard and they believed the family troubles were over." His hand tightened on the stock and his aura flared red once more, although he seemed more opaque. "But then things went wrong. Her little sister died. Came down with some fatal illness. My grandmother thought she was gonna die, as well. Said she saw the grim reaper when he came for the girl, and she knew he wanted her, too. She hid in the larder cabinet in their cellar, but she never forgot the icy chill of his breath."

If it had been her time, hiding would have been futile. "I understand that you wanted to save your sweetheart, but believe me, her contract must've been up. If you *had* saved her, someone else would've died in her place. That's how it works. The universe likes balance." Chalk up another round of sounding like my boss. "If you cheat Death of one soul, someone close to you pays the price." While he'd told me his story, he'd lowered the gun an inch. He flickered again, and I zeroed in on that, rather than the double barrels. "How did Stormfinger make you so...physical?"

A man in dark robes swept into the room and lowered his hood. "Good job." Stormfinger patted the man's shoulder. "My latest experiment," he said to me. "What do you think?"

I saw red, and it wasn't because of the ghost's aura. "I'm going to kill you."

This garnered a chuckle. "Very realistic, isn't he? I've been trapping ghosts and drawing on their souls to see what I can achieve. Vengeance spirits have a one-track mind, and because of it, seem to hold the highest output of energy. I can pull enough from the others to make the strongest of the vengeful spirits corporeal. Amazing." He flexed his fingers, staring at his hands with a touch of awe.

He wasn't just a sorcerer or necromancer. He was a power-hungry psycho.

And Death was right—Stormfinger *was* gunning for his job, because if he could control earthbound souls, along with their dead counterparts, he could control the living as well. He could make his own rules, amass fortunes, bring grims and other supernaturals to heel. If we didn't do what he wanted, he'd send one of his ghosts to kill us. "I knew you created The Ghost Lands."

He gave me a confident, goading smile. "I need a lot of spirits to accomplish my goals. I appreciate you playing along. Took the spotlight off me."

"You had two of the necklaces already."

"And my minion tracked down the others. All I had to

do was promise to teach him magic. Everyone wants something—revenge, magic, power. Makes them easy to manipulate."

"While you and your witch milk people of their life savings."

A modicum of surprise showed on his face at the mention of Blair, but he blew over it. "A man of my stature needs money. I can hardly work a regular job."

"You could save her with the amulets. Why sell them?"

He glanced over his shoulder and lowered his voice, as if she were in hearing range. "They can't save her. She's too far gone. But once she's in spirit, I can bring her back with my power. She'll walk around as corporeal as Charles, here."

Charles, aka Suit Man, nodded. "It's a second chance at life."

"Did you kill those two innocent women and mark them as witches, or did she?"

A piercing sharpness entered his eyes. "A soul for a soul, Grim Zero. You know the rules."

"You're not cutting deals with any grim. You killed those women."

He brushed at his sleeve. "I didn't kill anyone."

"But Blair did."

His astonishment was forced. He wasn't even a decent actor. "You're more clever than I gave you credit for."

"You gave me the hallucinations, too, didn't you?"

The confident smirk grew. He reached over to adjust the end of the gun so it pointed once more at my face. "Too bad I have to kill you, Grim Zero. I really thought we'd make a good team."

I needed to buy time, and it was no secret I wasn't a fan of Death's. "From what I've seen, my boss doesn't deserve to be in his position. I can help you take him down. He trusts me."

The archimagus seemed to think it over, but then gave me a regretful look. "Tempting, since I do believe your magic would supercharge mine. The problem is that you could become even more powerful. You're probably already more powerful than Death." He shook his head, then zeroed in on my collarbone. "Give me his amulet."

"I don't have it."

His face blanched. "Where is it?"

If I got him out of the room, maybe I could handle Charles. "My purse. In the foyer." From the corner of my eye, I caught the slightest movement and prayed it was Katarina. "And I don't want the power. I don't even like this job, and I detest ghosts. I'm happy to support you and stay in the background."

"Afraid I can't accept your offer." He patted his ghostly soldier once more. "Kill her. Blair and I will make sure the Rawlings' kid is framed for it."

"She's here? The witch?" I asked, desperate to get him out of his tunnel focus and keep him talking. "I heard she's a fang-banger. How do you feel about that? Sleeping with vampires?" I gave a fake shudder. "You hate them so much. I didn't take you for the type to share."

His magic flashed out hot and angry. Mine instinctively responded, and the two hit with the force of a freight train and the side of a mountain.

Fiery agony tore through me. The scene went into slow-mo once more: Stormfinger yelled a curse, the ghost began to press the trigger, and I grabbed the empty tray from the counter.

From behind the archimagus, a cat winged through the air, claws extended. She landed on Stormfinger's head, nails sinking deep into his skull. Veronica, the little hellcat, took the great sorcerer to his knees. He let out a blood-curdling scream, knocking an elbow into the shotgun and sending the barrels askew at the same moment the blast rang out.

I already had the tray in front of me. Pellets pinged against the silver, denting it, and I tried to command my magic to form a shield, but it was AWOL. Nada. Not even a trickle. I'd slammed the last of it into Neymar's wall of magic.

Staggering from weakness and the blast, I hit the edge of the breakfast bar and bounced. The ghost fired again, and this time I felt the sting of hot metal graze my cheek, neck, and shoulder.

I dropped to my knees, my back now facing the killer, as the archimagus wrestled with the cat. My skin burned and my blood ran onto the tiles.

"What should I do?" Rafael cried. "He's going to hurt my baby!"

The *thunk* of the ghost reloading the gun mixed with the cat screeching as she hung on for dear life. I staggered to my feet. "Get out!"

Rushing the vengeful spirit in an attempt to stop him was stupid, but I did it anyway. A final *boom* of the shotgun echoed in my ears, just as a blur of movement rocketed past me. My body was knocked through the air, hitting the fridge.

I dropped to the ground in a heap of white-hot torment and screamed.

FORTY-ONE

Killion had taken the shot.

His vampire was on full display as he shielded me, then turned on the gun-wielding ghost.

Lying on the kitchen floor in a pool of my blood, I watched it all play out like a movie. I'd been struck by multiple pellets again, but he'd taken the majority center mass.

Rafael pounced on Stormfinger, rescuing Veronica. The sorcerer was covered in scratches and blood, and luckily, the cat seemed fine. As Killion attacked the vengeance ghost, the spirit evaporated.

The master vampire, in a rage, clawed at Stormfinger and left him even bloodier. The archimagus' eyes rolled up in his head at seeing the monster and he passed out.

Killion sent a red-eyed glance over his shoulder at me, nostrils flaring at the scent of my blood, then he tore out the door, leaving a trail of his own behind.

Katarina appeared with a woman in thrall, who she dumped unceremoniously into a chair. JR followed, calling my name when he saw me. The room swam as both spoke urgently to me but my ears were buzzing and I couldn't understand either of them.

JR removed the shells still in the gun and set it aside. Rafael stared in wide-eyed horror at the blood, before cowering in the corner near the pantry door with Veronica in his arms.

Stormfinger revived. Katarina hauled him to a chair next to Blair and put him in thrall, too. With blank eyes, he stared at me, swaying ever so slightly in place. The vampire twitched her nose at my blood, and her irises went red. I saw the tips of her fangs descend into her bottom lip. She turned on her heel and fled as well.

JR grabbed dish towels and bent over me. Through the buzzing, I heard the sound of sirens. The fear on his face told me he believed I was going to die. I tried to tell him not to worry, I could heal myself, but I couldn't seem to form words.

The room went black, pitching me into a nightmare of fangs and blood and death.

When I came to, I was being wheeled into the back of an ambulance. One of the medical technicians was yelling about the fact I had no pulse. I opened my eyes and the poor man jumped away and let loose a scream of fright.

"It's okay," I mumbled through the fog in my brain and the pain in my body. "Even if I die, I won't stay that way."

It was meant to reassure him, but from the way he paled, I thought he might need the gurney more than I did. His coworker took several steps back, as well, and they exchanged a shocked glance, then delved in and began administering help once more.

The coppery scent of my blood filled the air. My chest, as well as my shoulder, burned fiercely, but I discovered my wrists were secured at my sides. Being restrained freaked me out and I jerked at the straps. When I turned my head, I caught sight of JR and his mother on the porch. Officers Rogan and Loomis escorted Stormfinger and Blair, each in handcuffs, to their squad car. Mrs. Banks was crying and JR was holding her. I called to them. "Don't worry. I'm fine."

My blood warmed in a different way, signaling Killion was near. "You are hardly fine." He stepped into view, the worry on his face beyond any I'd ever seen. He was his normal self again, both in looks and temperament. I knew it took every ounce of his willpower not to fall on me and feed. I also knew he would never do such a thing. "Now, be quiet and let the attendants do their job. I will meet you at the hospital."

As the gurney was lifted, I saw Katarina join JR and Kitty, giving me a thumbs up. They were in good hands.

The next few hours came and went in a haze of white coats, medication, and people asking if I knew who I was and what had happened. The facts that I spouted about being Grim Zero and how I'd stopped an archimagus was chalked up to blood loss, trauma, and pain killers.

Finally, an aging man with a head of thick hair and warm hands told me Killion had sent him, and I was going to be okay.

I was grateful he understood that I had self-healing abilities, and he didn't question my mental stability. He dug out the pellets, sewed me up, and made sure I had plenty more pain meds before he disappeared.

I woke briefly when Uncle Morty and Aunt Camille visited. My uncle swore a blue streak, demanding to know what had happened and threatening to kill the SOB who had done this to me. My aunt did her best to calm him and comfort me.

From them I learned the police were pinning the

shooting on Stormfinger, and charging Blair with crimes involving holding JR and his mother hostage.

Aunt Camille told me Kitty was also in the hospital, having experienced a nervous breakdown after what took place in her home. She mentioned JR would be by soon to speak to me. I begged her to put him off so I could sleep.

I waited for Killion, and also Death. Neither showed before I drifted into the land of medicated unconsciousness, even as my wounds slowly healed.

At some point, I woke to the feel of my blood warming. I blinked, letting my vision adjust to the shadows, Killion's glowing aura a spotlight. "About time," I groused. "Are you okay?"

"I needed to wait until the others left, and yes, I'm well." Even though I couldn't clearly make out his features, I knew he was still sporting the latest in thundercloud fashion. It was clear in his tone, as well. "What were you thinking, taking the two of them on by yourself?"

I pushed myself up on my elbows, but wooziness made me slide back down. In an instant, he was by my side, grabbing a pillow to support my upper body. Even with the painkillers, I was sore and discovered my ribs heavily wrapped. My skin itched under the tight bandages, and I tried to scratch it to no avail. "Don't for one minute believe you get to chastise me. You don't even know the whole story."

He laid his hand on my rib cage, brushing my fingers aside. "Tell me."

Instant relief flooded my torso and I sighed. I wanted him to climb into the bed and hold me, let me ignore reality for a little longer. That was a fantasy world, and this wasn't.

I told him how the ghost was impersonating JR, how Stormfinger had been trapping vengeance spirits and using them for his purposes. "I don't believe those two women were killed in some sort of sacrifice, because they bought the necklaces. They were simply targeted by earthbound spirits who wanted revenge, or Blair used them for her magic."

"And those ghosts are still out there."

"SMG needs to step in and take care of Stormfinger. If they don't, he may be able to use his ghosts to break out of jail and continue with his plan." I tried to sit up again, sucking in my breath at the sharp twinge in my chest. "I need to talk to Death. I have to cross those spirits so they can't hurt anyone else, or be used by Stormfinger."

"You're not going anywhere." He gently guided me back down. "I will speak to him about it, and we will handle it."

"But—"

"No arguing. You've done enough. Let us handle the rest."

I grabbed his hand. "Don't leave me."

I sensed more than saw him drop his chin. "It is my wish to stay, but it would be better if I don't."

"Why?"

"Seeing you on that floor reminded me of how fragile you truly are. How special. I thought my heart would..."

I entwined my fingers with his. "It would what?"

He shook his head, then leaned down to kiss my forehead. "I have not been that scared in a long time. It brought back memories I thought I'd buried."

Like he had buried his wife and child? "I'm alive, and I'm going to be fine."

"You exist in a mortal body. This vessel will not live forever, and I'm not sure I'm strong enough to witness you die permanently." He withdrew his hand from mine and stepped away from the bed. "I must go, and your friend is waiting to see you. He's a good man and he deserves your... attentions. He can give you a nice life."

"Wait. What?" That sounded like a goodbye. "Don't you dare walk out. I need you."

"Rest, Chloe. Things will look different in the light of day."

Against my protests, he did, indeed, walk out. The heavy door closed softly behind him. Flabbergasted, I stared at it in shock.

My magic ached from overuse, but my determination shoved the pain aside. Me: *What are you doing?*

Killion: ...

Really? He was giving me the silent treatment?

Me: *Come back. Now.*

Killion: ...

Me: *If you think I'd ever take JR over you, you're not as smart as I thought you were. This is ridiculous. Get back here.*

Killion: ...

I had to quit when JR slipped into the room, holding balloons. He was backlit, and spoke slightly above a whisper. "Hey, slugger. How ya doin'?"

I wanted to pull out the IV, grab my clothes, and go after the vampire, but I was too weak yet, and my old friend and I had a few things to discuss about the malachite necklace. "Turn on the lights and pull up a chair," I told him, and then I sent another message to Killion.

We are not done.

FORTY-TWO

I gave JR as much of the story as I could without sounding like I needed to be committed. Which was considerably harder than I anticipated—he had too many questions. I had to play dumb about a lot of things, and chalked it up to my memory being fuzzy, thanks to being shot and the drugs humming through my veins.

In turn, he told me what the police had pieced together and the charges they'd levied against Stormfinger and his accomplice. Detective Adams would be by once the doctor okayed him to get my statement.

I insisted he turn over the necklace to Killion. He argued vehemently, but I gave it to him straight. "It's cursed. Get rid of it now, before something bad happens to someone in your family." Like you.

Because even if Stormfinger and Blair were behind bars, the amulets were bad news.

By the time he left, it was midnight, and I fell into a deep sleep again, but it was tormented with dreams about someone trying to kill me. When I woke a few hours later, I felt heavy and hung over, as much from my aching heart as my body.

Nita, Vera, Aurora, and Mary Lynn had all sent messages and left voicemails. Although it was late, I replied to each, assuring them I was fine. I kept saying it, but I didn't feel that way, and I wasn't sure who I was trying to convince, them or me.

A male nurse came in at three a.m. to check my vitals. I pretended to be asleep, and as soon as he left, I forced myself out of bed and searched for my clothes. Aunt Camille had brought a fresh set, and I tugged on the pants, trying to ignore the restriction around my rib cage and the floaty feeling in my head.

My hospital gown was hanging open, bearing my backside as I hobbled around, tugging on the tight jeans. I heard a chuckle behind me—I yelped, whirled, and being the world-class klutz that I am, lost my balance and knocked into the wheeled cart holding a pitcher of water.

The cart, pitcher, and myself went down, the metal pole of my IV swaying dangerously over my head until Death grabbed it. He reached down to help me, and I slapped his hand away, the front of the thin gown now drenched and leaving nothing to the imagination.

"What are you doing here?" It was a dumb question—I'd been expecting him. I scrambled to my feet, jerking the pants up, while using the edge of the mattress for balance. "Knock first, remember? Then enter."

"Going somewhere?"

"I need to talk to Killion." I snatched up my shirt and motioned for him to turn around.

He brushed my jaw where a pellet had cut open my skin. It was healed now, but his finger traced where the injury had been. "You're lucky the vampire was there."

I shifted my face from his touch. "I'm well aware. Turn around and tell me what SMG is going to do about Stormfinger and the amulets."

Slowly, he dropped his hand and did as instructed. "He's taken care of. No need to worry about him anymore."

Keeping my eye on his back, I shucked off the hospital gown and pulled on the soft shirt. It smelled like my laundry detergent, and for some reason, that calmed me. I hadn't realized how much the antiseptic odor of the room, as well as the bleach of the gown and sheets, had affected me. "Taken care of how?"

"When he was being transferred to his overnight holding cell, the funniest thing happened—he was struck by lightning before they got him in the building."

Sounded like biblical-type justice. Couldn't say I was upset about it. "Blair, too?"

"She'll be brought to justice, just the normal kind."

"She killed two innocent women. Where's the justice there? Those families..." I stopped and swallowed the hard pit in my throat. "I want her to pay."

"I understand that, but I don't kill people."

"You're literally death."

"I *manage* death, and yes, I can choose to take a life if I deem it necessary, but the two women who died—their contracts were up, Chloe. It was their time." He must have sensed my extreme frustration. "I'm sorry. I know that's not what you want to hear, but it's the truth. Blair will be handled by the legal system."

"How deep will the cops dig before they close the case?"

"That hinges on your testimony. All you need to do is confirm that Stormfinger was the shooter and there was no other man."

"What about the ghost?"

He put his hands on his hips, continuing to stare at the door. "You and I are going to tackle The Ghost Lands and cross all of them, once you're back to work. Smudgy has okayed giving you a couple days of PTO."

I tossed the damp gown on the end of the bed. "Generous of them. What about the corpse road incident? How exactly did that happen?"

"Stormfinger was playing around with time and, like Aurora thought, he caused a fracture. It created a brief future timeline event where JR's ghost was able to portal through to you."

"It won't happen again?"

"Yes and no. As your grave sight grows, you may have more incidents where you see the future."

"Premonitions about people dying? No thanks." I was certainly staying off potential roads where that could happen. "You can turn around now. What about the shadow worm I saw on JR? There's another one in a man named Honus Sokoloff."

"I cleared those already. They probably would have died on their own once the necklaces were taken away." He sank into the visitor's chair where Killion had been only hours before. "As I suspected, that sorcerer was behind everything. I told you he was after my job."

"He admitted to being responsible for my hallucinations, too. If I could, I'd bring him back so I could kill him all over again." I was tired of discussing all of it, yet I needed to know more. "If you knew from the beginning he was after your job, why set me up with him to train?"

"I knew you'd get to the bottom of things, and once you had that premonition on the corpse road, you were an easy carrot to dangle in front of him. I knew he'd take the bait—a young, single, beautiful grim with necromancy abilities? He was salivating to touch your magic."

Gag. "Why didn't you tell me all this to begin with?"

"I needed you to just be you, not going cloak-and-dagger. It was the only way to keep my eye on him without raising his suspicions." Death smiled serenely. "That lightning strike was something. Not my doing, mind you, but impressive. Too bad you didn't get to see it."

"Whose doing was it, exactly?"

A shrug. "Does it matter?"

While my questions had been mostly answered, I still felt lost. "This has been fun and all, but I have to go."

He tipped his chin at the IV and monitor tracking my heart rate. "Taking those with you?"

"As soon as I unhook them, it will alert the nurses' station." I found my boots, sat on the bed, and tugged them on. "I need to be ready to scoot the moment I disconnect."

"Go home, Z. Give Killion time to process things. What happened last night shook him."

No kidding. "I don't need your input about my relationship, and please don't refer to me as Z. My name is Chloe."

His eyes went flinty. "I told you not to get involved with a vampire."

"None of your business."

He sat forward and placed his elbows on his knees. "It *is* my business. I am in charge of you, and your head isn't screwed on straight these days because of him."

Simmering anger flowed through my veins. "I'm not arguing about it. I'll handle Killion, and I'm allowed to have personal relationships. Doing so with a human who knows nothing about the supernatural world will never work. You know that."

"I don't disagree, but he does. In the past few months,

he's grown to care for you in a way he hasn't experienced in over a hundred years. His wife and son were human and he still blames himself for their deaths. Their contracts were up, it was their time to die, but he thinks he should have turned them so they didn't need to. His wife didn't want it, and he went along with her wishes, but he's lived with tremendous loneliness since. He shut his emotions down until you came along. Now, all of it has surfaced again. It's as though he's reliving it, and it's devastating to him. He submitted his resignation."

"He *what*?" I rubbed my temples. "I know he's struggling, but refusing to discuss it is immature and ridiculous. I'm not Eliza. I'm Grim Zero, and even if I die, I'll come back. He's not going to lose me."

"You're not immortal, and you've made it clear you don't want to be a vampire, just like she did. He *will* lose you."

"Okay, eventually, yes. But we still have sixty, seventy years. Even as a human, I'll be around until I'm eighty or ninety. He'll be the one leaving me, and long before that, probably. What vampire would keep an old lady around, right?"

Death gave me a flat look, firming his lips as if holding back an argument.

My skin prickled, one of those damn premonitions stirring. "Why are you looking at me like that?"

His gaze dropped to the floor and he sat back. "You need to understand that to somebody who's already lived for hundreds of years and thought that he had found the love of his life, then lost her to something that wasn't within his control, he's working through a lot of dark stuff. Leave him be, and let him do it. It might be good for both of you. Go out with this human moron, who obviously cares about you.

Act like a normal twenty-four-year old and have some fun. The vampire will come around."

OMG. "I'm not normal, and I don't want to date JR. Everyone needs to stop with the matchmaking and assuming they know what I want and need."

"You say that, yet, you keep clinging to your old self. You won't quit your jobs or put school on hold until your grim contract is up. You're determined to open the clinic, though you can't keep up with your studies, or carve out time for a love life. Killion knows there's no hope of turning you, so spending the rest of *his* life with you is out of the question. Even as a team, you're doomed since you won't consider continuing your employment with SMG beyond the required year."

The truth of his words hit me in the chest. It gutted me to admit it, but he was right. "I'll figure it out, and he should be willing to do that *with* me, not bail and leave me hanging." Arguing was a waste of time. "When is my contract up? You've seen it, haven't you?"

Like before, he wouldn't meet my gaze, toying with a well-placed rip in his faded jeans. "You know I'm not at liberty to discuss that."

I stepped in front of him and lowered my face to his, forcing him to look me in the eye. "Do I have sixty years?" When he set his jaw, I felt my stomach cramp. "Fifty? Thirty?" He refused to answer, and my breath hitched as realization sank in. "Reapers creepers, *twenty*?"

His face remained impassive. I righted myself and found my knees were weak. I leaned against the bed. He wasn't refusing to answer because of any SMG rule. He knew I didn't have anything close to a normal life expectancy. "How long? I deserve to know."

For a long moment, I could clearly see the war going on

inside his head. Finally, he held up a hand, five fingers splayed wide.

A chill swept through me. In this incarnation, I'd brought myself back from his domain three times already. "Tell me that means I have five more resurrections."

He shook his head.

"You're kidding, right?" I swallowed hard. "Five years?"

He lowered his hand. "I'm sorry, Chloe."

The enormity of it hit me like I'd been shot all over again. I had to lay back on the bed and stare at the ceiling to catch my breath. The wrappings around my ribcage were stifling. I couldn't expand my chest enough, get enough air into my lungs.

"There has to be balance, and you've been busy saving other people, extending their contracts. Smudgy doesn't like that, and they've been peeling off the years you've been getting for other people from your own contract. Killion's in particular cut deeply into yours."

I focused on a spot on the ceiling, trying to regulate my breathing. I reached up under my shirt to rip off the constricting bandages. *Five years.*

I wouldn't even make thirty. Never have a midlife crisis. Maybe never have kids. If I truly only had that much time, there was no point in bringing children into the world because I refused to leave them without a mother.

The two of us sat there in silence for a long time. Death was so quiet, in fact, that at one point, I glanced over to make sure he was still in the chair.

He was. His eyes were sad as they met mine. "Even if I wanted to give you my blessing, which I know you don't care about, I couldn't. It's not fair to Killion for you to lead him on and not be around for longer."

I forced myself up, gritting my teeth against the pain.

Against the awful rawness in my heart, and the truth of Death's words. I pushed off the mattress and grabbed my jacket. "Time is wasting. I better get back to work."

"Chloe..."

I held up a hand to stop whatever he was going to say. "Did you find the other necklaces? We need to make sure all of them are destroyed and can never be used again. I'll handle the spirits in The Ghost Lands. You don't need to come."

He stood and towered over me. "Aurora is taking care of the destruction of the jewelry. I gave her a sword that will render them inert. You don't need to do everything alone. I'll help you with the ghosts."

I needed time to think, time to plan. "Fine, but I have a few things to do first."

"I'm telling you, leave Killion alone."

I pulled the IV pic from my arm and tossed it on the bed, then ripped off the small heart monitor patch. "I'll meet you at the Undead church cemetery at sundown. Don't be late."

"It's Sunday. Don't you have a staff meeting at the clinic?"

The monitors were buzzing; the male nurse would be here in seconds. I headed for the door. "I'll handle it." Just like I did everything else. "Speaking of meetings, arrange one with Mei Han for me. I have something to say and she's going to listen this time."

FORTY-THREE

After I set things straight with the head of SMG, reminding her that even *she* was expendable, and if she didn't stop with the threats, I would make it my personal mission to take her down, I collected myself and did one of the hardest things I'd ever done.

Shepherd's Rest was still dark. The sun wouldn't rise for another hour. "Thought I might find you here. It's rude to not return my messages or calls."

Killion had brought a folding chair and lounged in it, his attention on the graves in front of him. A liquor bottle dangled from his left hand, and he worried a necklace between his fingers on his right. The locket was open, two sepia toned photos staring back at me. He couldn't have looked more out of place. Or grief-stricken. "In case I have not made myself clear," he rasped. "I wish to be alone."

I wasn't going to be deterred, and I poked the toe of my boot into the frosty ground. "And I'm going to honor that after I tell you something."

He was as unmoving as the statues dotting the landscape. His five-o-clock shadow was heading into full-on beard territory. "Say it, then, and be gone."

Ouch. His vampire side was fully in charge at the moment, determined to push me away. I tried not to take it personally, knowing he was in the depths of sorrow and remorse. I'd spent time in that bottomless hole and knew how desperately hard it was to climb out of.

"You told me once that working for Soul Management Group was the thing that saved you after your wife and son died. Please don't give that up because of me. You're the best investigator they have, and while I still want you for a partner, I understand if you prefer to work alone again. I've spoken to Mei Han and your probation is lifted. You're cleared of any wrong-doing. I've also requested they hire Aurora as my partner. You won't have to worry about me, and you will still have a purpose for your life."

The dead beneath the ground called to me, but I had control of my necromancy. Eliza wasn't in sight, and I hoped she stayed that way. I glanced at the headstone and saw that he'd brought flowers for her, and a teddy bear for his son. Seeing that nearly broke me and sent my "life giving" ability spiraling out like an explosion.

I took a step back, swallowed my feelings, and dug deep for a way to reach him. "You did the right thing by honoring her wishes, and you should never feel guilty about that. I'm sorry you've had to live all these years without her,"—I nearly choked on the tears clogging my throat—"and someday, I'd really like to hear about her and your son. You can tell me about them, and I'll tell you about my mom and dad. Dr. Maxwell assures me that keeping them alive in our memories, and talking about them, is the best way to heal. So the invitation stands, and when you're ready, I hope you'll find me so we can heal together."

While my eyes had adjusted, he continued to be the darkest shadow in the place. He said nothing, still totally locked down.

Heart in my throat, I turned and left.

DURING THE FOLLOWING HOURS, I kept myself busy. At my apartment, I related the facts to Vera and Nita about my experience, using them to rehearse what I would tell the detective later that morning. The hospital was upset that I'd left without being officially released, but I asked Uncle Morty to step in and smooth things over.

Between phone calls and my visit to the police station, I stripped my bed and did my laundry, playing with Ghost and Corvus as we made a dozen trips up and down the steps and allowed Vera to fuss over and feed us.

Since it was the weekend, there was no one in the registrar's office at the university, but I sent my counselor a note explaining that I needed to reduce my course load for the spring semester and asking him to remove three of the five classes from my schedule.

After the fiasco with Randy Jarvis messing up the report, Uncle Morty begged me not to quit, but we compromised. As originally planned, I agreed to hang around until they found my replacement, who I would train, and I would continue on as a backup when needed, doing a weekly review of the new office manager until we were all sure he or she could handle things.

I picked up a variety of sweets from Aunt Camille's shop, and made sure there was plenty of coffee to go around. While I was there, she told me she'd talked to Piedmont and they'd agreed to go in fifty-fifty on a food truck, once he was ready to work again.

At the appointed time, I was at the clinic where I spent twenty minutes scrubbing the employee kitchen from top to bottom. It felt good to get my hands dirty with something other than ghosts and death.

When the others arrived, I greeted each with the best smile I could muster. Once again, I had to answer questions about the incident. Everyone in town had heard about the shooting, but I found it was becoming rote for me to offer the same story.

JR assured me his mother was doing better and that she wanted me to come for dinner once her home was back in order. He told me the necklace had gone missing, and he was worried about her cancer surging back. I did my best to reassure him, and I had to force myself not to obsess with finding a way to extend her contract.

Patty had handouts, and I went over the major things on her agenda, as she gave all of us a folder with our first week's itinerary, a few general guidelines for the office, and a detailed map of where the supplies were stored. To my delight, she'd already labeled the cabinets and drawers with their various contents.

She questioned my white strip of hair, and before I knew it, she'd decreed she was dying it purple for me.

I kept hoping Killion would show, but he didn't. Life felt flat without his presence. After they left, I found myself standing in the room staring at the spot where he'd kissed me. I heard the back door open, and my heart leaped. It was only JR.

He stuck his head in. "You okay?"

The memory of his spirit on the corpse road flashed in front of me. Regardless that Stormfinger had been screwing with timelines, I didn't know when JR's contract might be up. "You really should call Nita," I told him.

"Better yet, go see her at The Bean. She's working tonight."

"I know you broke up with your boyfriend, and I know it may take some time, but I'd rather wait for you."

"We didn't break up," I argued lamely. Who was I kidding? "Look JR, you and I are friends, but that's it. If last night taught me anything, it's that none of us have a guarantee that we'll wake up tomorrow. You don't have to marry Nita, just go see her. Share a coffee. It may be the best thing you've done since you got back."

My rebuff caught him off-guard. He didn't argue, though. "What about that other friend of yours? Katarina? Is she free?"

Holy reapers. "She's not what I'd call a friend, and please stay away from her. She's not..." I couldn't come up with anything but the truth. Sort of. "Normal."

He gave an impatient frown. "Sure you don't want to come?"

"I have something else I need to do."

He left, and I downed the dregs of my cold coffee. Death was waiting. It was time to play reaper and shut down The Ghost Lands.

FORTY-FOUR

The first week the clinic was open was both disastrous and exhilarating. By the following Friday afternoon, we were booked for the next six weeks, and Dr. O'Leary and JR had established specific days when they could batch procedures, just like Patty wanted.

After a couple missteps, she and I found a rhythm for working around each other while assisting the doctors, and when our software program crashed, we took appointments and payments old school until help arrived.

That came in the form of Megan and Mason. Megan, who'd shaved one side of her head and pierced as many visible parts of her body as possible, was already at the clinic, decorating the front window with paw prints. Mason, looking a bit gaunt but smiling, happened to be bringing us cookies. He claimed Nita had sent them, but I knew they weren't from The Bean nor my aunt's bakery. Nope, these were the work of Pennyworth.

While I hoped the butler's boss might be behind the gesture, I suspected otherwise. I missed the vampire who was akin to the perfect house elf; I hoped he missed me, too. Maybe he'd keep sending food.

The high schoolers instantly annoyed each other, insisting each was a more capable computer expert than the other. I didn't care either way, as long as they got the system fixed. They did, and I later found them in the kitchen laughing and flirting. I asked Megan to refill the intake forms, closing the door for privacy once she'd left. "Has Killion spoken to you about relationships with humans?" I asked Mason.

It was good to see him out and about, but my live-and-let-live side had taken a vacation.

He toyed with a cookie. "This sounds like the beginning of a lecture."

"No lecture. I just know he feels strongly about it."

"My mom has told me to stick to supernaturals. I know the drill."

"Megan is human."

He seemed confused about my point. "She died and came back. She sees ghosts. NDEs can cause that, you know."

"She does?" While my near-death experiences were slightly different than hers, I was all too familiar with the side effects. I should probably talk to her about them. "Still...she's human. She's not like you or me."

"She's cool with me being a hybrid. Besides, it's not as if I'm going to go all *Vampire Diaries* on her."

My mouth hung open. "You told her?"

"She can see it in my aura."

The girl saw those, too? Definitely needed to speak to her. "How could she tell by your aura?" This was a trick I needed to learn.

He shrugged and bit into the cookie. "She told me the

Undead look like a checkerboard of energy, some of it alive, some dead. Shifters have strings of different colors woven together. At least to her, that's how they appear."

"And grim reapers?"

He swallowed. "I don't know about all grims, but she said you're like me—a hybrid. A mix of sunlight and moonlight."

Interesting. "Just be careful, okay?"

"*You're* giving me relationship advice?"

His tone was condescending. "Hey, I may be terrible at it, but I'm trying to save you—and her—from ending up in a no-win situation."

"Like you and Killion? Why did you break up with him, anyway? I thought you two were, you know, in love or something."

Or something. "Who told you *I* broke up with *him*?"

"He hasn't been around much, and when he is, he's *super* grumpy. Katarina said you're the reason."

I was tired after the long days at the clinic and nights spent at the morgue. It pissed me off that the Undead Nation thought I was the cause of Killion's foul mood. I was, but not because I'd done anything to provoke it. "It's complicated. He told me to leave him alone, and I've done that. I respect his wishes."

Mason rose and stretched before opening the door. "Some things are worth fighting over, and some worth fighting *for*. Killion told me that. Seems like you need to decide which he is."

Now who was being lectured? Watching him leave, I sat in his abandoned chair, thinking it over. The sounds of him and Megan flirting again in the hall made that ache inside my chest take front and center. I rubbed my hand over the spot—it felt deeply bruised—wishing I knew how to fix things.

Dr. O'Leary called my name. I returned to the commotion and he told me he needed Mrs. Crabtree's wiener dog x-rayed. I let myself get lost in the work, imagining my father's steadying hands on mine as I positioned the canine, heard my mother's voice offering gentle guidance when the animal tried to bite me. Twice. It didn't bring them back, but it soothed my heart.

Aurora stopped in and left a tea concoction for JR's mother. "You know I can't cure cancer, but this will boost her immunity, give her blood cells a fighting chance."

I thanked her, even though I wondered how bad it tasted.

Another unexpected visitor brought me odd, but happy news. Right before closing on Saturday, Patty called me up front.

Jimmy Haskell and his mother stood at her desk.

Mrs. Haskell nodded at me. "Hi there. Sorry to bother you. My name's Marge, and this is my son, Jimmy. He found a bird feather and we wondered what kind it might be. I sent photos to the wildlife service and the bird sanctuary, but neither could identify it. They said it was fake, but I don't think it is." She motioned for Jimmy, clutching a large plume in his small hand, to show it to me. "I wondered if one of your veterinarians might know."

The aura around the thing glowed with a certain magic I was all too familiar with. I could practically taste stardust on the back of my tongue. "Where did you find it?" I asked the boy.

"An angel gave it to me."

Mrs. Haskell placed her hand on the boy's shoulder.

"Jimmy's been through a lot recently. Our whole family has."

This was said as if to offer a reason for the boy's claim. He looked like a healthy kid, even though he no longer wore the necklace. I crouched and pointed to the item he held in a death grip. "That's a magical feather from a mythical creature. I've read about them. Very powerful."

"It came from an angel," he said matter-of-fact, and with the slightest edge of condescension, as if I were as dense as the other adults who didn't believe him. "At first it sparkled. Now it doesn't."

I sent a tiny pulse of magic out and scanned his system. I detected no disease. *Thank you, Death.* This was a better apology than an official written letter any day. "That's because the sparkle is inside you now."

Mrs. Haskell sent him to a vacant chair near the window. "So it is fake? It seems so real. Very...ethereal. I know it sounds looney, but I thought maybe it was a sign from my sister. She passed recently, and I was hoping... Oh, I don't know." She glanced between us and laughed, embarrassed. "Silly, isn't it?"

"Not at all," Patty said. "I believe in angels and signs from beyond."

I sensed Mrs. Haskell's emotions and the real issue behind her worries. "It's good to see Jimmy is healthy. I saw him on the news," I told her. "You wouldn't happen to be looking for a job, would you?"

Her surprise at the change in subject caused her to step back. She cocked her head. "How did you know?"

I knew a lot of things these days. "The hospital is looking for a part-time morgue office manager. I know it sounds morbid, but it's easy work, fairly flexible hours, and you can use the hospital's free daycare for Jimmy when you need it."

"I thought the daycare was only for full-time employees," she mumbled, still in disbelief.

"I'll pull some strings. I have an in with a certain pathologist."

Her pause was brief, desperation overriding any wariness she had regarding my out of the blue offer. "I'll take it." She blinked, and a tremulous smile grew on her face. "If it's really available."

"It is. I'll let my uncle know I've hired you. Can you start training Tuesday night at six?"

"Who are you?" she asked.

"Chloe Frost." I held out my hand. "Nice to meet you. And the feather isn't fake. Your son is right." I winked at her with a conspiratory smile. "It's from an angel."

An angel who had come through for all of us.

FORTY-FIVE

When I made it home a few hours later, I went to my bathroom, turned on the water, and cried good and long for the first time since my parents' funeral. Ghost licked tears from my face and Corvus paced and flapped, squawking out, "Happy New Year" every time he crossed the floor.

Once I was out of tears, I shut off the water and put on my Harry Potter sleep shirt with the words, *I solemnly swear I am up to no good.* I didn't care that it was early and I hadn't eaten. I was numb.

The moment I climbed under the covers and got comfortable, wrapping my magic around me like a cocoon, a quiet knock sounded from the exterior door. I groaned. It had to be Nita. She and Vera had been hovering nonstop since the shooting, but I didn't want company. My eyes were swollen, my nose red. I debated pretending I wasn't home.

Of course, the dog barked and the bird squawked. I stared at the ceiling, holding my breath. What were the chances she'd believe I wasn't there?

My cell rang with a familiar song, *Graveyard* by Halsey. Even before I heard that, my blood heated. Pulse skipping, I scrambled for the phone and the message waiting for me.

Killion: *I do not want to alert your landlady. May I come in?*

Me: ...

What could I say? I'd hoped for the best, but planned for the worst. This could be nothing more than him chiding me about lecturing Mason or telling me something ridiculous, such as he was leaving town. If I didn't go to the door, I could put off the inevitable, right?

Me: *I'm in bed. Come by tomorrow.*

Killion: *What are you wearing?*

Me: ...

Was he *flirting* with me?

The bruised place in my chest bloomed with hope, like one of the flowering houseplants I'd revived at the church. I left the bed and walked to the door. Reining in my galloping pulse, I opened it slowly.

We stared at each other, neither of us moving or saying a word. He was dressed in his usual suit and trench coat, and the scent of his magic—warm caramel and old libraries—washed over me. I couldn't even breathe, soaking him in.

He held the peace lily I'd resurrected, and my heart pounced on that tiny thing like Miss Pickles on catnip. Was this an olive branch? A request for a do-over?

"I was only trying to help with Mason," I blurted.

A dark brow quirked. "What has he done now?"

He didn't know? *Whoops.* "Nothing. He was quite helpful today, actually. You should be happy he's getting out again and back to normal."

"The purple strip is...nice."

"*Nice?*" The amethyst color reminded me of his eyes when he was lusting after me. "I think it's awesome."

"Why were you crying?"

"Don't be silly." I ran my hands over my face, wiping at my puffy eyes. "I have allergies."

The other brow rose. "It felt like extreme grief to me."

Busted. "You felt that?"

"I have, unfortunately, felt much of your despair since my deplorable actions last weekend." He handed me the plant. "Congratulations on a successful opening of the clinic. I regret letting my emotions get in the way of supporting you."

I accepted it, dumbfounded again, and stepped back to allow him in.

The dog and bird greeted him like they hadn't seen him in years, rather than a few days. I tried to decipher whether he was only there to wish me well, or resume our relationship.

"I missed you being there." It was true, and while my head warned me to tread lightly, my heart demanded I be honest. "I thought you would show up and help out. Not because we were involved, but because you're my friend."

"Chloe?" Vera called up the inside stairs. "Is someone here?"

"I'm on the phone," I yelled back.

He waved a finger and a curtain of silence fell around us. "I *should* have been there. I'm sorry, and I hope you'll forgive me." He looked me in the eyes and I saw his contrition. "Her name was Gertrude Grace Elizabeth, as you saw on her headstone, but she preferred Eliza. When I wanted to annoy her, I called her Gerty. She hated that." He chuckled. "She was a nurse. It was her calling, this passion for saving people. You are nothing like her, except in that manner."

A breakthrough—he was taking me up on my offer. After setting the gift in a shaft of sunlight, I scooped a pile of laundry off a chair and motioned him to it. "She sounds like my kind of woman."

We spent the next hour telling each other about our loved ones. We laughed and got a bit teary-eyed at times, but Dr. Maxwell was right—it helped to talk about them.

I got us both a drink, while he smiled over his son's antics. "I never thought I'd be able to have children. Wasn't sure I wanted to, considering my...situation. But he was amazing. A wonder to me. Eliza insisted we would have a girl, too. She wanted to name her Clover. I must confess, I didn't care for that name, but I would have given her anything she desired."

A question had been bothering me for some time. It was still a sensitive thing to ask. "Your blood—a few drops like you gave me, could it have saved them?"

He deflated and self-reproach hit me hard. "They were on the mend, or so I believed. Eliza said it was true, and though I'd offered my blood to assist their recovery, she'd adamantly refused, claiming it wasn't necessary and their natural immunity would rally. They would be stronger for it. Right before she fell ill, she'd made me purchase a Victorian home behind King Street. We were going to fix it up and had already moved into the east wing. She loved that awful place. Total money pit." He shook his head. "But I couldn't talk her out of it. A storm hit that night and a section of the roof over the library was ripped clean off. I left her and Marius to take care of it. Most of her prized books were damaged, but Katarina came and we placed tarps over the opening and cleaned up the water as best as we could. The wind was against us, and it took hours. By the time I returned to Eliza's side, they were both gone. Cold. It was too late for my blood to revive them, even if I'd tried."

I handed him his beverage as I sank into the chair next to the sofa. "I'm so sorry. I know this doesn't help, but Death told me it was their time. Their contracts were up."

"He's told me the same. Changes nothing for me."

After a brief silence, we told more stories again until we'd talked ourselves out, and both the dog and the bird fell asleep, Ghost in his lap, Corvus, feet up in the air, in mine.

"I wish to court you," Killion said, the sun now gone and night in full swing. "Properly."

"*Court* me?" I laughed, rousing the bird so I could turn on a light. "Is this a Jane Austin novel?"

"Good god, no. I find those terribly ridiculous, however, the word 'date' doesn't seem accurate, and I abhor the term 'hooking up.' I don't want a passing, short-term dalliance. I want you to feel cherished, desired, and honored above all others, and I want it to last as long as it makes you happy."

My heart thudded hard, dumbstruck. Corvus squawked and I had to set my glass down. "I would love that, but..."

His brows dipped at my hesitation. "Do not hold back. What concerns you? Have you renewed your affections for JR?"

"Good god, no," I mimicked. Reapers, this was hard. "I need to tell you something, but you have to not freak out."

He went very still. Ghost peeked her eyes open, yawned, and hopped down to play with the bird. "With that opening, I'm already, as you say, *freaking out.*"

"You look exactly the same as you always do."

He scowled. "Tell me."

His magic wove around me, protective. I wiped moisture from the glass with my thumb and considered how to phrase my next words. "Are you going to work for SMG again?"

"I find it taxing not to have an investigation to occupy my mind. In truth, you were all I could think about for the past week, and while I enjoyed certain fantasies, it drove me mad not to have a puzzle to work on. Why?"

A certain level of satisfaction made me smile at the fact he'd fantasized about me, but only briefly. "What I'm about to tell you is going to affect our relationship, and I want you to know that I totally understand if you don't want to undertake a romantic future with me."

He sat forward, reached across the space, and clasped my knee. "Nothing you say will keep me from wanting that."

I was about to test his commitment to that. "Okay, here goes. Ninety isn't going to happen, like I'd hoped. I only have...five years."

"For what?"

I took his hand from my knee, holding it firmly in mine. "To live."

He drew back. "*Doamne,*" he swore in Romanian. "This is truth? How do you know?"

"Death broke the rules and told me—my contract runs out before I'm thirty. It's a shock, and I'm still processing it, but I can't ask you to commit to anything beyond friendship when I'm not going to be here long-term."

Pulling me out of the chair, he drew me into his arms. I melted into him, yet braced myself for his response.

All he did was hold me. It felt so good, so right to allow his solid body to support mine. "On the other hand," I added, "I'm going to make the most of the time I have left. I was hoping you might do that with me...?"

His hold was steady and strong. He stroked my hair and rested his chin on the top of my head. Then, "It would be my pleasure."

I raised my face to look at him. "You're sure? It's okay if you don't want to. I know the pain all of this has brought back up for you."

"A lot can change in five years."

I knew what he was suggesting. I'd negotiated with Mei Han, but I had no guarantees. My reaper job, as well as Killion's contract, could still be revoked at any time. "While I have no desire to become a vampire, who knows what deal I can finagle out of Death?"

He kissed me, deeply, tenderly. My toes curled. Stardust had nothing on that kiss. "Perhaps I can seduce you to come to the dark side."

His voice was as warm as melted chocolate and I felt like giving in right then and there. "Might be fun to let you try. You did say something about pleasure, right?"

The next kiss was erotic, his fangs raking gently against my bottom lip. He caught my surprised exhale with his mouth, and my resistance grew weaker. When we finally broke apart, I was clutching him desperately. "Are you sure, Chloe?"

"I am if you are."

The third kiss felt like a contract—solely written in my favor. "What do you wish for?" he asked when he finally let me up for air. "I will grant it."

"You. You're my wish. I'm ready to get on with the whole *live life to the fullest* motto."

He grinned wickedly. "I promise you will not regret spending your days—and nights—with me."

Magic sparked between us. A bargain had been struck. Promises woven into the words. Another line crossed.

There was no coming back from this one.

I was in deep—too deep.

I didn't care. "Maybe we should stay at the penthouse tonight. We can be more...uninhibited there."

"Indeed." He chuckled and glanced at my well-worn shirt. I thought he might rip it off me. Instead, he helped me into his wool trench, securing it around me. "You just want me to feed you."

Chuckling, I gathered the sleeping dog and he carried the bird in his cage. "Want to know a secret? Food porn. Promise me unlimited Pennyworth-made meals and I'm likely to cave to your every demand."

He brought his mouth close to my ear, lowering his voice to that melted-chocolate octave once more. "I will feed you by my own hands."

My breath caught, the image he telegraphed into my mind so scandalous, it nearly singed my hair. It involved me naked on his massive dining room table surrounded by decadent desserts that he fed to me one by one. He was also, *ahem*, enjoying his own snack—me.

"Promises, promises," I taunted on a whisper.

He caught me around the waist and tugged me to him, crushing Ghost and making me laugh. "It *is* a promise." He nuzzled my neck. "And I am anxious to fulfill it."

This time I kissed him. Not a promise—a vow. I had five years. No more treading water, scared to accept who and what I was. I'd accepted my magic, and although I needed practice, it was flowing quite easily for me now, just like he'd told me it would.

Happy new year to me. It was time to jump into the deep end.

I was ready.

. . .

DON'T MISS *The Vampire's Kiss,* An Accidental Reaper Exclusive Short Story, releasing August 2nd, and ONLY available in Misty's Direct Buy Store, to find out what happens next when Killion and Chloe seal their personal soul contract with each other. (*Please note, dear reader, that The Vampire's Kiss is for those 14+, and is not intended for younger readers.*)

Paranormal Urban Fantasy

<u>The Accidental Reaper Series</u>

Grim & Bare It

Killin' It (short story for newsletter subscribers only)

Reaper's Keepers

In too Reap

The Vampire's Kiss (August 2022 exclusive in Misty's Store ONLY)

Grave Girl (January 2023)

<u>The Kali Sweet Series</u>

Revenge Is Sweet, Kali Sweet Urban Fantasy Series, Book 1

Sweet Chaos, Kali Sweet Urban Fantasy Series, Book 2

Sweet Soldier, Kali Sweet Urban Fantasy Series, Book 3

Sweet Curse, Kali Sweet Urban Fantasy Series, Book 4

Paranormal Contemporary Romance

Witches Anonymous Step 1

Jingle Hells, WA Step 2

Wicked Souls, WA Step 3

Dark Moon Lilith, Witches Anonymous Step 4

Dancing With the Devil, Witches Anonymous Step 5

Devil's Due, Witches Anonymous Step 6

Dirty Deeds, Witches Anonymous Step 7

Wicked Wedding, Witches Anonymous Step 8

Paranormal Romantic Suspense

Soul Survivor, Moon Water Series, Book 1

Soul Protector, Moon Water Series, Book 2

Cozy Mysteries (writing as Nyx Halliwell)

Sister Witches Of Raven Falls Mystery Series

Of Potions and Portents

Of Curses and Charms

Of Stars and Spells

Of Spirits and Superstition

Confessions of a Closet Medium Cozy Mystery Series

Pumpkins & Poltergeists

Magic & Mistletoe

Hearts & Haunts

Vows & Vengeance

Cupcakes & Corpses

Tea Leaves & Troubled Spirits (September 2022)

Sister Witches of Story Cove Fairytale Mysteries Series (coming fall 2022)

Cinder

Belle

Snow

Ruby

Zelle

Deadly Intent

Deadly Affair, A SCVC Taskforce novella

Deadly Attraction

Deadly Secrets

Deadly Holiday, A SCVC Taskforce novella

Deadly Target

Deadly Rescue

Deadly Bounty

Deadly Betrayal

Deadly Threat

The Super Agent Series

Operation Sheba

Operation Paris

Operation Proof of Life

Operation Lost Princess

Operation Ambush

Operation Christmas Contraband

Operation Sleeping With the Enemy

The Justice Team Series (with Adrienne Giordano)

Stealing Justice

Cheating Justice

Holiday Justice

Exposing Justice

Undercover Justice

Protecting Justice

Missing Justice

Defending Justice

SCHOCK SISTERS MYSTERY SERIES w/Adrienne Giordano

1st Shock

2nd Strike

3rd Tango

The Secret Ingredient Culinary Mystery Series

The Secret Ingredient, A Culinary Romantic Mystery with Bonus Recipes

The Secret Life of Cranberry Sauce, A Secret Ingredient Holiday Novella

MEET MISTY

USA TODAY Bestselling Author Misty Evans has published over seventy-seven novels and writes romantic suspense, urban fantasy, and paranormal romance. Under her pen name, Nyx Halliwell, she also writes cozy mysteries.

When not reading or writing, she embraces her inner free spirit and loves music, movies, and hanging out with her husband, twin sons, and three spoiled puppies. She's a crafter at heart and has far too many projects to finish.

Don't want to miss a single adventure? Visit www.mistyevansbooks.com to find out ALL the news!

Check out her humorous pen name Nyx Halliwell for magical mysteries https://www.nyxhalliwell.com .

Hello Beautiful Reader!

Thank you for reading this story! It is an honor and a privilege to write stories for you.

I hope you enjoyed this book, and I'd like to ask a favor – would you mind leaving a review at your favorite retailer? I'd really appreciate it, and reviews help other readers find books they will love too.

If you'd like to learn about my other books, sales, and special promotions, please sign up for my newsletter at www.readmistyevans.com.

Grab special edition box sets and get new releases before they come out at retailers by visiting my direct buy website www.mistyevansbooks.com. I have sales and offer NEW RELEASES early and at a discount!! Check it out.

Last but not least, if you enjoy clean, cozy mysteries, visit my pen name www.nyxhalliwell.com to see those books!

Thank you and happy reading!
Misty